THE
S·T·A·R·S·
PROJECT

LEE ANDREW TAYLOR

CONTENTS

PROLOGUE

S.T.A.R.S (Scientific Testing aimed at a Rat's Survival) is a project set up by the government to increase the population of rats in the town of Aaronsville, North of England.

In today's society, rats have become a lifeline for people, and their blood is used to heal the sick. But a worldwide virus killed off most of the population a few years ago. This virus was known as the rodent killer.

The local government set up a lab to help maintain the rats and to mate them for the future. The lab was safe from the virus.

Now, a few years later, a change has happened; a change within the rats has arrived. They have grown wise to people and want out.

Scientists have been studying these rats for a long time, but now the rats have begun to study them. They sit and watch the humans from behind their glass cages. They sit and plan an escape. They will flee from the lab tonight, taking revenge on the human race who thought it best to cage them.

Tonight, the town of AARONSVILLE will once again be awakened by the scurrying of rodents, but this time the outcome will be different.

THE RATS ARE COMING!!

CHAPTER ONE

Monday *7:00 am*. The sun shone brightly on an early April day, over fields near a house where Mr and Mrs Palmer lived; a loving, elderly couple who ran a vegetable farm on the outskirts of Aaronsville.

Raymond Palmer was sixty years old, a stocky man whose weight was increasingly slowing him down to maintain the farm. For the past few months, he'd been struggling to pick vegetables to sell to the local market traders and store owners while his wife, *Norma*, a thin and frail lady in her late fifties, was unable to help. She had told him time and time again to hire someone, but he'd remained as stubborn as a mule on the subject, telling her he was fine, everything was fine, and all will be fine. Eventually, she just submitted to his words.

Raymond rose in bed, turning off the alarm clock as Norma stirred beside him. He smiled at her as she rubbed her eyes. He got up, placed on his dressing-gown, and entered the en-suite bathroom; the sound of Norma shouting, "Are you cooking breakfast today, Raymond?" whistling around the room as he shut the door.

"When don't I?" he shouted back.

Norma lay in bed smiling after listening to the water escape from the shower, her smile broadening after Raymond began to sing until a small giggle escaped her mouth.

Here he goes again, thinking he's a rock star.

Raymond always sang when taking a shower, but his tone was so bad that it always made Norma laugh. Every morning she would lie in bed listening to him, knowing that his silliness would motivate her to face another day. It made her love him more.

A thin beam of sunlight appeared through the gap in the curtains, shooting across the room to land on Norma's face, her eyes adjusting to it as it warmed her skin. She reached out and grabbed a bottle of pills from the bedside table, staring at it like it was telling her to take one. So, she did, swallowing a pill with water left in a glass close by. She looked at the bathroom door as her heart melted, knowing that Raymond was the reason she kept taking them. If he wasn't with her then she would have given up on life, given up because of a broken heart and the loss of her daughter.

Raymond dried himself and placed on some clothes before brushing what was left of his hair and returning to the bedroom. He smiled at Norma again as she exited the bed to put on her slippers, but she just laughed. Raymond knew it was because of his singing, or lack of it, so he laughed back.

"Tell me you love my singing, or I won't cook breakfast."

"Raymond, stop it, you know I can't lie."

They laughed even louder as Raymond exited the room.

Norma sat on the edge of the bed to place on her bathrobe, listening to the last step creak after Raymond reached the bottom of the stairs before walking towards the window and pulling back the curtains. She opened it to breathe in a burst of fresh air before looking across the fields, soaking up the silence to smile as the peaceful quiet excited her.

She closed the window and walked towards the bathroom.

What a beautiful day.

———

Raymond stared at his vegetable patch from the kitchen window, becoming emotional within seconds as something ran amongst the cabbages, carrots, and parsnips. But he couldn't pinpoint what it was.

He stopped making breakfast and opened the door, walking outside to place his bare feet on the dirt upon inspecting the closest vegetables; his face fuming after seeing a few bitten cabbage leaves. He touched one as he looked ahead, knowing that an animal was the culprit, but the teeth marks embedded in the leaf weren't that of the local fox or rabbit because they were too small. It confused Raymond, even though he knew the farm *did* have its fair share of smaller animals.

What's going on around here? I hope field mice aren't to blame.

Raymond froze, leaving just his heart racing after a glimpse of the thing he saw ran between the vegetables. But again, it was too fast for him to recognize. He looked at the door, wanting to go back inside, but his feet wouldn't move. He was eager to find out what the culprit was, hoping to catch a glimpse that would answer his nagging question: *What is out there?* But whatever it was, it was very cunning, and he couldn't see it.

He was interrupted by a bang coming from inside the

house, the sound almost causing him to fall over as he glared at Norma rapping on the bedroom window.

"What's up with you?" she said, pointing at him.

Raymond tore off the bitten leaf to show her, but, as Norma looked on confused, a cat jumped out of the vegetable patch almost giving Raymond a coronary. Norma laughed as the cat raced past him, but stopped after seeing a group of rats get closer, slipping in and out of the vegetables unnoticed. She banged harder on the window until it came close to breaking, but Raymond paid no attention after her laughing had annoyed him.

He turned to re-enter the house, but a rat spooked him. It didn't frighten him but it had been a while since he'd seen one in the open, so stayed as calm as he could to not scare it off. He wanted to catch it and claim a reward from the lab, but, as he entered the kitchen again to find something to catch it with, sighed after seeing dirty footprints on the floor.

No! Norma will kill me.

But the excitement at catching a rat was too strong, outweighing the possibility of him cleaning the floor.

Raymond ignored the mess and picked up the bin, but a vision of Norma moaning like a crazy banshee because he was using it to catch a rat shook him. He wiped it from his mind and opened the fridge, grabbing the cheese he would use to put on Norma's toast before running to the door, but the rat was gone as he entered the outside. Raymond felt miserable, but, after Norma banged on the window again, shouting out that a rat was seen, he was back to smiling and setting up his plan. He placed the bin on its side near the door before throwing bits of cheese into it, hoping the smell would attract the rat's attention so he could catch it. But, as he stood with the bin lid in his hand, looked up to see Norma nervously smiling at him.

In her teenage years, long before the rat virus spread, Norma encountered an experience with some rats that she'd rather forget. Her school had some, and one day when she was waiting in the classroom for the teacher to arrive, a few bullies forced her into the stockroom, locking the door. Not only was this traumatic for her but there were also six rats running around by her feet. The bullies had let them out of their cage. Norma had screamed at least a dozen times before someone came to rescue her so has been frightened by rats ever since. Raymond waved to her, knowing the feeling she felt.

He re-entered the house to look out of the kitchen window, silently waiting for the rat to show. It did within seconds, its nose twitching as it neared the bin. Raymond smiled as he held the lid ready before moving with caution to avoid being seen, nearing the doorway to smugly smile after seeing a few rat tails waving from inside the bin. He counted them as the thought of earning more money pleased him before rushing to turn the bin upright, seeing the rats drop to the bottom to carry on eating the cheese as he laughed. But, as he pushed the lid down, a rat pounced and scratched his face. It shook him as it landed by his feet, his left cheek bleeding to leave him stunned as the lid fell to the ground.

The rats escaped the bin to stand next to the other one as Raymond nervously touched the scratch, fear racing through his veins after noticing the rats watching him look at the blood on his finger. They twitched their whiskers and attacked his ankles, leaving his screams after every bite echoing all around him. But Raymond gritted his teeth and moved to the side of the house, breathing heavily as thoughts of Norma's fear entered his mind.

The rats followed after smelling the blood leak out of his

wounds, avoiding the house to chase him until he reached a wall before savagely biting him to leave him cringing in pain.

Raymond swung fists at them, yelling even louder as the punches connected, but his surprise fast turned into shock at what the rats were doing. Gone was the vision of how useful they were, and in its place was anger, but Raymond could only watch on as the rats shook off his punches to carry on attacking. He limped to the other side of the house, moving along the wall to leave a blood trail, watching them through watery eyes before suddenly becoming still. He hoped they would turn and run away, but the sound of his breathing and the smell of blood caused their noses to twitch even more.

Raymond cried when they jumped on him, his body slamming against the wall as one rat attached teeth to his chin and another bit into his stomach.

These aren't normal rats, he thought, shaking. *Normal rats don't attack people for no reason.*

He tried fighting them off, but again he couldn't do it.

Norma waited for him to shout again, but nothing arrived. She listened and listened as tears streamed down, the sound of her watch ticking the seconds away reminding her of how quiet her husband was. She knew she had to find out if he was okay, but the rat sighting still had her hypnotised with thoughts from the past, so wasn't strong enough to break free to help him.

Raymond tugged at the rat on his stomach, cringing as he pulled it off to throw it onto the ground; his belly bleeding as the rat ate his flesh. He placed fingers over the wound but blood seeped beneath them to turn his trousers red; his heart beating faster after feeling the warmness of the liquid with his feet. He spat some over the rat on his chin as it ripped at the bone, punching it as the others jumped on his back to force him to his knees as his chest tightened. He panted for air as sweat dripped off him, feeling more pain as they bit deeply before finding the strength to crawl along the pavement, getting further away from the house to prevent the rats from attacking Norma. But his breathing became erratic as all signs of a heart attack dropped him.

He lay face down as more bites tortured him, his screams sounding more like yelps as he tried lifting, but his arms struggled to generate power, his elbows trembling instead of locking. He tried again but a rat bit two fingers clean off, leaving him crying as the others forced him onto his back. They smothered and choked him with their weight until his strength was gone, the only effort to try and push them away now coming to nothing as he lay with tears dripping off his face. Raymond felt every bite from the savage rodents as they attacked him over and over again, but they stopped when he moved no more.

Norma stood nervously by the bedroom door, waiting for Raymond to say that everything was going to be okay, but deep down knew he wasn't as she plucked up the courage to go downstairs. She walked towards the bannister, clutching it tightly, her eyes staring at the bottom of the stairs as each step felt harder and harder to achieve. She saw the door open, feeling scared to slump against a wall as thoughts of a rat being inside the house freaked her out, now tempted to just shut the door and hope they hadn't invaded. But Raymond's silence overpowered her mind, so she couldn't rest until finding him.

"*Ray*mond!" she shouted, entering the outside.

She walked past the bin, the smell of the cheese still strong in the air as she peered inside.

I hope that wasn't mine.

But the disgusting thought was brushed to one side as she followed the path that Raymond had recently taken. She breathed deeply as she reached the corner of the house, turning it to find him lying motionless on the ground, feeling shocked as she stared at his blood-soaked body. But she failed to notice the bite marks covering him. She moved closer but froze after seeing his fingers sitting in a pool of blood.

Norma didn't scream. She *tried* to scream, but all she managed was a gulp as the hairs on her arms stood up after remembering why her husband was unconscious. She saw his stomach violently move up and down, making her smile to release a happy tear because he was alive, but, as her silent footsteps neared him, her slippers became soaked with blood. She bent down to witness his stomach move again before laughing nervously as it moved once more.

"Hey, baby, I'm going to get you some help."

She touched his face, it was cold, and it scared her, but his stomach was still moving. Norma felt lost as she reached out to grip his bloodstained shirt, lifting it to suddenly jump out of her skin after seeing a few rats inside his ribcage tear at his flesh and organs.

One of them pounced, sinking teeth into her neck until tearing the jugular, leaving Norma's eyes widening as blood sprayed over Raymond's body. She slapped hands at the rat until it let go before wrapping hands around her neck like a scarf to walk in a daze, but struggled to escape as the rat teamed up with the others. She tried to run but her throat stung from the blood pushing against the wound, wobbling to fall to the ground to pull herself across the concrete slabs to close in on the house as her hands became soaked in the sticky liquid. She tried to get up, but gurgled and fell again, her body now still as the blood flow ceased.

One of the rodents sniffed her face as another bit flesh from her neck, the others watching on with glowing eyes before diving in to feed.

CHAPTER TWO

In the kitchen of a farmhouse, about half a mile away, sat *Sean Riley*, the widowed husband of Norma and Raymond's daughter. He stared at the clock as the time reached *7:30 am*, another spoonful of cereal rushing into his mouth to remind him he needed to do some work. He had lived alone on the farm for the past two years since cancer finally won and destroyed his wife. He remembered the last words spoken to him before she died, a deal that he would promise to never give up on the farm. He hadn't. Her words were the motivation behind everything he did on the farm and were the reason why he expanded the business. He smiled as another mouthful of cereal was eaten.

He looked at the clock again and scrunched his lips, muttering as he waited for *Chris Bloomfield*, one of his workers to arrive so the milk can be delivered from the expanded business. But Chris was late. Sean had a few part-time staff working for him, with most working on the fields and arriving about *9:00 am*, but at *7:15 am*, Chris was meant to be doing the milk round.

He appeared as Sean was washing up.

"Sorry about being late, but my baby kept me up all night."

Chris was twenty-four years old, tall, thin, and straggly. His girlfriend gave birth to a daughter a few weeks ago, so was still adapting to fatherhood.

"No worries. So, how is life at home?" Sean asked, replacing the mutter with a sympathetic smile.

"Sound. Sound...Rachael's trying her best but it's harder than we thought."

"I bet it is."

Chris sat at the table. "Is there any more tea in the pot?"

"Yeah! You know where everything is. Just help yourself." Sean walked towards the door after checking the clock for the third time in minutes. "I need to sort the fields out before the others arrive," he said pointing. "The milk is ready, and the delivery list is on top of the microwave. I'll see you later."

Chris watched Sean leave before staring out the window to see him climb up on a tractor, hearing it roar to bring a smile as it headed towards a field. He stared at a cupboard door before counting to ten, checking to see if Sean would return as he opened it to retrieve a packet of biscuits, grabbing a cup from a stand-up rack to sit down again to pour tea into it. But he yawned several times as he dunked the biscuits.

He left the house minutes later with the delivery list in his hand, smiling at the dairy cows on his way to the milk float. But his smile turned to concern after noticing they were quiet. Chris usually received a 'moo' as he walked by, but today there was nothing, not even when he clapped. He shrugged it off as he reached the float before placing the list next to his seat as he started it up, but stared awkwardly at the cows as he drove away.

———

Sean steered the tractor along a field, but his concentration faded after witnessing a flock of crows act strangely in front of him. He saw they were fighting over something on the ground before glaring towards his homemade scarecrow, seeing a dozen birds perched on it to make him think they were mocking him. He shook his head at how useless the scarecrow was as the birds flapped their wings, their feathers hypnotising him as he drove past. But they flew off to team up with the others.

He stopped the tractor a few yards away, but the birds ignored him to feed on something. *This doesn't look good*, he thought, standing in his seat to see more clearly. He watched them flap at each other, their squawks echoing around him as they smothered the thing to stop him from seeing it. He cursed after getting down from the tractor, but a strange burst of nerves raced over him as he tried counting them. He walked closer with his finger moving at speed as they moved too fast, watching them fly over each other before landing to snap at what he still couldn't see. But, as he counted around twenty of them, another twenty arrived.

Sean panicked as the crows flew towards him, his arms covering his face in fear they were about to attack. But they didn't, they just scattered and flew off into the morning sky. He removed his arms to face the thing on the ground, breathing heavily as he neared. But after five steps he was screaming, tears flowing after seeing what was left of a dog, *his* Collie dog. Sean had let it outside like he always did when getting up, with the dog doing its usual routine of running through the fields as he got ready for work. It always came home when hungry, so he rarely saw it during work time.

"Trigger!" he shouted. "What's happened to you, T....rig....ger?"

If it wasn't for the dog collar, Sean wouldn't have been able to recognize it. Birds had ripped out one eye; its hind legs were only attached by the skin because something had tugged at them, and numerous bites covered its body. Sean was worried, thinking maybe the tractor did it but knew that couldn't be possible seeing as Trigger was in front of him.

His legs weakened as an avalanche of vomit splashed down his clothing after staggering back to the tractor. He rested against it, his body almost crumbling after seeing rats run around on it. Sean could only stare as one jumped on his head to bite him, his squeals grabbing the attention of the others as blood slid past his eyes. He gripped the rat with a red-covered hand, the dark liquid also clinging to his clothing as it bit into his scalp again. Sean screamed even louder as it bit his hand, his teeth gritting in anger as he threw the rat at the ground. He watched it scurry under the tractor, but he was jumped on by others before making his escape. He tugged, punched, and kicked out at them, but couldn't scare them away. He was frightened by them; their viciousness sent his mind into meltdown as he lunged back on the tractor to start it up. He shouted at the rodents after feeling blood pour from the recent wounds, the tractor rolling over the body of Trigger as he tried to get away. Sweat began to mix with the blood on his face to sting his eyes, his vision now a problem as the tractor steered off course.

His hand felt numb, useless to hold the wheel; his other hand fending off the rats still glued to the tractor. He swung at them as they attacked from all angles, losing control of the tractor to stall it. He jumped off screaming; rats clinging to him as he raced through the field at a speed he didn't know he was capable of. He remained fighting them, but others caught up to snap out at him. He weakened quickly after each swing took energy from him. It was like the rats knew. They waited until he was close to falling; his body drained from the blood loss as they covered him. He fell to his knees, as they tore at his eyes, bit his hands again, and attacked his ankles. He was now an easier target. An easier kill.

Sean whimpered as a rat ripped at his mouth; the pain on his lips stinging as it savagely ripped out his tongue. His face bled like a red waterfall as he attempted to escape again, seeing his house in the distance to raise a tiny smile of hope as a chance to be saved washed over him. He tried returning to his feet but they snapped beneath him, the tendons on his ankles giving way after being viciously attacked. Sean screamed until he was heard no more. After that, all was quiet again, with Sean dead, along with his dog.

CHAPTER THREE

Aronsville's rat sanctuary was stationed deep in the heart of the university. It was home to science students wanting to learn more about the rats and the virus that almost made them extinct.

The first sign that they disappeared occurred around *5:00 am*.

Two hours before the first murder took place. A security guard laughed it off at first, thinking he had been pranked by one of the students, but, after seeing no sign of anyone on the security video, knew that it probably wasn't. The only rats left in the building were the ones in the incubator room, all newly born and fragile. The security guard noticed them because they were closely monitored, but had scratched his head a dozen times before calling the police about the others. That call was made at *5:15 am*, a call he wished he hadn't made after hearing how unconvincing the police officer on the other end sounded during the conversation.

Arriving at the university in the early hours was police sergeant *Adam Sayer*. A forty-year-old, attractive male who was physically fit and a hit with the ladies. Beside him was his nephew, *Brendan Sayer*. A twenty-two-year-old constable of just five-feet-four, who didn't take after Adam in looks or stature. He was overweight, had a tooth missing, and his lazy eye made him shy around women, but he was top of the class at the academy in the written exams. Adam always reminded Brendan of how brainy he was, and how much he knew about the role he played in the police force, especially when Brendan was having one of his low days.

The security guard had explained all he knew during the thirty-minute tour of the crime scene, with the officers writing notes as they followed him. The glass from one of the rat cages was smashed as if by some blunt force, its pieces scattered around the floor. But the other cages had been opened electronically to leave Adam and Brendan thinking it was an inside job.

But why was just one glass smashed and not the others? Adam thought as he circled the words - the mystery behind the broken glass – in his notepad.

Those words got to him and haunted his mind, but, after hearing what was inside the cage, Adam was left stunned. It belonged to a larger rat, nearly *twice* the size as most of the others. A brown one with white dots and a piece of ear missing. Brendan had sniggered after hearing that, but the security guard explained why. The rat was labelled a troublemaker, a vicious rodent that never acted the way the others did. That was why it was caged alone. Many times, it had escaped the play area it roamed around in, even disturbing classes after running through classrooms, but it was in the testing room that the ear incident happened. It tried escaping during one of the experiments on it but ran into a lit Bunsen burner, setting fire to its left ear. The rat had been the most tested on during the past year, but the university professor wasn't able to conclude why it was larger than the others and why it didn't react in the same way when experimented on.

But Adam's only thought was aimed at *why would someone steal it, unless for profit.*

He had sent out a request to all local police stations to keep an eye out for anything suspicious, like a lorry container moving at speed, but nothing was reported back to him as the time reached *6:00 am.* For the next two hours, he and Brendan sat typing up their report, with both lost for words as to how the rats disappeared undetected. Adam had viewed his notes several times before coming back to the smashed glass cage, but each time had no answer. There was no other indication of vandalism. The other cages had been opened in the usual way, and the door to the lab room was locked before the security guard opened it. No windows in the room had been tampered with, and no one was spotted on the security camera leading to the room where the rats were kept. Adam had noticed there were no cameras in that room but figured no one could get inside without being spotted, so never questioned it.

He looked over at Brendan, huffing whilst typing on the keyboard and twirling a pencil through his hair.

"Grab us a coffee," he said, as Brendan looked up from his computer screen. "This paperwork is doing my head in."

"Tell me about it," the reply came, as Brendan left his chair. "It's nearly eight-thirty. We've been writing this report for ages."

"Hey! You wanted to be a policeman." Adam laughed, as Brendan left the room.

He watched as Brendan returned, but a look of concern gave away his state of mind as he placed down a cup of coffee.

"What are you thinkin'?" Brendan asked.

"I'm thinking the security guard is full of shit. That's what I'm thinking."

"My thoughts precisely." Brendan returned to his seat and carried on typing. "How can one-hundred rodents disappear without a trace?"

Adam scratched his head. "That's what the security guard said, but we honestly don't know how many there were."

"He wouldn't lie about it, would he?"

Adam smiled. "No, he wouldn't. But in this job, you have to think the worst in people sometimes."

"Yeah, like maybe it's an insurance claim and the rats were worth a lot of money?"

Adam finished typing. "They possibly *were*." He printed off his statement before saying, "Have you done yours yet?"

"Yep! Just on the last line now."

Adam grabbed a folder to place his report into it before walking over to Brendan. "Just pop yours into here."

"What do we do about the security guard?"

"Nothing! For now, we just take his word for it."

"And what now for *us*?" Brendan asked.

"Now we investigate."

CHAPTER FOUR

The time approached *9:00 am* when local man *Peter Adams* entered the store. He was thirty-seven years old, extremely tall with a ponytail that reached the middle of his back. He was there with his twelve-year-old daughter, *Cortney*; a bright girl with long, brown hair. She'd always say that her brain wouldn't work properly unless she had a good breakfast every morning, so here they were shopping for supplies. Peter was sucked in by her ritual, but it was her puppy dog smile that worked on him the most.

He'd lived in this town all of his life, but Cortney hated it, there was nothing for children to do here. It was a farming town, so most people just farmed. The usual places to shop were here, but there weren't any shopping centres of any kind. Also, there was no fun stuff like bowling or the cinema, meaning people had to go out of town for entertainment.

He left Cortney to wander around the store, as she was more likely to choose what to eat, while he walked over to a troubled-looking storekeeper.

"Hey, John, you okay?" he asked.

John Davis was Peter's best friend. They'd grown up

together, went to school together, and Peter had been part-owner of the store before changing job roles and becoming a lorry driver. Driving a lorry was the perfect job for him as he could escape the town for a few hours, and sometimes a few days. But, the few days weren't greeted well by Cortney. She knew her father had to work so he could supply her with the gifts she would receive on his return, but she still hated it. She would pretend all was okay, but all *wasn't* okay with her and Peter knew that. However, he didn't want to swap job roles again.

"Hey, Peter. She's growing fast," John replied, avoiding the question.

Peter stared over at Cortney as she picked up a packet of bacon from a shelf.

"She sure is. And she's got a good head on her shoulders. I'm hoping she uses her smartness and makes a good career for herself after school."

"I heard that," Cortney replied, reaching out to grab a box of eggs.

"Did I say she was very nosey too," Peter said, laughing.

John also laughed.

"Dad! I can still hear you."

"Then turn the volume off on your ears and you won't anymore."

The men remained laughing when Cortney brought the items to the counter.

"Ears don't have a volume switch," she said, grunting.

She moved away again to gather more items, so Peter asked John the same question.

"I'm fine, Peter. Truly, I am. It's just that I keep hearing this loud scratching coming from the stockroom. It's been on and off for the past hour."

"Have you taken a look?"

"Only a quick peek. I've got a store to run."

Peter knew John was having a dig at him for bailing on the business but didn't want to bring it up.

"Why don't I come over later, when you close? We can have a look together. I don't have work tonight."

"It'll be okay. I'm sure it's nothing to worry about."

Peter sensed that John was indeed worried, and the little macho speech wasn't convincing him otherwise.

"But you are worried. I can tell." Peter placed a hand on John's shoulder. "I'll be back before you close."

John relaxed a touch before thoughts of dread climbed back inside his mind. He knew if the scratching sound increased it would be heard by customers, evidently leading to him losing their business, but he couldn't just shut the store and check the stockroom as questions would be asked as to why he did it. He hoped all would be quiet until Peter turned up again.

Cortney had gathered a large supply of edible items, but Peter knew she was testing him.

Most of this stuff wasn't needed, so why is she putting them on the counter?

"We don't need more cereal, and we don't need more chocolate or biscuits, so take them back."

"But Dad. I'm hungry."

Cortney gave out another puppy dog smile, but this attempt didn't work.

"I know you're just trying to get me back for laughing at you, but it won't work."

"It will!" she snapped back.

John found this rather interesting. He was glad of it because it kept his mind free of the stockroom problem.

"Your move," he said to Peter.

Peter sighed before gathering the unwanted items.

"It definitely won't!" he shouted at Cortney, sending her one of his very rare glares. "If you keep this up you'll have no breakfast today or tomorrow."

"But that's child cruelty."

John was close to laughing again as Peter tried replacing the items, but Cortney was tugging at his coat.

"But please, dad, I need them!" she shouted, crying fakely.

She tugged harder until Peter dropped most of the items, his face now red with embarrassment as he bent down to pick them up.

"Leave it, mate, I'll do it," John said.

"No, no, she's my daughter, so she's my problem. I'll sort it out."

"So, I'm a problem now, am I?" Cortney said, huffing.

John was loving this situation.

He had no children so was thankful to see someone else's child entertain him for a while. He watched Cortney storm off out of the store, muttering to herself as she left.

"Wow! She's got one on her today," he said.

"She's just pissed at me because I've got another long run tomorrow night. This time, I'll be gone for a week."

"But I thought she was okay with all that?"

"She is and she isn't. It's her birthday this week and I won't be here."

"That's understandable as to why she's annoyed. Can't you swap runs?"

"I've tried, really I have, but it's a busy time, and I need the money." Peter glanced over his shoulder to see Cortney outside the store door. "She'll be okay, eventually." He watched John bag up the items. "I'll be back later. Promise."

Peter paid before grabbing the shopping and catching up with Cortney.

CHAPTER FIVE

Chris re-entered the farm after finishing off his milk round, parking the float in its usual spot before walking over to the cows. But they seemed startled. "Hey, girls, it's *me*. You don't need to be frightened of me."

He spotted fear in their eyes but couldn't work out why? until witnessing something race off inside the cowshed.

There's fuckin' vermin in here.

He couldn't let it rest without reporting it to Sean, so made his way to the house, but, after noticing the tractor wasn't back from the field assumed Sean was still working.

He'd normally have a break around now.

He turned a corner to find one of the workers nearby.

"Have you seen Sean?" he asked, approaching.

But *Marie Noble* had been working inside the greenhouse ever since starting her shift so never knew where Sean was. Every morning at about nine, she would enter the farmhouse, grab a coffee and then go to the greenhouse to attend to the tomato plants, cucumbers, and anything else Sean wanted to grow inside. She hardly saw him on her shift. The only possible times would be during her break or if Sean visited the greenhouse for a chat, but that was pretty rare.

"No, I haven't. Isn't he on the field?"

"He must be, but it's ten in the morning. He's normally on a break at this hour."

Marie gave out a lost sigh. She really couldn't help Chris.

"He's probably just finishing off. He'll be here in a minute."

"Yeah, you're right, he's probably just got a lot on."

Marie knew Chris had something on his mind, something he needed to tell Sean urgently.

"Why do you need him so badly?"

"It's nothing. It can wait."

She watched him bite his nails like someone trying to quit smoking, so knew he was worried.

"Come on, Chris. What's wrong? You can tell me."

Chris looked worryingly inside the greenhouse, and to Marie, it looked like he was searching for something.

"Have you seen any rodents running around inside here recently?"

"What kind? Do you mean field mice?"

"I don't know what kind, but something ran inside the cowshed. The cows are spooked by it."

"Sorry, Chris, but I've not seen anything in here with me." Marie pulled a funny face to relax him, but it wasn't working. "Chris, it'll be fine. If there are mice in the cowshed then we'll just get rid of them."

Chris knew he was being stupid and probably worried over nothing, so shook the thought of the rodent from his mind.

"You're right. I'm sure it's just a one-off. I'll find out how it's getting into the shed then board up the hole."

"But what about Sean?"

"I'll tell him what's happened when I see him."

He left Marie to carry on with her job but changed his mind about looking for vermin after remembering he was needed back home. He decided, that if any holes needed boarding up, he would come back later.

Chris walked past the cows again, now happy because they didn't seem spooked by his presence. He smiled at one flapping its tongue in front of its face, listening to it calmly moo, so knew that whatever was running around inside the shed was gone.

He walked towards his car, opened it, and climbed inside. Then, after taking another look at the closest cow, started the engine before waving at it as he drove away. But, seconds later questioned himself as to why he did it. It wasn't like the cow would be waving back.

———

Marie looked up from inside the greenhouse to see a flock of crows acting crazy in the distance. She knew it was the area where Sean was meant to be working, so took it as being serious, but, as she placed down her trowel to walk in their direction, found them fighting with each other, snapping beaks as feathers fell to the ground.

She saw the path the tractor had recently taken, following the tread the wheels made in the dirt until a minute later finding it parked bizarrely and way off course. She reached it before looking around to see where Sean was, but he wasn't to be seen, sighing as she climbed into the driver's seat to see the keys still in the ignition.

This is weird...he must've gone back to the house as I walked here.

"Sean! Sean!" she shouted.

Marie watched the chaos unfold in front of her until noticing the crows fighting over something stuck inside a large mould made by the tractor. She couldn't make out what it was because the birds were in her eye line but knew something wasn't right.

What's going on?

She stood up, leaning on the tractor to gain a clearer sighting, but it spooked the birds into flying in her direction. Some hit her at speed, almost knocking her off as they fell into a semi-conscious state on the ground, but, before being able to check on them, they were gone, leaving behind just a pile of feathers after rats had snatched them in their teeth.

Marie saw thin lines of blood near her feet as she got down off the tractor, the sight causing her mind to be fearful as she shouted out to Sean again. She shook nervously as she scanned the area to find him before awkwardly walking towards where the birds had been fighting, and there she too saw the mangled body of Sean's dog.

"AAAAARRRGHHH!" she screamed.

She turned, rushing back to the tractor to place a foot on it as a swarm of rats raced from the crops, but Marie was so nervous that she failed to spot them. They were so close to touching her, and biting her that she was lucky they narrowly missed. One of them pounced as she sat in the seat again, missing her trailing foot by inches as she started up the tractor to drive the machine she wasn't supposed to drive, turning it around and heading for the farmhouse as the rats scurried off again into the crops.

CHAPTER SIX

Adam Sayer spoke to *Troy Bentner* again, the security guard from the university; a thirty-year-old man who was probably only employed as a security guard because of his mean-looking appearance. Brendan sat next to them to listen closely, smiling to himself at gaining more knowledge for when it was his turn to interview someone.

Troy had been asked to visit the police station after his shift to give a full statement of what he'd witnessed. Even though Adam had his version of what was said and done at the university, it was still necessary for Troy to have a signed copy for himself.

Adam watched him sign the statement, but, as Troy got up to leave, Adam's phone rang. He answered it as Troy nodded his head, returning a nod as Troy left the station.

"Hello! This is police sergeant Adam Sayer speaking. How may I help you?"

It was Marie. "There's been a death at the Riley farm."

Adam bit his lip as the word 'death' rattled his brain.

"Someone's been killed on the farm?" he asked softly.

"No!" Marie replied quickly. "But the dog's been killed."

"Not Sean's dog?"

Adam knew all about Sean and his trusty dog, and so did almost everyone because Sean was one of the nicest people in town. He'd often invite Adam around from time to time for a coffee. The invitation was never refused because the farm was relaxing, leaving the stress of work to wash from Adam's body within minutes of just sitting outside. He would look out towards the fields and become lost inside another world for a while; a world full of joy and peace.

"Yes, it's Sean's dog," Marie replied.

Adam could tell from her distraught voice that she was keeping something back, but what?

"Is this the only reason why you're phoning the station?"

"No! Sean's gone missing."

"What do you mean by missing? And whom am I speaking to?"

Marie hit herself for not telling him who she was. "It's Marie Noble. I work on the farm with Sean."

Brendan eagerly listened in on the conversation as his mind tried hatching a story of what was happening.

"Hi, Marie. I know you," Adam said quietly. "Tell me what happened."

Marie explained that she went to look for Sean but found the gruesome remains of his dog instead. And, because of the mangled state, it was in, thought it best to notify the police.

"Do you think someone did this to his dog?"

"I seriously don't know, but it looks like the tractor ran over Trigger."

"And you think Sean's in shock because he killed his pet?"

"Maybe. I'm not sure." Marie momentarily went silent. "Do you think you can send someone here? I'm getting a little spooked by all this."

Adam knew that other officers were due about ten-thirty, so promised to send them out to see her. Then his phone went silent again.

"What was that all about?" Brendan asked, sweating nervously as excitement took over.

He had a bit of a crush on Marie. She was a few years older than him, but he thought she was the cutest thing he'd ever seen.

"...Are we going to the farm?" he asked in hope.

"No, mate. We're knocking off in a bit. I'm letting Louise and Jack sort this one out. They should be in soon."

Brendan sighed. He hadn't spoken to Marie off duty before but always chatted with her when in uniform. When he was off duty he was just the small man who was shy to women, but when he was at work he felt like a God. His uniform made him invincible. He prayed that Adam would change his mind but knew he wouldn't.

Louise Browser arrived on time. She was nineteen years old and a novice to the police force. She had red hair and a nose ring so wasn't the usual type, but her timekeeping was impeccable and she learned fast. The inspector liked professionalism in his staff, and Louise was very professional, but rumours had escalated that he only hired her because she was a great pole dancer at the strip club he visited. However, until someone *saw* him there, it was going to remain a rumour.

"Morning, Lou," Adam said, watching her walk towards his office.

"What's up?" she replied, blowing a bubble from the gum she was chewing.

"The sky," Brendan said sarcastically.

"You need new material, mate," Louise snapped at him.

But Adam broke up the attempt at the usual morning

quarrel that happened on most days between the two. Working with them every day wasn't a blast for him so he was glad to see *Jack Foster* arrive, a fifty-year-old retired nurse from the city who was probably too old to re-train as a police constable. But his nurse training and life-saving skills were a welcome addition. Adam always partnered Jack and Louise together because he hoped the knowledge the man obtained would wash off on her. So far it hadn't, but Adam still had faith.

"Morning, Jack," everyone said.

He unzipped his jacket but stalled after seeing Adam's head shake. "Morning! And why are you shaking your head?"

"I have a job for you and Louise, so keep your coat on."

Louise's face lit up. "What are we doing? And where are we going?"

"You're going to the Riley farm," Adam replied.

"Not *there*. He's boring. He's always too fuckin' nice!"

The others all laughed.

"He won't be nice today, Lou, because he's gone missing."

She shut up, feeling embarrassed.

"What do you mean?" Jack said.

"I mean what I just said. Marie Noble's just phoned from the farm. She's worried because she can't find Sean anywhere."

"But it's a large farm, so why is she worried?"

"She's worried because his dog's been killed, so thinks maybe Sean's gone off somewhere to do something stupid."

"Killed?" Louise asked.

"Sean may have run over it and feels sad. So go to the farm, remove the dog and please find him."

"Will do!" Louise and Jack replied.

It wasn't long before they reached the farm, with Marie meeting them as the police car drove down the pathway leading to the milk float.

"He's not returned still," she said, almost in tears.

Jack moved towards her while Louise stared at the cows.

"We'll find him. Don't you worry," he said, calming her down.

They followed Marie past the house but halted once reaching the greenhouse. Marie pointed out that she'd seen bloodstains on the field near the tractor before driving it back to the farmhouse, but Jack questioned it by saying the stains could easily belong to the dog and wasn't proof to indicate Sean was in trouble. He looked into Marie's eyes, noticing she was extremely nervous as Louise noticed also.

"Show us where the dog is," she said, waiting for Marie to start walking again.

She did.

They followed her through a field, scanning for signs of where Sean could be, near Marie as she closed in on Sean's dog. But she slowed down to almost stopping again as she reached the area before rapidly switching her vision from left to right as if searching for something she'd lost. Jack knew something wasn't right.

"Okay, Marie, what's wrong?" he said, touching her arm.

"It's gone!" she screamed. "It's bloody gone!"

Louise raced over to her with confusion in her mind. "What's gone?"

"The dog! The dog was right *there*."

Jack watched Marie frantically point to where she last saw it until seeing a blood trail leading away from the tractor mould.

"Maybe the dog got up and walked off?" he said.

But Marie burst into tears, catching the officers off guard.

Jack stared at Louise as the moment became tough for her. He knew she didn't do the 'touchy-feely' thing so hugging Marie when she needed it, seemed harder for her than seeing a dead dog.

"Come here," he softly spoke, hugging Marie tight. "It's okay, we'll get to the bottom of this."

"What do we do?" Louise asked curiously.

"We look for the dog." Jack stared at the blood trail again. "Follow that to see where it leads."

Louise was quick to do this. The action side, even if it *was* just following a creepy-looking mush of congealed blood was perfect for her. She raced off with excitement in her eyes, searching the field as Jack kept Marie close, but Louise sighed as the trail ended too soon, the field going back to its original colour.

Jack scratched his head before smiling at Marie, now believing her story about the dog. But Louise wasn't as convinced.

"If Sean had killed it as you suggested, then one, where is it now? And two, how come there are no broken pieces of corn if Sean ran away from the scene?" Louise snapped a piece with her foot. "He would've done the same if he'd gone back to the house this way."

"I don't know," Marie replied, sniffing.

Jack was impressed with Louise's theory but not with her execution. She needed more practice on her people skills, but he hadn't thought of what she had just done. It was true, if Sean *did* go through the field after seeing his dog then he would've left a trail.

"Well done, Miss Sherlock Holmes," he said, smiling.

For a split second, Louise felt like a queen, but then reality kicked in and she was back to remembering the missing man and dog.

"So, where is he?" she asked.

But Neither Jack nor Marie had an answer.

Marie slowly turned around before asking if they wanted a drink at the farmhouse. It was her way of bringing some normality back to the situation.

"Sure," Jack replied. "We'll have a brew and a good think about where Sean could be."

"And don't forget his dog," Louise said, grinning.

Jack glared at her as they slowly followed Marie back to the house.

CHAPTER SEVEN

John Davis looked at his watch as the time drifted to *11:00 am*. He seemed fidgety to the point of panic, so couldn't wait any longer for Peter to arrive. He needed to find out what was making the constant scratching sound now.

He worryingly watched a close neighbour and friend enter the store, his nerves racing as she browsed the shelves to pick up a few tins of soup before slowly reaching him and placing them on the counter. But the scratching sounds made John itch and the woman noticed.

"Ants in your pants?" she asked.

"If only it was just that," John replied, scrunching his lips. "Are you busy right now?"

"Why?"

"I need a little favour." John turned quickly after another scratching sound annoyed him. "You couldn't keep an eye on the store while I check out the stockroom, could you?" He watched her think about it. "You'll be okay, Mrs Smith. If there's a problem then just shout out."

Mrs Smith, or to her friends, *Tess*, was a retired sixty-five-year-old woman who had become a housekeeper for John since living next door to him. Being a single man with no family around had made him rather lazy outside of work. He wasn't very good at looking after himself or keeping his house tidy. Tess had come to his rescue on numerous occasions, so John offered payment for her services. She refused of course, but he wouldn't take no for an answer. Tess did his washing, ironing, and cleaning, and sometimes brought cooked food around for him on the nights he worked late.

"Don't worry about me, John, I'll be alright." Tess smiled, allowing the lines on her face to stretch. "You go and sort your problem out, but don't take *too* long mind as I need to be home at half-past."

"Why?"

"Loose Women is on television."

John had never seen it but knew this wasn't the time to discuss it.

"Okay! I'd better rush then."

He thanked Tess with a smile before opening the door behind the counter. And, as she moved to the other side of the till she felt very important and in charge. It brought back a memory of authority for her, a reminder of her last job. She missed it sometimes. Tess watched the door shut and waited for a customer to arrive.

John entered the stockroom as sweat escaped him before nervously looking around the room to see nothing.

What's wrong with me? It was only a scratching noise. It's probably someone's pet, that's all, and it's got trapped in here.

He moved around the room, stopping at some tampered boxes as a cold shiver raced over him, spooking him after thinking something was there. But the idea of not knowing what it was made him jumpy to the point of leaving.

But where was the culprit?

He examined the boxes to find teeth marks embedded, with some boxes torn open, so knew that whatever was there was looking for food.

Bloody mice...

It wasn't unusual for the store to be overrun with field mice, especially at this time of year, but John wasn't looking forward to paying someone again to get rid of them. Last year had cost him a small fortune, he couldn't forget that. He also couldn't forget the five callouts he'd made to the vermin catcher, the vermin catcher who was supposed to be brilliant.

Fucking brilliant? ...The hell he was!

For John to call the man out five times was a disgrace, but each time the man would have a great excuse as to why the stockroom was overrun. John flashed a memory of how easy it was for him to be sucked in by the vermin catcher, so wasn't going to be caught out again.

I'll have a word with Peter. Maybe he'll help me this time?

He reached out and grabbed the broom from behind the door, gulping as he smashed it against the boxes. He was eager to see signs of mice running out from behind them, but none did.

Where are they?

He hoped he was wrong about mice being there, but the memory of last year's fiasco and how the store was overrun by them made him think it could happen again. The store floor was covered with field mice. He remembered having to turn customers away because the vermin catcher was laying traps everywhere. Cereal boxes had been shredded as bread, biscuits, and anything else the mice could get into were thrown away. John was left in debt for a while after that.

He picked up a box and placed it behind him, doing the same with another two, but stopped after seeing half of a dead mouse. After removing another box, he saw two more, both savagely torn apart.

"Holy shit!" he shouted.

He heard Tess shout back, "John, are you okay in there?"

"Yes, yes, I'm fine," he said, leaving the stockroom again.

Tess waited for him to return before saying, "Why were you shouting?"

"I've just found out what was making the noises back there."

"And what was it?" Tess slowly asked, knowing from the look on John's face that he wasn't happy.

"I've got mice again."

Tess knew he wanted to carry on talking but somehow was holding back.

"Are they running around in there?" She asked, nervous in case one ran past her leg.

"No, they're dead," John replied, stony-faced.

Tess freaked out. "John, what's wrong?"

But he never replied so she shook him.

"They're dead, Tess. Torn to pieces!" But she still wasn't with it. "Something bigger did this."

"Something like a cat?" she asked.

"Maybe! But I've seen no cats in this store." John's stony expression faded. "I would've seen a *cat* in my stockroom."

"What are you going to do?" Tess felt disturbed.

"I need to get this mess sorted before I'm overrun by something other than field mice. I don't want to shut my store again. I need the business."

Tess had a feeling that he wanted her to keep this quiet, so smiled as she waited for him to ask, happy that no more vermin was seen inside the stockroom.

"Of course, I'll keep this to myself, John. You'll get this

sorted. I just know it." Tess looked at her watch. "It's time for me to go home."

John relaxed as he bagged up her shopping, offering it to her for free as Tess shook her head.

"Come on, John, I was only here for a few minutes. I don't need my groceries for nothing."

"You don't, but I'm letting you have them all the same."

Tess knew the main reason was that she agreed to keep quiet over the dead mice but she didn't want to hang around and argue over it, because in five minutes her programme was on. She accepted the gift, or bribe, and slowly left the building.

John waited a few seconds before picking up the phone, staring back at the stockroom as he dialled Peter's number.

"Hello!"

"It's John. Are you busy now?"

"Busy?" Peter replied, acting confused because he'd seen John less than three hours ago.

"Yeah! I was wondering if you could come to the store."

"Sure! Cortney's just gone to see her mother so I'm free for a bit. I'll see you in five."

Just as he said he would, Peter arrived within five minutes. "What's the emergency?" he shouted.

But John shuddered as he pointed to a customer browsing through magazines. Peter closed in on John to whisper 'Sorry' after realising the customer wasn't meant to hear, as they silently watched the person give up on the magazines.

"...What's going on?" Peter asked after the customer left the store.

"The scratching noises have ceased."

"That's great news, so why did you call me in?"

"Take a look inside the stockroom then you'll know."

41

Peter didn't hesitate and walked past John to enter the room.

"Fuckin' hell! What's happened here?" he said, as John closed in. "You've moved all the boxes."

"What? Don't worry about the boxes. Just take a look over there." John pointed.

"Have you got a friggin' cat?" Peter asked, after seeing the remains of the mice.

"No! You know I haven't."

"So, what did this?"

"That's what we need to find out."

John held off from speaking again like something was stalling him.

"Are you okay?" Peter asked.

"Yeah! ...Have you seen Ted recently?"

Ted Dalton attended school with them but had moved out of town a few years ago to better himself. He was overweight and had been most of his life, so concluded that he needed to escape this crappy town to find the right path. He was only living in the city, so wasn't too far away.

"I spoke to him a few weeks ago. Why?"

"Didn't he train to be a vermin catcher recently?" John asked.

But Peter laughed at the question. Just imagining Ted chasing vermin was funny to him, but it was true, he did train to be one.

"Yeah! He told me he got a certificate and everything. He's qualified."

"Do you think he'll come and put some poison down, or traps?"

The reason why John asked Peter about Ted was that he never got on with him. John had bullied him about his weight during their school years and, after he left, was in a gang that targeted Ted every chance they got. If it wasn't childish taunts about his weight it was something else. Sometimes Ted would have mud thrown at him and sometimes it was worse, *much* worse, leading to him being assaulted. Ted had been hit a few times and was once knocked out, but John wasn't there when that happened. He had punished himself many times over it as he grew up, even apologising to Ted on many occasions, but Ted wasn't having it. John knew that part of the reason why Ted left town was that he wanted to forget about what happened to him, what happened all those years ago at school, and what happened after.

Peter had kept out of gang life but wasn't able to protect Ted from the bullying. The taunts finally stopped once the gang separated, with some joining the army while others moved away. Now, the only person left was John. Peter seemed unsure of giving John the right answer but promised he would ask Ted.

"You *do* know he can't forget, don't you?"

"I know." John bowed his head in shame.

"Hopefully, this is your chance to finally persuade him to forgive you. I'll call him today."

"Thanks."

John asked Peter to keep it quiet, hoping Ted would do the same. That's if he helped. To hire the local rodent catcher again would not only piss John off but would also be an advert to the residents of the town that the store was full of vermin again. That would mean another quiet spell of shoppers for a while. John couldn't let that happen, not again.

Peter patted him on the arm as he walked back to the store entrance. "Leave it with me."

CHAPTER EIGHT

It had been seven hours since the rats escaped their home of the past few years, the home where they had received numerous days of experimental torture from the mad, university professor. Not only was he doing the usual experiments of extracting blood from one rat and mixing it with the blood from another to see if it became more powerful in regards to healing the sick quicker but was also doing experiments behind closed doors on them. The professor knew that what he was doing wouldn't pass with the board of science superiors, but he was trapped inside his work. He strived to be the best, but for him, being the best meant taking chances. He needed to find more ways of increasing the capability of the blood to help fight more illnesses in the future.

———

Tess Smith was snuggled in her armchair as the time drifted past noon. Her favourite daytime programme was keeping her entertained so never noticed what was happening outside her home. She did her usual ritual of arguing with the television programme at every chance she had. For Tess, talking to the TV seemed more natural than talking to *real* people these days, and her visit to buy groceries and help John was mainly all she did outside of her home. He was probably one of only five people she saw on a daily, or sometimes a weekly basis, so to keep her mind fresh she would have conversations with every person on every TV show. Some were social, while others would see her shouting at whoever was talking at that time. This was one of those times. The 'Loose Women' ladies were having a debate on men, and if they were or were not useful.

"They're ruddy useless!" she shouted, as sounds coming from her back door were unheard.

But if she could hear then she would've opened the door to six ravenous rodents attacking the wood, tearing strips off with their teeth to reach the inside.

Tess was lost in the moment of her TV fantasy life as the rats extracted more wood, aiming at the same area until a small hole was formed.

The rats, a combination of three brown, a grey, a black, and an albino squeezed through the hole in the door, their noses twitching as they scurried across the kitchen floor. But the albino rat found the short journey to the living room door a struggle, its poor eyesight the reason it crashed headfirst against the base of the fridge before finally reaching it.

Tess exited her chair as an advert break came on but the scratching sound coming from behind the door worried her.

"What's going on out there?" she shouted.

She waited for a reply, but it went silent.

Her hand trembled as she gripped the door handle, but, as she slowly opened it a pain ripped at her chest. But it wasn't physical pain, it was more like a sign that something bad was about to happen, a feeling clawing at her mind. She shook after seeing five rats race into the living room, but the sixth, the albino one, was still gnawing at the bottom of the door. It hadn't noticed the others leave its side. Tess looked down at it with caring eyes, her nerves thrown to one side after seeing the cuteness of its face. It had been a while since she witnessed a breed in this town, and to witness one so beautiful in colour, with pink eyes, had her hypnotised from excitement. She leaned over to touch it, but the rat snapped at her hand. It bled, the smell sending the others wild. Tess started to sweat as she pulled her hand back, her legs becoming stiff like she was standing in quick-drying cement. Her mouth quivered as two rats ran at her, feeling petrified as they used her body as a climbing frame to reach her face. She cringed when one bit her cheek, the blood spilling as she opened her mouth to scream. But no words escaped.

Tess' legs were bitten, forcing her to fall over, the carpet now bloodstained as she pulled herself across it to reach a lampstand. She stretched for it, but the pain from her wounds slowed her down. She cringed again after searching for the rats, shedding a tear after seeing them huddled together like they were hatching a plan before gripping the lampstand to be bitten on the back of the neck, the bone-cracking to leave her head slumped.

She lay on her stomach, unable to move, frantically scanning for the whereabouts of the rats, but the pain from her wounds caused her to cry hard. She swallowed fast, trying to speak, pleading with the rats to stop, but only silent gurgles were heard as they circled her, teasing her like a pack of hyenas before a kill. Tess closed her eyes as one rat clawed at her face while another stomped its dirty feet on her head, digging claws into her scalp. She gritted what was left of her teeth as another rat slipped underneath her to bite into her sagging breast.

Tess lay in a pool of blood as the TV show ended, the credits appearing on screen as a rat bit savagely into her eyes, popping the orbs over her face.

And seconds later she was gone.

CHAPTER NINE

L ouise became restless from being stuck in a situation she wasn't comfortable with. Marie had poured her and Jack two cups of tea within a short amount of time whilst trying her best to talk about Sean and his dog, but Louise hated being stuck with nothing to do. She liked her action and needed some soon. And Jack noticed as she left her seat at the kitchen table.

"I'm off to take a look around," she said to him.

"You do that. I'll talk to Harvey; tell him what's going on."

Harvey Nickels was the Chief Inspector. A man of sixty years, with forty of them working in the police force. He was a people person, a great listener, and a very good negotiator. He had arrived at Aaronsville police station for a midday briefing but wasn't aware of where Jack and Louise were. But that was about to change once he took the call.

Louise moved away from the house and headed towards the cowshed.

"Hello, girl," she said, approaching the nearest cow.

She placed a hand on top of its head and rubbed it. It felt

like therapy for her. Louise had received a fair share of counselling over the past five years for her to say she was an expert at sitting on a couch and letting her feelings out to a stranger but rubbing the cow's head soothed her mind much easier than any of those sessions did.

"...You're very lucky not to be human." She smiled at the cow as it tried to lick her. "I hope that when I die I'll come back as a dairy cow. You have a peaceful life. All you *do* is eat, shit, and produce milk. Perfect."

She couldn't stop herself from laughing. Of all the things she could wish for, returning to earth as a cow shouldn't be her first choice. But here she was laughing and rubbing the head of a black and white beast. The cow slapped its tongue in the air again as Louise removed her hand. She waved goodbye and walked to the other side of the shed, but something caught her eye that made her slightly nervous.

This shed needs a good repair job, she thought, after spotting thin pieces of wood lying next to a six-inch hole.

The thing she spotted had run away from the cowshed. It was too quick for her to identify, but she was pretty sure it came from the hole. She glanced all around before continuing with her walk, her eyes on full alert in case it came back.

This is much better than sitting in a house with a boring ex-nurse and a woman who claimed her boss had vanished. More like she'd taken something and so imagined seeing a dead dog.

Louise constantly peered over her shoulder as she made some distance between herself and the cowshed, as the thought of a small farmyard animal nearby charging her from behind occupied her mind.

———

Jack remained sitting at the kitchen table watching Marie wash the cups. She wasn't as talkative now, not like when he first arrived, but Jack knew she was still worried about where Sean was. He had not long finished the conversation with Harvey on the phone, with Harvey telling him that he was on his way to the farmhouse. So, Jack braced himself for his visit.

"What are you growing in the greenhouse?" he calmly asked Marie.

She looked at him as she dried her hands on a towel. "Sean wanted me to try out some new ideas, so I've got a line of tomatoes, cucumbers, peppers, and several types of herbs. Plus, my usual plot of cannabis."

Jack shot out of his seat after hearing the C-word, but after seeing Marie's comical attempt at laughter realised she was just messing with him. But, as he smiled, his mind fought over the word, leaving him stuck in the middle of - *was she growing cannabis? or was she joking*? Marie noticed him fidget as he glared in the direction of the greenhouse, so knew she had gone too far with the joke.

"I was only kidding," she said, worried she would be arrested. "Seriously, I was."

"I know. You wouldn't be stupid enough to admit it if you did."

Jack felt relaxed again, laughing as he opened the door to the outside. He knew Harvey would be arriving soon so wanted to be alert when he did.

"I'm just going to wait out here for the chief."

Marie just waved at him.

———

Louise turned to see no sign of the cowshed, pleased that the thing she saw escape was not seen again as she followed the path leading to the other side of the house. She turned a corner, reaching the edge of the nearest field, smiling as she saw the greenhouse fifty meters ahead.

———

Harvey turned onto the slip road that led towards the farm, glancing at the time as it reached *12:30 pm*. He wasn't rushing because he thought it was a hoax. He knew Sean well so knew how attached he was to his dog. He thought the same as the others that Sean had gone off to have a good cry somewhere and wasn't missing, so hoped that when he pulled up to the house Sean would be there.

He drove past the main gate, seeing the other police car in the distance, with Jack waiting for him by the house. But a sudden rush of rats dashed out of a field to attack his car, jumping at it as Jack watched on. Harvey lost control of the wheel and accelerated into the side of the other police car before bouncing off to crash into the milk float.

"What the?!" Jack cried out, rushing towards Harvey's car to see ten rats race to the roof of the vehicle, attempting to bite into the metal casing.

Harvey shook his head as blood poured from it. He wasn't badly hurt but the shock of the crash stunned him. He heard the rats frantically claw at the roof, their squeals annoying him as he reached for the button on the car radio. But, as he turned it off the rats stopped attacking. He stared at some on the bonnet, becoming confused as their dark eyes stared back at him before cursing as he turned the radio back on. But the rats switched back to crazy mode, joining in with the ones on the roof to bite and claw at the car.

Harvey looked over at Jack closing in as the radio was

turned off again, shrugging his shoulders as the rats calmed down.

"Harvey! Are you okay?" Jack shouted, trembling as he eyed up the rats.

Harvey slowly grabbed a handkerchief from his breast pocket, nodding back as he placed it over the cut.

"...I can't get to you." Jack pointed at the rats on the roof. "You've got rodents on your car."

But Harvey sarcastically mimed the words - 'You think so?' to leave Jack embarrassed for mentioning it.

"Do you think the robbers dumped them here?!" Jack shouted, stirring the rats to hiss at him.

Harvey just shrugged.

Louise and Marie arrived at the scene, their mouths open wide as they stood next to Jack.

"What's going on?" Louise asked him. "Why are rats on Harvey's car?"

Marie shivered.

She cowered behind Louise as the rats violently tried getting inside the car again, their loud shrieks scaring everyone into stalling. Jack stared at Louise as thoughts of her being the courageous one because she likes danger entered his mind, but she was struggling to move.

"Go on," he said. "According to your CV, you were an adrenaline junkie and a daredevil, so this should be easy for you."

"I'm going," she replied, frowning as she stuck up a middle finger.

"When?"

Louse stared at Harvey. "Soon!"

But Jack didn't know whether to laugh or cry.

Harvey listened hard as he tried pinpointing where the rats were on his roof, but he was struggling. He produced hand signals towards Jack in the hope of finding out, needing the rats to be away from his side door so he could escape, but what came back wasn't good news. He sighed and banged his baton against the roof, but the rats ignored the noise and instead focused on the people watching them. They could hear Jack talking to Marie as he tried telling her to go back inside the house, but either she was mesmerised by fear or was mesmerised from seeing something she hadn't seen in a while, so wasn't budging.

"Just get back inside while we handle this!" Jack shouted at her.

The words hit Marie like a hurricane wind blasting through a wooden building, almost knocking her off her feet. She shuddered, running back towards the house as Jack repeated himself.

"...Remove your baton," he said to Louise. "I think you're going to need it."

Harvey watched on as their movement kept most of the rats entertained, but the rest attacked the car again to annoy him even more. He banged his baton against the roof even louder as a rat sprang off the car and headed for Jack, leaving Louise fearing the worst because of his age and his reflexes. But Jack locked onto the rodent, gripping his baton like a baseball bat as it swiftly closed in. And, as it leapt at him, the bat connected perfectly against its head. The rat flew back towards the car as Louise stood in awe, but, as it smashed against the windscreen, Harvey jumped back in his seat. He grimaced at the sight as blood trickled down the pane, the glass cracking as the rat fell on the bonnet.

"Why'd you kill it?!" Louise shouted.

"What would *you* have done?"

Jack tensed up as he waited for another rat to strike, but Louise just looked at him, unable to answer. She held her baton out in front, scanning the rats spitting at her before one screeched and a few jumped off the car. They ran at her to send shudders down her spine, her nerves kicking in as they approached at speed, but the thing Jack waited for finally arrived. Louise had found her *kick-ass* adrenaline. She acted like Wonder Woman – her baton colliding gracefully against the nearest rodents to leave him nodding at the speed of her attack. He was thankful she had found the courage to fight because he was tired after hitting the rat against the car, but he wasn't going to let her know that. He stood behind her as she cracked her baton against two rat skulls within a second of each other.

Harvey removed the handkerchief to see it full of blood, frowning after noticing the rodents on the bonnet sniff at him. He was about to open the door to escape when the crack in the windscreen extended, the rats twitching their ears to make him shriek. They leapt headfirst into the glass to smash it to pieces, leaving him covering his face to avoid being struck by flying particles. But, as he removed his hands, the rats were inside the car. Harvey became like Indiana Jones, pushing his baton into the mouth of one as it tried to bite his face before shaking the baton hard to send the rat spinning towards the backseat, as the other one scurried beneath his feet, forcing him to frantically kick out at it. He struck it with his boot to send it screeching over to the passenger side, but, instead of staying to finish it off, he opened the door and raced out of the car before quickly slamming it shut. He took a few deep breaths before looking over at the officers, trying his best to smile after seeing they had control; happy that the remaining rats were fleeing back into the field.

"Are you okay?!" Louise shouted.

"I'm fine, just fine!" Harvey shouted back, as more blood leaked from his wound.

"What's going on here? Why are they attacking us?" Jack asked nervously.

"I've no idea, but I'll find out." Harvey cautiously neared them, waving a hand towards the farmhouse. "Let's get inside."

"But what are we going to do about the rats in your car?" Louise asked.

"Lou, just let me take some time out, please. I'll figure out what to do with them after."

Jack and Louise followed him to the farmhouse door before Marie frantically opened it.

"Did you sort them out?" she asked.

The others smiled and laughed at her, but deep down they were on edge, feeling blessed for not being bitten.

"I'm going to get hold of pest control, see if we can catch the little suckers that are in my car," Harvey said.

He knew he needed the rats alive to be tested to see why they reacted as they did, but had a feeling that Louise would disagree with him. And she did.

"Forget pest control, you saw what they tried to do," she said, glancing at a worried Marie. "What if it were the rats who attacked the missing dog?"

"Marie said the pet was pretty much unrecognizable so could've been run over and killed by Sean? He could've gone back and removed it himself, maybe burying it somewhere," Jack replied.

"I am *here* you know," Marie said shyly.

Jack smiled sheepishly before apologising to Marie for making her think she was invisible, but she just smirked at him and put the kettle on.

"Right now, we need those rats alive. We need to find out why they've gone a bit crazy," Harvey said.

"Gone a bit crazy?!" Louise shouted. "They've gone utterly crazy!"

She received no disagreement from anyone as Harvey vigilantly entered the outside again. He stared at the nearby fields, knowing the rest of the rats were probably watching him, but none appeared as he released his mobile phone.

CHAPTER TEN

The time had gone past *1:30 pm* when Peter re-entered the store. John was pleased to see him back so quickly, but Ted wasn't with him.

"Where is he?" he asked.

"Be patient, mate," Peter said, smiling. "He's coming in from the city. He'll be here soon."

"Did you tell him that I needed his help?" John asked bashfully.

He had a feeling the reply would be a negative one, but Peter told him that Ted knew why he was needed.

"Look! This is your chance to put things right with him."

"I know." John bowed his head as if to cry, but he breathed deeply before a tear fell. "Do you fancy a cuppa?" he asked, changing the subject.

"Go on then." Peter moved to the other side of the counter. "I'll watch this place while you make it. It's not like I don't know where everything is."

John smiled. "Tess helped out earlier. You sure you can do a better job?"

"Watch me."

John laughed before saying, "And anyway, I might have moved some things around."

"I doubt that." Peter laughed back. "You're too fucking lazy!"

Now they were both laughing.

"True! So true," John replied, as he disappeared to make the drink.

Peter looked up to see a female customer arrive.

"Where's John?" she asked, placing some items on the counter.

"He's having a lie-down."

"I heard that!" John shouted from behind the back wall. "I'm in the kitchen!"

"Oh!" replied the woman. "You stay where you are. Peter's better looking than you and he's giving me twenty-per cent off."

John raced out of the other room, bringing spilling cups of tea with him.

"Hold on," he said, looking the woman up and down. "Is he better looking than me?"

She laughed out loud. "And here's me thinking you would be more upset about the discount."

"To be honest, I was stunned after hearing the bit about Peter being better-looking than me, so didn't catch the rest of what you said." John winked at her.

"John, you're a funny man," the smiling woman replied.

"Did he give you twenty-per cent off?"

"No! I was joking."

John wiped a hand across his brow as Peter bagged the items. "I knew that," he replied.

Peter looked at the woman like they were thinking the same thing, both smiling, knowing John was lying. Peter then handed her the shopping and she left.

"You should've seen your face," he said, sipping his tea.

But John nudged him, almost causing him to spill it.

"Woah! mate," Peter shouted.

They broke into laughter again as the door opened.

"Is someone going to make me a cup of tea?" Ted shouted, moving towards the men.

But John couldn't look into his eyes. The years of not speaking and not sorting the problem out with Ted had left him shattered emotionally, leaving him now struggling to look at him.

"It's okay, I forgive you," Ted whispered.

John slowly made eye contact as Peter entered the kitchen.

"I'm glad this day has arrived," John said, hugging Ted.

"Me too."

Peter stirred Ted's cup of tea, feeling pleased with himself on the progress so far. He searched for some biscuits, finding some in a jar nearby before taking the jar and the tea back to the counter.

"Get this down ya," he said, passing the cup to Ted. "You guys got it sorted then?

"We sure have," Ted replied, glancing towards the doorway Peter just came through. "I take it the problem is back there?"

"Problem?" John asked.

"Yeah! The rodent one."

"Oh yeah, that one."

Ted walked past him, knowing he looked worried. He took the cup of tea into the stockroom, puffing out his cheeks after staring at the dead mice, shaking his head at how unrecognizable they looked.

"Is this all you found?" he asked, sipping the tea again as the others caught up.

"I've only checked this room," John replied.

He explained about the constant scratching from earlier as Ted scratched his head.

"You got a cat?"

Peter smirked, as John replied, "No, I haven't. Do you think there's a stray cat in my store?"

"What else could've chopped them up?"

"That's why you're here, to find out," John finished.

Ted walked around the room, placing the cup on a shelf as John, and Peter returned to the front of the store. He removed some boxes to find a hole in the wall below a window, figuring it had been there for many years to allow mice to go through before staring at it to wonder if any were still inside. But assumed something larger than they had scared them away.

But what?

He placed on some latex gloves before picking up one of the left-over mice, studying it until convinced that a larger rodent was probably responsible. The idea of there being a cat faded quickly after seeing the bite marks up close, the size too small to be one. He knew that the way the bodies were left had something to do with an ambush. If a cat had pounced on them then only one would've been killed, as the others would've escaped through the hole, but this looked like a planned attack from something smaller than a cat, something that had the stealth and accuracy to strike in a pack. Ted didn't want to suggest a pack of rats, but all the clues were aiming in that direction.

He threw the mouse on the floor before exiting the room and meeting back up with the others.

"It wasn't a cat," he said.

"Why wasn't it?" John asked, confused.

"For one, the bite marks were a lot smaller. And two, a cat

would've played with its catch, teasing it for a while before going in for the kill. The other mice would've escaped if it was a cat."

"So, what happens now?" Peter asked.

"Now I get some traps, put them around the room to see if I can catch the suckers that did this." Ted walked toward the main entrance. "They'll be back. You have my word on that..."

He left the store and walked to his car, picking up his pest control bag before making sure no one was watching as he returned.

"...This won't take long," he said, walking past the men again.

John followed him into the stockroom. "So, have you an idea of what it could be?"

"Oh yeah, but you won't believe me."

"Why not?" John seemed astonished.

"I think you've been invaded by rats, and they're hungry."

"How hungry?"

"Very hungry! They've already slaughtered three mice."

John interrupted him. "Do you think they were blind?"

Ted smiled but didn't know why. "Blind?"

"Yeah! Were they three blind mice?"

Ted laughed, closely followed by an outrageous roar from John.

Peter overheard it, so rushed back into the room. "What's up with you two?" he said, feeling lost.

He saw John almost fall over from laughing too hard.

"Sorry, bud, but John's just made me giggle," Ted said.

Peter was let in on the joke, but the idea that a bunch of rats could be the killers stopped him from laughing.

"But you can't kill rats. They're a rare species now. The government needs them for their blood."

"Peter, I know that." Ted opened his bag to show him the

type of trap he would use. "Look, as far as we know no rat has been seen outside the lab for years, so it may not be them. But, as a precaution, I'm going to use these special traps. I'll set one up in each corner. When a rat nears it, or any other rodent, it will set off an alarm that releases an infrared beam. And, once they cross it the trap will drop on top of them."

"A bit like the old 'mousetrap' game."

"Yes, Peter, it is. There's no death with these traps. It just catches them."

Peter nodded as Ted set up the traps, John looking on excited like a child on Christmas morning, feeling pleased with the idea that this could be over before it began.

"I'm off back to my counter," he said, walking back to the door.

Peter slowly followed as Ted placed down another trap. "Looks like he's come to the rescue," Peter said to John.

"Mate, I'm glad you called him.

Ted left the stockroom minutes later, feeling chuffed at the thought of his traps catching something.

"All done?" John asked.

"For now...Just keep out of that room as much as possible. If you hear anything then let Peter know. I'll be at his house."

John agreed before watching his friend, and the man he was now friends with again exit the store.

CHAPTER ELEVEN

Marie was making a habit of supplying the officers with drinks. For her, this was keeping busy, but for the officers, it was another cup of tea they didn't want. However, none of them seemed brave enough to let her know.

They sat around the kitchen table waiting for someone to arrive from pest control.

"They should be here soon," Harvey said, checking his watch and scrunching his nose.

Louise shrugged her shoulders as she fought with boredom again, while Jack nodded at Marie, thanking her for the fifth time.

———

A pest control van slowly entered the farm, but the occupants, a seventeen-year-old trainee apprentice, and his boss, *Barry*, a pest control expert of twenty years, had forgotten to let Harvey know they were nearing the house. To them, this was just a routine job, a quick in and out before returning to base. The mention of rats being on the farm did stifle them, but it was more in excitement than fear.

"There's the inspector's car!" the apprentice shouted.

"*Craig*, how do you know that's his? I bet you've spent some time inside it." Barry laughed.

The van pulled to a standstill beside Harvey's car. Barry exited to gawp at the broken windscreen before opening the back of the van, grabbing a pair of rubber gloves and a large trap.

"Harvey said there were a couple of rats in the car," he said, as Craig exited.

"Do you think they'll still be in there? The glass is broken so they've probably escaped."

"There's only one way to find out..."

They walked towards the front of the car but Barry slowly moved to the back to peer through the window.

"...Nope, I can't see anything in there," he said, looking annoyed.

"Maybe they're underneath the seats?" Craig's eyes danced from left to right in excitement at the prospect of seeing a rat.

Barry put down the trap to place on the gloves before opening one of the back doors, bracing himself for the rodents to flee from the car. But nothing happened.

"Looks like the little buggers took a dump and fucked off!" he shouted, leaning inside to see rat droppings on the driver's side floor.

Craig couldn't hold back from laughing at Barry's outburst.

"So, what happens now?" he asked.

"Now, my friend, we place the trap inside..."

Barry walked back to the van to mix some powder with

food before returning to pick up the trap, adding the mixture inside before placing it between the front and backseat.

"...Okay. We'll just sit and wait for them to come back."

"Why do you think they'll come back?" Craig asked.

"You don't know much about rats, do you." Barry sniggered. "The food that's inside the trap is a favourite of theirs, or it was before the virus. I'll leave the door open, so they'll smell it easier. They'll be back."

"But why mix the food with a sleeping drug if you're going to trap them?"

"In case the trap doesn't work. That's why."

They smiled as they returned to the van, but Craig's smile broadened after seeing a rat running towards them. He nudged Barry as the rat climbed inside Harvey's car, feeling pleased as they snuck up to the door to not scare it off, but a swarm of rodents appeared from nowhere to circle them. They hissed at the men as the circle tightened, acting like hunters attacking an enemy. Craig started to sweat, his smell causing the rats to frantically twitch their whiskers to leave him on edge.

"It was a set-up!" Barry hollered, shaking his head in disbelief after seeing the rat inside the car calmly leave to join the circle. "The little shit was sent out to keep us off guard!"

"Why?" Craig asked.

"So, the others could come."

"But I thought Harvey said there were only two?" Craig wiped the sweat from his brow, flinching every time a rat moved.

"He did."

"You sure he didn't say twenty-two?"

Barry shrugged his shoulders. "Maybe. But it doesn't matter now because they've all come to say hello."

He stamped his feet as the circle of rats remained strong,

but his non-nervous approach to what was now glaring at him left Craig too frightened to stay. He ran towards the van as a few rats chased him, his face now pale as they closed in fast to attack. He wasn't given the chance to open the door.

Barry suddenly panicked as Craig kicked out at the rats. He wanted to help, tried to help, but the rats in the circle watched him like guards on duty, hissing at every move he made. He was scared, fearing for his life, his legs feeling like they were in a block of ice after seeing the others bite into Craig's flesh. He cried as Craig's tortured screams left him urinating down his trousers.

———

Harvey appeared in the distance, closely followed by Jack and Louise, but the screaming coming from the trainee was constant to make them feel sick, the noise acting as a magnet, pulling them in to take a look. They saw the trainee fall to the ground, now extremely weak as he tried shuffling underneath the van to stop the rats from biting him, but the shuffling suddenly stopped as one rat ripped at his face; the blood escaping, attracting others to do the same.

Barry looked sadly at the officers, as the rats guarding him ran towards Craig.

"Hey! Are you okay?!" Harvey shouted, closing in a little more.

But Barry shivered as he pointed towards the dying trainee.

Louise and Jack removed their batons, gulping as they stood next to Harvey to wait for him to say something, but he just stood there transfixed, watching the chaos unfold, ignoring them as though they didn't exist. Jack slapped the baton against the palm of his hand, his mouth ready to speak, but Harvey turned and smiled at him before releasing a taser gun from beneath his jacket.

"Cool!" Louise said, after spotting it.

"Cool indeed," Harvey replied, acting like a child showing off a new toy.

There was no hope for the trainee. He was dead, hidden beneath the blood-covered rats.

They turned to glare at the others, their eyes glowing red like rodent vampires satisfied with a kill upon leaving Craig's body, as Harvey moved towards them. But his courage faded after a few steps. Jack and Louise watched him cautiously approach with the taser held firmly, his trigger finger ready to fire, but he found the moment hard. Louise frowned, ready to grab the taser from him, but Jack stopped her.

"But!"

"No!" Jack snapped at her. "*He* is the chief, not you, so let him do his thing."

"His thing is sucking big time right now." Louise sighed. "Those rats will be on top of us soon if he doesn't pull his finger out his bum hole!"

They watched Harvey suddenly rush the rats, but he regretted his decision after a few of them jumped on him. He shook them off but the taser accidentally fired two electrodes into Barry, leaving him shaking violently until falling to his knees, the rats now attacking him as Harvey turned the taser off.

"Go help him!" He shouted.

Louise and Jack charged the nearest rats, swinging their batons at speed, but the rodents were quicker this time, avoiding being hit as they ran around the officers, tiring them out.

Harvey cringed after seeing a rat hang from Barry's face before quickly recharging his taser to the sound of muffled cries. He saw another six rats jump at Barry's face and neck before hearing him YELL out for help, feeling sick to his stomach as he looked away. But a second later, he re-fired the taser into the man, seeing the rats drop off to twitch violently on the ground.

"Get back to the house. Now!" he shouted, shedding a tear as Barry lay still.

Jack and Louise retreated as the rats fed on the dead men, with Harvey catching them up as they reached the farmhouse door. Marie smiled, pleased they were safe, but her smile faded after noticing their distraught faces.

"...Quickly! Grab that table and tip it on its side," Harvey said, slamming the door shut. "We need to push it against this door..."

Jack and Louise did what he said, clearing everything from the table before flipping it on its side and forcing it against the door.

"...Marie! I want you to close all the blinds," Harvey told her.

"How long are we going to be here for?" Louise asked.

Harvey glared at her. "Why don't you go outside and ask the rats how long they plan on tormenting us?"

Marie closed the blinds in the kitchen before leaving to do the same in the next room, as Louise was made to feel like a stupid child. Jack smiled at her, but she refused to look at him. He knew she was only asking a question, but it wasn't the right time to be asking that one.

Harvey wanted everyone to remain quiet, knowing that noise was a pure giveaway of why the rats attacked so quickly. They were safer inside the house he told them; they just had to wait it out. They sat with their backs nestled against the kitchen table, breaths held with anticipation, waiting for the slightest sound to come from the rats.

CHAPTER TWELVE

Chris Bloomfield paced up and down inside his house as the time reached *2:00 pm*. And *Rachael Haydock*, his girlfriend, noticed. It irritated her. She tried her best to avoid it, but it was now one too many times over her patience limit.

"What's up, love? If you keep this up, you'll wake the *baby*."

Chris didn't need a lecture right now, especially one on ways to wake a newborn child.

"Sorry, Rach, but I'm worried about Sean. He's not spoken to me since I began my shift this morning."

"And?"

Her reply shocked Chris and it felt like she didn't care. But he knew she was unsure of why he hadn't spoken to Sean.

"I told you earlier that he wasn't at work when I got back from delivering the milk. Do you remember?"

"I thought you said he wasn't to be seen, not wasn't there."

"Well, Marie hasn't been in touch to let me know that he's arrived at the house yet..."

Rachael stared at him with the look of a green-eyed monster. She was jealous of Marie and had been since giving birth. Her lack of self-confidence and the fact she thought she looked like a fat hippo made her think Chris was more into Marie than her. Deep down she knew he wasn't, but Marie's name still got her blood boiling.

"...Stop looking at me like I've just fucked a nun!" Chris said. "I know that look. She was meant to pass on a message to Sean, that's all, but seeing as he's not got in touch I thought she would've."

"Message about what? How big your cock is?" Rachael was close to slapping him. "I know what she wants from you and so does that Sean..."

Chris smiled, but the smile was short-lived once he knew she was being serious.

"...Are you listening to me? I said that skunk bitch wants your dick inside her."

"So why did you mention Sean's name?" Chris said.

"Because he wants it too. That's why."

"Sean's not gay."

"Isn't he?" Rachael walked around the room. "Do you remember last Christmas?"

"Of course."

"Well, he was checking out your rump as you put the star on top of the tree."

Chris broke into a fit of laughter but stopped after realising *Rose* could wake up.

"Stop it! You're having me on."

"Am I?" Rachael walked over to the window. "I even overheard him telling someone that he wanted to fuck your poop-hole."

Chris wiped tears from his face. *Wow, this woman is a comedian all of a sudden.*

"Who was this someone?" He knew she was making everything up. He could tell. "See, you don't know, do you?"

Rachael admitted defeat. "Okay, so I made that bit up, but I'm not wrong about Marie. I know she likes you."

"Everyone likes me, but I like *you*." Chris now felt Rachael's paranoia lessen slightly. "I've liked you from the first moment I laid eyes on you. I wouldn't have had a child with you if I wanted someone else."

"Then you need to make sure she knows that too." Rachael put her hand on his mouth. "Promise me you'll tell her to back off."

Chris removed her hand. "Back off? She hasn't said or done anything for me to think she likes me, so please put your knives away..."

They heard Rose crying, and in a way, Chris was thankful because of it. He hoped Rachael would back down, but knew she was very tired and extremely stressed.

"...Why don't you get some sleep. I'll look after Rose."

He was very surprised to see Rachael agree so easily. For the past few weeks she'd been like a mama bear protecting her cub from the world whilst keeping everyone at arm's length from Rose, but today she was too tired to fight, and Chris could prove himself.

He followed Rachael into the bedroom, watching her slip off her shoes to get into bed before removing a wide-awake Rose from the cot in the corner. She watched as Chris nestled Rose into his arms, her wet nappy soaking his shirt to bring a giggle from Rachael. Chris stuck out his tongue as she got comfy in the bed, her eyes closing as he took the baby out of the room. He was going to take advantage of this rare father and daughter moment but first needed to change her nappy. He found it easier than how Rachael described it, with her version sounding more like disarming a bomb, but Chris knew it was because Rachael was trying to keep Rose with her. He entered the kitchen and prepared her feed before sitting down to cradle her in his arms, looking into her big blue eyes and smiling as her cute little mouth drank from the bottle. Chris felt relaxed; blessed to have such a beautiful and precious child in front of him. To him, she was a gift sent down from heaven. He thought he couldn't have children because of what the doctor told him after his motorbike accident, but here he was looking at a baby he had made with Rachael. Rose was a living miracle.

He lay her down on the sofa after her feed, sitting by her side while reaching for his phone before scrolling down and pressing Sean's number.

———

Inside the kitchen of the farmhouse, where four on-edge figures sat, a low sound of music was heard.

"Can you hear that?" Harvey whispered.

"I can," Louise whispered back.

Marie focused on the tune. "It sounds like Sean's phone." She got up off the floor and searched for it, finding it inside the living room to answer.

"Hey! Sean! Did you get my message about the sighting of a rodent in the cowshed?" Chris asked.

"It's Marie," She said, shivering. "Sean's gone missing."

Chris accused her of messing with him, but her tone never wavered. "Don't kid around. Where is he?"

Harvey had banned everyone from mentioning the rats as he didn't want to make the situation worse, so Marie was limited to the information she could pass on. But she knew that whatever she told Chris still meant Sean was missing. Rats or no rats.

"And you drove the tractor back?" Chris asked, frowning. To him, Marie was just the goofy nerd who tended the greenhouse, so he was surprised to hear it.

"Yes, I did."

"Wow! I'm very impressed," Chris said with excitement in his voice. "What did it feel like? Did you honk the horn?"

"Yeah! I honked the horn many times. It was awesome."

Those were the words Chris assumed were going to be said back to him, but what he received was different.

"Chris! Listen to me. Sean's not been seen since this morning. He's disappeared. You understand?"

Harvey arrived, holding out a hand for Marie to pass him the phone.

"Who's this?" he asked.

"It's Chris. I deliver the milk for Sean."

"And you called because of him?"

"Yeah! Marie just said he was missing."

"I wouldn't say missing, just misplaced." Harvey looked over at a still-shaking Marie, smiling at her before returning to Chris. "I don't want you to worry. I'm sure he's fine."

"Okay."

"But why did you want to speak to him?"

"It's nothing."

"Seriously, I need to know."

Chris felt stupid now but told Harvey about what he saw in the cowshed.

"I don't know if there was more than one, but I needed to let Sean know so he can secure the shed."

There was more than one, Harvey thought.

He told Chris he would be in touch if any news on Sean arrived, with Chris doing the same if he heard from him. Then Harvey disconnected.

At least now I have a rough timescale on how long the rats have been here, Harvey thought, looking at Marie again. "You hear that?"

"Hear what?" she replied.

"We are talking normally, not whispering, so why can't I hear those rats trying to get in...Can you hear them?"

"No," she replied, as they walked back to the others.

Harvey placed Sean's phone on the table as Jack and Louise waited for positive news.

"Right! I think the rats may have gone away, so I'm calling in some backup to get us out of here."

"Are you calling in the army?" Marie asked, frowning.

Harvey sniggered. "Nope! I'm calling in Adam Sayer." He sighed after seeing the faces of the officers. "But I think he'll be pissed off coming back to work so soon."

"You're going to ask *one* man to come to rescue us?" Marie shrugged.

"That's right, one man."

"But you've seen what those rats can do. We need people with guns and many of them!"

Harvey knew Marie was panicking to the point of screaming so needed to keep her as calm as possible.

"I know you feel let down, but what happened to those pest control guys happened. There's nothing we can do to change that." Harvey rubbed his chin. "But I can't wave the white flag so they bring in the army to save us when there's a good chance we can do the saving ourselves."

"This isn't the time to act like a stubborn moron. We need help and you know it."

Louise and Jack were on Marie's side over this, but Harvey wouldn't listen. He remained on course to do things his way, even if it *was* a suicidal one.

———

Adam's phone rang, disrupting his sleep. He tried his best to ignore it before placing it under his pillow, but, after the tenth ring, he tiredly picked it up.

"Hello?" he said, sounding worn out.

"It's Harvey..."

The tone of his voice slapped Adam around the face, waking him as quickly as if someone threw cold water over him.

"...I need your help."

"Help? Now?"

"Yes, now." Harvey looked at his watch. "Sorry, did I wake you?"

"No, I wasn't asleep. I don't need it," Adam said, cursing under his breath. *Of course, I need to sleep. I'm fuckin' dog-tired!*

"Good! That's what I like to hear. A sergeant capable of being on top of his job."

"What can I do for you?"

"I need you to go to the Riley farm, but you need to be careful."

"Careful. In what way?"

"Just trust me. And bring Brendan with you."

Harvey told Adam to wear riot gear, including a helmet, and to use a shield for protection in case of an ambush.

"I didn't even know we had those things," Adam said, shooting out of bed. "It's not like we've ever used them before."

"We *do* have them, and you and Brendan are using them today." Harvey peered through the kitchen blind, happy not to see a rodent. "When you get here, look out for rats."

"Rats? You have to be joking!"

"It's no joke. The rats from the university are here on the farm. Don't ask why, they just are. They've killed two people from pest control, so suit up."

"Holy shit!" Adam put the phone on speaker as he quickly dressed. "So, what are you suggesting? Did they escape? or were they taken from the lab?"

"I don't think that matters right now. All that matters is they are here, they are dangerous and they're stopping us from leaving the farmhouse." Harvey took another look through the window. "I can't see any outside, but I'm not risking leaving here so they can jump out on us. You got that?"

Adam understood everything. "I'm on my way. You just stay where you are."

"Very funny," Harvey replied.

He disconnected and looked at the others, knowing none were impressed with what he was trying to do. He watched them on the floor with their backs against the table, their vision burning into him. All they could do was wait.

CHAPTER THIRTEEN

John served a few more customers as the time drifted to *2:30 pm*, but the scratching sound had returned, leaving him thinking two things. One: excitement that the traps will catch the culprit, and two: worry that the customers will hear the scratching and tell others. He stayed as calm as he could as the latest customer approached the counter, watching the person stare past him. John waited for the person to confront him over the noise, but the customer just smiled and asked for a packet of cigarettes. John sighed, feeling thankful, but the customer stared past him again.

"What's going on back there?" the customer asked.

John sweated as he fumbled for a reply. "Nothing is going on."

The scratching was constant now, becoming a nuisance, as the customer ignored John to listen closely to the sound. John panicked, about to tell him the truth, but the person said, "Sounds like you've got birds nesting back there."

"Really? You may be right." John felt relieved.

He quickly handed over the cigarettes, took the payment, and waited for the customer to leave. But, as he walked back to the store entrance said, "You need to check it out before you get loads of chirpin' chicks."

John waved nervously as the person left before rushing to phone Peter again, cursing under his breath as he waited for him to answer.

"Tell Ted to get over here. They're back."

Before Peter could utter a word, John had put down the receiver. But, within minutes, as he placed the CLOSED sign on the shop door, he smiled at the familiar faces approaching, ushering the men inside before shutting it.

"Have you been inside the room?" Ted asked.

"Nope!"

"Then how do you know they're back?"

"Just listen," John replied, pointing towards the stockroom.

Ted did, and sure enough, the sound of rodents scratching proved John was right.

Ted walked towards the room, slowly opening the door, expecting to find the culprits behind the dead mice caught in the traps. But his face dropped after seeing none had been touched.

"...You okay?" John asked, closing in on him.

Ted nervously faced him as he placed up a thumb, slowly stepping inside the room to close the door to stop John from witnessing the sad news.

"You fancy a cuppa?" John asked Peter.

"You sure know how to charm a guy." Peter laughed as he walked towards the kitchen.

Ted stared at the traps as he paced angrily around the room.

You may have won this time, you fucks, but it's not going to stop me from finding out where you are.

He opened his bag and took out the more traditional type

of trap that snaps on its victim. He knew he was meant to not harm the rodents, especially if they were rats, but, without evidence of there ever being any, he decided to get nasty. He kicked one of his new traps, cursing as he lay down the smaller, wooden ones, cringing as he removed a torch from the bag. He turned it on to hover the light over the hole in the wall as a faint scratching noise confirmed the creature's whereabouts before smiling and sinking to his knees, shuffling closer to see the torchlight suck inside it. But he struggled to see what was behind the wall because the hole was too small. He reached into his jacket pocket to retrieve a small mirror before inserting it inside, lying on his belly with one hand holding it while the other held the torch. He angled the mirror but couldn't see a rodent before angling it again to find rat droppings nearby. He smiled once more, knowing now that something larger than field mice had been inside the store. He breathed deeply and remained in position.

John and Peter listened out for Ted, but he was silent.

"Do you think he's forgiven you for the past?"

John rubbed his chin. "Nope. I just think he's being nice. You know what Ted's like better than anyone. He's just being his usual, nice self."

"Yep! My thoughts exactly. But at least he's here now."

Ted angled the mirror again, shivering unexpectedly after catching a glimpse of fur disappearing into the wall to his left. He got up and rushed over to it but was blocked by a stand-up unit, so cursed under his breath again as he removed boxes from the bottom shelf. But, after he pulled away the final box was happy to see another access point, the hole large enough to fit his hand inside. He picked up the trap and got back into position, holding the mirror as he placed his hand inside the hole whilst gently laying some food on the trap. But, as he slowly put it inside, YELPED after something bit him.

"Fuck! Fuck! Fuck!" he shouted, jumping back from the shock to stare at teeth marks embedded into his bleeding hand.

The other men raced into the room to find him sweating.

"What happened?" John asked.

"I've been bitten by something," Ted replied, squirming as he wrapped tissue paper around the cut. "That's what happened!"

Peter laughed. "I thought you were a pro at this?"

Ted laughed back. "I am! This is the first time I've been bitten by a rodent."

"Yeah! Yeah! Yeah!" Peter replied, unconvinced by the words.

"Did you see what bit you?" John asked.

Ted pointed at the hole behind the unit. "How long's it been like that?"

"I don't know," John replied, surprised by the size of it. "The boxes haven't been touched for a few months, so it could've been there for that long."

"Whoops!"

"Why whoops?"

John hoped Ted wasn't questioning his health and safety. He knew it was a serious issue but he honestly didn't know how long the hole had been there.

"I said whoops because if it's been there for months then you could well have a family of vermin living inside the wall cavity of your store. Not a good thing for you."

"You're right. It's not a good thing, not a good thing at all..."

Ted stared at the hole in the hope that the mystery biter would show itself. It didn't, but that didn't mean it wasn't still there.

"...Do you want me to fetch the first aid kit?" John asked.

Ted removed the tissue. "Nah! It's okay. I'll pop to the hospital for a tetanus jab after I catch the little shit! ...A plaster will do for now. I have some in my bag."

"Okay. We'll leave you to it then."

"Nice one, John."

Ted watched the others leave the room before returning to his bag to fetch a plaster, his face red with rage as he glared at the hole. But nothing was seen as he placed the plaster over the wound. He shook his head and got back into position, trying to ignore the blood seeping through to drip onto the floor as his nerves took over.

Get yourself together. It's only a rodent!

He shone the torch back inside the hole as he reached in to retrieve the mirror, but a large rodent sprung out to attack his face, snapping teeth down on his nose to bite off the tip. Ted shouted in agony as he pressed the tissue paper onto the wound, but the blood gushed through it to slide down his chin, soaking his clothing as it landed on the floor. He glared at the rat as it landed nearby but his vision blurred quickly as painful tears streamed down his face. He felt faint as the now blood-soaked paper fell onto the puddle of blood, the image of the rat watching him causing him to freak out as he remained struggling to see. He rubbed his other hand over his eyes to gain more vision, but the rat's size shocked him, causing him to sigh after seeing its damaged ear. He was amazed by its courage. It didn't seem frightened by him at all as it sat covered in filth, blinking as it licked the red juice from around its mouth.

Ted was in awe of the rat.

He was in extreme pain but didn't scream upon spitting out blood and returning to his bag, grabbing more tissue paper to feel it soak quickly once placed on his nose. He dropped it to do the same routine several times, as the rat gathered the bitten-off piece to eat in front of him, twitching its whiskers as each blood-filled tissue fell before squeaking so loud to confuse him. But, as he held the latest tissue against his nose, nine more rats raced from the hole to jump him, and this time he screamed. His hands shook as he tried pushing them off, but they bit him before he had a chance to break free.

The large rat watched on as the others clawed at Ted before it suddenly lunged at his privates, biting hard into one of his testicles to make him scream louder.

"What the f--?!" John cried out, entering the room to see a rat aim for him.

But Peter grabbed it and threw it against a wall before sighing as it attempted another attack.

Ted frantically tugged at a rat on his chest, as the one biting his testicle made him cringe, leaving him struggling as Peter rushed over to help. He tried pulling the rats from Ted, but every time he grabbed one, another would snap out, forcing him to let go. He watched on in fear as Ted's face was ripped open.

John kicked at the rat that still wanted to attack him. He swerved after it lunged at him again before reaching for the broom that was in the corner, swinging the broom head at it to catch it cleanly in the face. But he knew it was only dazed as he stared at it rolling around on the floor. He moved in to finish it off but he couldn't do it.

"Peter, we need to get out of here!" he shouted, wanting out of the room.

"Not without Ted I'm not," the reply came, as Peter angrily fought with the rats.

John swung the broom again, kicking his way through the rodents to reach Ted, grabbing his arm swiftly as Peter punched the rats still attached to his body. But they hissed at him as the large rat released its grip on the testicle. It dropped to the floor squealing until the others jumped from Ted to line up next to it, leaving John and Peter looking on in shock. They grabbed onto Ted but his legs were weak, so, they carried him to the door, with John opening it at speed as they rushed him out of the room covered in blood. But the rats appeared in front of them.

They must've found a route through the wall, John thought.

They closed in on the terrified men with bloodlust in their eyes, but John and Peter weren't going to let them take Ted without a fight.

"Get inside there!" John cried out, pointing toward the kitchen.

It was a tight squeeze to fit all three men inside the room, especially when one was spread out on the floor, but it was accomplished before the rats struck, with John kicking the door shut on the large rat as it lunged.

"You do know they'll get in here too," Peter said.

"Then we'll just have to stop them," John emotionally replied.

They trembled as they looked down at Ted, cringing as the floor tiles changed from white to red, John grabbing some kitchen towel. He needed to plug up the holes but had a feeling it would take more to stop the blood from escaping, knowing if help didn't arrive soon then Ted would die.

CHAPTER FOURTEEN

Another police car arrived on the outskirts of the Riley farm, coming to a stop at the main gate. Adam and Brendan sat in the front seats, both unsure of what to expect, but eager to help in any way they could. Adam didn't need to ask Brendan twice for him to go with him; the rat speech had him hooked. But it was the chance to rescue the woman he loved that made his heart beat faster right now.

Adam observed the chaos through a pair of binoculars before concentrating on the police cars and the pest control van, his face showing many emotions as the binoculars went from left to right. But it was the evidence of Harvey's close encounter with the milk float that made him nervously gulp. He looked over at Brendan, passing him the binoculars to stop his boredom.

"Was Harvey drunk when he smashed into it?" Brendan asked, confused at what he saw.

"I told you already; some rats attacked him. That's why he crashed the car."

"Oh yeah!" Brendan moved the binoculars from side to side. "But where are the rats he mentioned?"

"That's where *we* come in. We must find out where they are. Harvey said they weren't near the front of the house when he phoned me, so they could be close by. The question is *how* close?"

'How close' wasn't what Brendan wanted to hear, but the words - I can't see them so let's get the hell out of here - were.

"Are you saying we have to go down there to find out?" he asked, pointing towards the damaged car.

"No! You can stay here if you want, read a comic or play on your I-phone. But I've got a job to do. Harvey, Louise, and Jack are stuck in that house waiting for us to let them out." Adam smiled at Brendan. "Oh yeah, and that woman you fancy is there as well."

"No! I don't fancy her." Brendan blushed.

Adam nudged him. "So, let's leave *her* there and just rescue our team."

"What? We can't leave her there with those rats."

"Why not? You don't like her, and think there aren't any rats anyway, so why act worried about them now?" Adam watched Brendan lose it inside, his words had him utterly confused. "I'm just messing with you. Of course, we're going to rescue your sweetheart."

Brendan punched him in the arm. "Shut up!" he shouted, still blushing.

They exited the car and stared at the main gate, sighing upon seeing the distance between that and the house. Adam knew there were many hiding places for the rats, especially where the vehicles were, so told Brendan to be on full alert. He walked to the back of the car and opened the boot, leaving Brendan sadly staring at the protective police uniform.

"I can't wear that. I'll look stupid!"

"This isn't a fashion show, you need to wear it." Adam gave Brendan a helmet. "I don't want anything to happen to you."

Brendan wasn't used to seeing his uncle's angry side. Adam was usually a placid and humorous character but Brendan knew he was only looking out for his welfare. He stopped moaning and grabbed a uniform, placing his feet inside before pulling it up to his chest, but he still felt stupid. To him, it looked like he was wearing a costume ideally used for those fun nights out, the dark-coloured, padded suit making him look a bit like Batman. But he didn't see it like he was a superhero. All he saw was an image of Marie laughing at him for looking silly.

Adam watched on as Brendan zipped it up. "Now grab your shield, release your baton and wait for me to do the same." He put on his suit as Brendan looked through the binoculars again. "See anything?"

"Nope! Just fields, vehicles, the farmhouse, and cows."

Adam sniggered. "Doesn't mean the vermin has gone, so put on your helmet and pick up your shield."

He watched Brendan do it before finally doing the same.

"Why don't we just drive up to the farmhouse?" Brendan asked as they walked towards the gate.

"Because I don't want another incident like what Harvey had." Adam raised his shield. "This way we get to see them more clearly."

"That's if they're still here."

Adam nudged Brendan upon reaching the gate, pleased to find no sign of the rats. They headed down to the vehicles, the quietness causing their skin to crawl as a pair of legs were seen next to the pest control van. A few steps later and the tortured bodies were witnessed, leaving Brendan to kneel and vomit. Adam looked away after seeing the faceless men, concern over his and Brendan's safety rushing to his mind. He stared in horror at the house as Brendan returned to his feet, wiping vomit stains from his mouth.

Adam shook him. "Are you okay?"

"I've got to be," Brendan replied, raising his shield as if an invisible enemy was coming.

Adam heard the cows mooing frantically as if something had disturbed them, so raced towards the shed to investigate.

This isn't right. They shouldn't be smacking into each other like this.

He saw a cow whack its hind legs against the wooden shed, its face filled with fear. He tried to calm it down, but it wasn't working, the cow's scared vision locking onto him as it bashed its legs over and over. Adam saw the shed weaken until a panel gave way, the sight worrying him because the cow could create an escape route if it didn't stop.

Brendan caught up with him to witness a rat running beneath the cow; a challenge to scare it off now feeding his ego. He climbed on the wall that separated the top and bottom parts of the shed but slipped over the side into a pile of cow dung.

"Fuck! Fuck! Fuck!" he shouted.

Adam saw him kick out at the darting rat as the dung stuck to the bottom of Brendan's boots flung in his direction. But Adam just ignored it.

The cow quietened down to stop kicking the shed, but two panels had now split before Brendan's craziness forced the rat to hide in a pile of hay.

"Did you get it?!" Adam shouted.

"Nope! But I scared it off."

Adam lowered his visor and scanned the shed, but no rats were seen.

"Lower yours too, then help me find something to block

up the hole before we have more than a *few* rats to round up..."

Brendan wasn't stupid, he knew if the cows were spooked again then they could smash out of the shed and stampede away from the farm to possibly cause a traffic accident, so he searched for something quickly, finding a wooden pallet before dragging it over to the hole. Adam was pleased that he was taking it seriously. He smiled as Brendan pushed the pallet against the broken panels before climbing back over the wall again.

"...Right, let's get to the others. I'm calling Harvey to let him know," Adam said.

———

Nerves had reached a boiling point for Louise and Marie, but Harvey remained as calm as he could, keeping a close watch on the outside. There was still no sign of the rampaging rats, but he stayed grounded, not risking walking out until Adam had given the all-clear.

He reached into his pocket and answered his phone. "Where are you?"

"We're by the cowshed, so pretty close."

"Have you seen any of the little monsters?"

"Just one inside the shed."

"They're cunning, so don't let your guard down." Harvey peered over at the women who were now frantically shouting. "Jack! Sort them out. They're starting to annoy me. Can't they see I'm talking to Adam?..."

He sighed as a tired-looking Jack tried to quench the situation.

"...You are wearing the protective gear?" Harvey said to Adam.

"Yep! We're both padded up."

"Then come get us."

Harvey finished the call before rushing over to help Jack.

"I can't stay here any longer!" Marie screamed, running into the living room crying.

Harvey chased after her as Louise sucked her bottom lip. She wasn't panicked like Marie was, but being stuck inside a stranger's house was annoying for her.

"Jack, I need to get out as well."

He held Louise's arms. "Hey, it's nearly over. Adam's just outside. He'll be here soon. We can remove the table from the door and go home."

Jack was grateful for his nurse training, as his soothing tone and kind words helped calm the situation.

"Sorry," Louise said, smiling in appreciation at the effort Jack made.

He smiled back as she took a breath.

———

Adam and Brendan cautiously walked away from the cowshed, but their nervous breathing steamed up the visors to prevent them from seeing properly. They aimed towards the front of the house, wiping the steam away from their visors, but frenzied moaning sounds halted their movement to leave them staring towards the damaged vehicles.

"What's that?" Brendan asked; his tone jumpy after seeing rats feeding on the dead pest control men again.

"Shit!" Adam shouted.

They were *so* close to running away and hiding somewhere, knowing that if the rats saw them they would be next on their list, but another twenty rodents raced from underneath the hay in the shed, and like a burgeoning tsunami, slammed into them to almost overpowering them. If it were not for the shields, the vicious rodents would have succeeded too. Adam and Brendan swung their batons aggressively, but the rats kept attacking, trying to find a way past the shields. Adam's eyes bulged in horror as the ones eating the men stopped to run at him. Stunned with fear, he became helpless as they clung to his suit to scale up his shaking legs, but he lashed out at them, knocking them back to the ground.

"...We need to get to the house!" he shouted.

"But what if they get in?" Brendan yelled back, slamming his baton against a rat.

"We have to hope they don't."

A rat clung to Adam's visor to scare him, but it was quickly pushed off to fall to the ground before pouncing on him again. Adam felt thankful towards Harvey for the heads up on the protective gear because none of the rats had been able to penetrate it, as he and Brendan wildly swung their batons and shields. But, even though they were stopping the rats from clinging to them, they were struggling to keep up the tempo. More and more of the rodents were reaching their helmets now, climbing on to snap teeth at the thick, plastic visors to make it almost impossible for them to see anything.

A trail of injured and killed rats lay on the ground as the men, still with some hanging from their visors, moved closer to the door leading to the kitchen. They were shattered once reaching it, as another frantic effort was made to rid the ones from their helmets. Adam hit the last rat *so* hard off Brendan's visor that it smacked against the door, causing Louise to jump as blood and brain matter slid down the glass.

"Chief inspector!" she shouted, looking out of the window.

"What's up?" Harvey replied, rushing into the kitchen.

Even though Louise was still shaken up from hearing the bang against the glass, she almost smiled after remembering what Brendan's response was to the same question from earlier that day. But she regained her focus and said, "Adam's outside, and so are those pains in the ass."

Harvey raced to the kitchen door. "Move the table!"

Jack helped Louise remove it while Harvey stood by the door, holding his taser as he slowly opened it.

"...Get inside!" He shouted towards Adam and Brendan.

A rat sprung at him, but the taser zapped it before it got close. Louise and Jack rushed to the doorstep, swinging their batons like they were swatting flies, as the attacked men threw themselves across the floor, but Brendan's adrenalin prevented him from seeing a rat still clinging to him. It bit into his leg, forcing him to look down from the intense sharp pain before gritting his teeth as a kitchen knife slammed into the rat's body. He slowly looked up to see a tearful Marie holding the blood-dripping knife.

"Thank you," he whispered, cringing as the rat fell to the floor.

He returned to his feet and removed his helmet before hugging Marie, as the others replaced the table against the door; all hearing the rodents scratching and biting it to fear the worst. They knew it was only a matter of time before the terrifying creatures penetrated the door to get inside.

Marie dropped the knife and pinched her nose. "Wooooohhhheeee!" she shouted. "What's that *smell?*"

Everyone sniffed the air before staring sickly at Brendan's uniform and boots.

"Come on people, it's only a bit of cow shit," he said.

"Go and clean that off!" Harvey demanded; his tone causing Brendan to feel embarrassed again.

He walked over to the sink and grabbed some kitchen roll,

wiping the muck from his clothing before removing his boots to wash what was stuck to them down the drain. Harvey took a binbag from a cupboard to kick the dead rat into before Brendan dropped the cow shit pieces of roll on top, but Harvey grunted at him as he closed the bag. He left the room and walked up the stairs, opening a bedroom window to throw the bag out, but seconds later something intense caught his eye. He witnessed something he'd never witnessed before; the rats were burying their dead in the dirt!

They're acting as if they're soldiers, he thought. *It's like they're burying the fallen heroes from a battle. It's so weird!*

He closed the window and headed back to the others, but his phone rang on his way down the stairs. It was a message from the station, saying there'd been an incident in town. A man was attacked by rats. Harvey felt useless because all his officers were with him. He never wanted to call in help from another police department but now had no choice. He ended the call as he reached the kitchen.

"Is everything okay?" Jack asked.

"Nope!" Harvey replied, rushing over to a window. "More rats have attacked a man from the local store. We need help, and we need it quick."

He looked at the others in turn, seeing Brendan standing next to a tearful Marie, Adam by the kitchen sink, with his helmet resting on the work surface, and Louise walking miserably up and down the room. They were unable to help the injured man in the store. It was futile, Harvey knew that, but he didn't want to believe it.

CHAPTER FIFTEEN

John and Peter stayed close to Ted like they were guarding him against an invisible evil. He remained on the floor covered in blood, but the bites to his face, body and private parts were too deep for the makeshift first-aid to work. John sighed, nervously checking his watch to find it was just after three.

"Can you hear them?"

"No, John, I can't," Peter whispered.

"Do you think they've gone?"

"No. Why would they?" Peter brushed a hand over his face. "Holy shit!" he shouted.

"What?"

"Did you lock the store?"

John stared hard, almost bursting into tears. "No! Do you think someone's inside?"

"I don't know, but the rats don't seem to be outside the door now." Peter stared at it. "Maybe they've found someone else to attack?"

"I put the 'closed' sign on."

"But you never locked it," Peter bluntly said.

John didn't need reminding again. "I know, but I wasn't expecting this to happen." He looked down at Ted before saying, "You need to find out."

"I'm not going out there," Peter replied, sweating from the thought. "It could be a trap."

"A trap?" John angrily snapped. "Do you think they're that clever?"

Peter felt foolish as the nerves got to him. "All I know is, they've been inside a laboratory for years so shouldn't be wild, but they are." He too looked at Ted. "So, what happened at the lab for them to be like this? To do that to Ted? They could've developed skills unknown to us, and those skills could've included thinking."

John didn't argue. "This isn't right. We shouldn't be scared of a few rats," he said, glancing at Ted again. "But if they *can* do that to him then they can rip into us as well."

They prayed that no one was visiting the store, but their prayers weren't answered because someone was now inside.

"Hello, John, where are you?" a female customer shouted.

"Get out of the store. Get out NOW!" John screamed back.

But the woman thought he was joking. "Shut up! Get out here so I can give you some money."

She heard scratching coming from one of the aisles, intriguing her to know more, so moved towards it, but three rats ran across the counter to grab her attention. She jumped back as the sight of their dirt-covered bodies shocked her senses, but she didn't fear them, she was just curious to know why they were there.

"Yuk!" she said, pinching her nose. "You guys need a good wash. You smell like a sewer…"

She became sucked in by their calmness.

"…Since when have you been selling rats?" she shouted, as a sharp pain ripped at her calf.

She cringed as the large rat dug its claws into her again, the sight of it frightening her as it climbed up her body. She became frantic, turning to run away, but the rat sunk its teeth into the top of her head. She felt the blood slide down her face, the wound stinging, causing her to scream before running around the store to the shouts of "Get out!" coming from the trapped men, but their constant banging on the door to attract the rats came to nothing. They chased the woman, deliberately running beneath her feet until tripping her over, leaving her head to sound like a hammer slamming down at an auction as it crashed against the side of the counter. She wasn't moving as John, and Peter listened closely, but the silence frightened them to bang some more.

"Do you think she escaped?"

"Peter, only time will tell. If we hear the sound of helpers then she got away." John gulped. "But if not then we need to be ready for when the rats come for us."

"Call the police again," Peter said.

John wiped blood-soaked hands over his trousers before reaching for his phone. "Fuck! The battery is low."

"How low?"

"Very low."

Peter watched him call the station again as they waited for the battery to die; their eyes narrowing, anticipating its demise. The receptionist transferred the call to Harvey's phone as the battery symbol flashed, leaving both men thankful to hear someone on the other end.

"Hello!" Harvey said.

"My phone's dying so I have to be quick. I need someone at my store!"

"Is this you, John?"

"Yes," John sighed with relief. "Just get here soon."

"I can't get to you right now," Harvey awkwardly said.

"Why not?" John snapped, as his face raged with anger.

"Because I'm trapped in the Riley farmhouse. That's why."

"Then send someone else."

"I can't. All my staff are here."

John told Peter the news, but Peter fumingly reached out to grab the phone.

"We have an injured friend here," he raced out of his mouth, staring at the battery life to see it was almost invisible. "Just send someone before we're attacked!"

"My advice is to just hold tight. I'm working on it."

Peter sighed. "Are you havin' a laugh? Hold tight? What do you think we were going to do? Invite the rats in for a party?"

"I'm not laughing. It's the same for us here, but……"

The phone went silent as Peter shook his head. He turned to John as the scratching noise returned, but this time it was more rapid.

"Fuck! John, they're trying to get in!"

"We need to be ready for them. Just breathe and don't let me down."

Peter took a deep breath. "Have you got anything in here that we can use as a weapon?"

"The extinguisher."

Peter ripped it off the wall bracket and held it firmly.

"What am *I* going to use?" John asked, worried.

Peter glanced around the room. "You can use the wooden spoon that's on the draining board."

John looked at it, feeling unimpressed at how useful it could be, but, after hearing Peter crack a nervous laugh, he did the same.

"Screw that!" John rushed to the cutlery drawer as the

rats squealed, pulling it open to grab two knives. "These will do."

He slammed the drawer shut and stared impatiently at the door. Peter did the same, knowing that soon a rat's head will break through.

Ted stirred, waking up to extreme pain rushing through his body. He tried to move but screamed and coughed up blood before touching his face and screaming again, shivering at the sight of so much gore. John went over to comfort him, sitting next to him to wrap an arm around his shoulders, but Ted cried after resting his head on John's arm before coughing up more blood as the pain became more relentless.

This was my fault, thought Peter, fighting back tears.

He rubbed his eyes as he stared back at the door, angry with himself for Ted's pain; the moment when the men finally pushed aside their differences, when they became true friends again was not meant to be like this, in this situation. He turned back to see John cradling Ted, his clothes darkened with blood.

The door started to shake to leave a nervous Peter holding the extinguisher above his head as John closed his eyes.

"You stay with Ted. I've got this covered," Peter said, smiling nervously at the sound of his heart racing.

The door shook faster and louder as the rats' aggression to get inside the room intensified. They scratched, bit, and tore wood from the door, hungry for flesh! Heads banging together in their wild hunt.

Peter stared at the door with sweat dripping from his nose, splashing to the floor like exploding balloon bombs as time seemed to slow down. But suddenly a hole appeared at the bottom of the door.

"Get off the floor and arm yourselves!" he shouted.

"But Ted's too weak."

Peter glanced at John. "Then you need to be his bodyguard."

John gulped hard. "I will!"

Ted shuffled along the floor to crawl into the space underneath the kitchen sink, sitting with his knees raised to his chest as his heart bounced around inside him. He was close to crying after spotting the blood trail he'd made as John stood up again, but his knees weakened as he gripped the knives tight. He looked over at Peter, but he remained solid, the only sound heard was his heavy breathing as a rat bit at the hole.

"It's now time!" Peter shouted, slamming the extinguisher down on the rat's head as it appeared.

But its eyeballs popped from their sockets to land a few feet away from Ted, leaving him puking as the dead rat was moved aside by others entering the room. But their speed caught Peter off guard and he wasn't able to land another death blow. One jumped at John, narrowly missing him as he lashed at it with the knife, but, as it landed, it jumped at him again, landing on his thigh. He quickly elbowed it off but squirmed as another rat sunk its nails into his calf.

Ted cowered into a ball to cover his bites, but the smell of his blood sent the rats into a craze. They closed in on him, hovering with their mouths wide open.

Peter kicked out to stop more rats from getting inside, but seven were now in the room before the extinguisher blocked up the hole. He saw John fight with two of them as the remaining five viciously bit into Ted; his body too weak to fight back as his moans echoed around the room.

"John, are you okay?!" Peter shouted, racing past him to be stopped by a rat.

But John never replied.

Peter swung a foot at the rodent and kicked it against the wall, but it shook it off and snarled at him.

Fuck! he agonisingly thought as John handed him a knife.

He was quick to stick it into the rat's ribcage, dropping it to the floor as the other one raced up John's body. It aimed for his neck, but he thrust his knife into its mouth to leave it falling next to the other one before rushing to help Ted, as the remaining rats hissed at him.

"He's going to die if we don't save him!" he cried out.

"Then let's save him!"

They watched Ted struggle to stop a rat from biting his face again, his screams rocking them as tears flowed before Ted sadly stared into space.

"Fuckin' wet the floor. And do it now!" he yelled, cringing in agony as blood poured from the recent wound.

The rats attacked him again, biting into two fingers to leave them hanging from the joints as his words slowly sunk in. But, as Peter rushed to fill a bowl with water, John kept trying to rescue Ted. He was struggling to agree with what Ted wanted.

"John, do what I ask...Please!" Ted screamed at him.

John gulped as Peter threw the water over the rats on Ted, but they hissed again to scare him. The men watched Ted slowly point at the toaster, but a rat bit off his damaged fingers to leave him sobbing loudly. He pleaded with the others, but John squirmed and shook his head.

"What are you doing?" he shouted, as Peter reached for the toaster.

"I'm doing what needs to be done."

Peter unplugged it and slid it over to Ted before grabbing John firmly to pull him onto a work surface, but the extinguisher shook and toppled over as two more rats raced inside. They aimed for Ted to make his eyes bulge, as he wearily pulled the toaster towards him, waiting until they were on top of him before plugging it into a nearby wall socket. But one of the rats halted and ran back through the hole as Peter held back tears to fill the bowl again. He stared sadly as Ted clutched the toaster against his chest before throwing the water over him to see him welcome it as it splashed him, the rats shaking to die as Ted's head lowered. But the smell of burning flesh almost caused the men to vomit.

CHAPTER SIXTEEN

Harvey ordered the others to patrol different parts of the farmhouse, with Louise and Jack staying in the kitchen, Marie, and Adam in the living room, while he patrolled the upstairs with Brendan. Everyone stood nervously next to the windows, searching for a sign of the rats.

"I see you have an admirer," Adam said to Marie.

"Who's that then?" she replied, shaking.

She knew he was just trying to keep her calm, so any distraction was welcome.

"You must know who it is?" Adam smiled, but the smile worried Marie because it made it seem like it was *he* who liked her.

"I don't want to sound ungrateful, but you're a bit old for me."

Adam burst out laughing. "It's not me, it's Brendan."

"Oh!" Marie laughed back. "Really?"

Before her rescue attempt with the knife and the hug from Brendan, she wouldn't have guessed it to be true. But that moment changed the way she looked at him. It may have been because she felt terrified and didn't know what would happen, but that hug switched on a light inside her heart.

Adam nudged her. "You like him as well. I can tell."

Marie sucked her lips. "Shouldn't we be looking for rats?"

The rat word stopped all efforts at Adam's attempt at playing cupid. "You're right. Sorry!"

But Marie smiled to give him the answer he waited for.

Jack watched Louise closely, knowing she was about to lose it again. He knew the signs well now with her. She bowed her head and muttered to herself like she was two people, as her constant pacing up and down the room worried him.

"You okay, Lou?" he said, holding out a hand to stop her.

But she wasn't listening.

"...Hey, come back to the window. Some of the rats are moving away. They may be leaving," Jack said.

Louise stopped pacing and looked at him. "I hope they're going back to the lab so we can leave here. I'm pissed off being stuck indoors." She carried on pacing but stopped within seconds. "You know me, Jack, I can't do this. I can't stay here. I need to get out!"

Jack laughed nervously at her pleading attempt to let her outside, knowing from staring into her eyes that she was losing control. Her emotions changed swiftly, and it spooked him.

"...I've got to get out!" Louise screamed, racing towards the kitchen table to pull on one of the legs.

"Louise, NO!" Jack tried stopping her from pulling on the leg, but it was futile. No matter how authoritative his tone nothing was going to stand in her way of freedom.

She aggressively pushed him away before removing the table, watching him mime the word 'No' as she opened the door to disappear.

"What happened?" Adam shouted, rushing into the kitchen.

"Louise went crazy and went outside. That's what happened."

Adam aimed for the door in the hope of seeing her, but the only thing catching his eye was a dozen screeching rats racing towards him. He panicked and slammed the door shut.

"I can't see her!" he cried out, staring hard at Jack as they put the table back. "What did you say to her?"

"Nothing! She just flipped and ran outside."

Adam sighed before leaving the room to stand at the bottom of the staircase. "Harvey! Can you see Louise from where you are?" he shouted.

"No! She's not up here."

"She's running to the side of the house!" shouted Brendan. "Why is she outside?"

"There's no time to work out why. We just need to rescue her!" Adam shouted back.

Brendan placed on his helmet, grabbed his shield, and opened a bedroom window. He saw the conservatory extension below, the drop to it only a few feet, so climbed out of the window to stand on the edge; shaking as he walked along the ledge to see the glass roof inches from his boots. He knew he couldn't risk sliding down the glass in case it broke from his weight, so, as Harvey glared at him in disapproval, reached the end and climbed down the side to land on the ground.

"Your fuckin' nephew has gone after her!" Harvey yelled out to Adam.

Marie overheard, and her heart skipped a beat.

———

Louise had been lucky so far, no rats had found her, and none were nearby. But she knew how quickly that could change. She heard Brendan shout out to her, the words muffled because his visor was down. She looked for him but shuddered after reality slapped her in the face; her mind mentally kicking her for making the stupid decision of leaving the house before almost stopping in her tracks.

She saw an old outhouse nearby with the word 'toilet' scribbled on it. It was only a few feet in width and six in length, but she knew it would do to hide inside until coming up with a plan on how to escape the farm without the rats reaching her. She moved slowly towards it, her vision darting from left to right as the terrible stench of dampness and faeces almost knocked her off her feet. She held her nose and opened the door, stepping inside to see a few rats running towards the house, but she avoided staring at the toilet, knowing the reason behind most of the horrid stench was probably still there. She peered over the top of the door, hoping that the smell would distract the rats.

Brendan's face burned with rage as he too avoided them, but his search was coming to nothing.

"Louise!" he shouted again. "Where are you?"

He waited for the coast to clear before racing towards the cowshed again. It was the only place he could think of to find Louise, but she was now cowering behind the outhouse door like she was playing a dangerous game of hide-and-seek. Brendan prepared himself to battle the rats, holding his shield and baton like a warrior upon reaching the shed. He took a deep breath and looked around him, spotting the outhouse in the distance upon listening to the cows 'moo', feeling pleased because it meant no rats were disturbing them. He climbed over the wooden wall and approached a cow.

"It's okay, girl," he whispered, patting it as he walked past. "I won't hurt you."

He searched behind a pile of hay whilst calling out Louise's name again, but his shouting spooked the cows more than the rats did.

Where are you? he thought, exiting the shed.

But Louise remained where she was as curiosity overtook her.

Why has he stopped shouting my name? she thought, standing up again to open the door, her face wet with perspiration as she surveyed the yard.

She couldn't see him but did see the milk float, its height making her decision to climb it. She raced towards it, jumping onto Harvey's car before leaping onto the float, but the sound was heard by the rats and they ran in her direction. She sat on top of it, resting against the metal bars that surrounded the crates to watch the rats below stare up at her like she was their next kill.

Brendan heard her shouting as she tried scaring them away, but he was now more annoyed with her than before. He raced towards her, but the sight of the rats stopped him, so lifted his visor and shouted, "What the *fuck* are you doing?!"

Louise stood up after the rats stayed on the ground, her adrenaline buzzing to bring out her crazy side as Brendan glared at her. He knew she was in extreme danger, so had to rescue her before she turned the terrifying event into a circus.

"This is fun!" Louise shouted back, but her words rattled the rats into action and they began to climb the float.

And Brendan looked on horrified as they raced amongst the milk crates.

"Louise, you need to get back inside the house. It's dangerous out here!"

He knew the more he spoke, the quicker it would be for

the rats to give up on Louise and aim for him, so shouted again to attract their attention, knowing he felt safe in his padded outfit.

The rats glared at him, but Louise was too pumped up to let him deal with them alone. She felt free like she did before joining the police force, back when she was a bit of a wild child. She was well known in town for her anti-social behaviour, and from the age of twelve-to-seventeen had been in more trouble than most kids of the same age. Many times, the judge had threatened to send her to a young offender's prison because of her stupid antics, but she mellowed after working at the strip club. She felt the burn to act all crazy again, not caring for her or Brendan's safety as she stomped her feet on top of the float.

"Brendan! It's okay. They won't hurt us!"

He never replied but found it hard to ignore her. He scowled at her and lowered his visor, charging the rats to the sound of her laughter, seeing her dance as he rammed his shield into a dozen of them before squashing two against the metal shell of the float.

"Get down off there!" he hollered, swinging his baton.

The chaos unfolding below now shook Louise's confidence, leaving her worried as rats pounced on Brendan. But, after he crashed into the float to shake them off, she almost fell off.

"I can't get down. There's too many of them," she said, shaking nervously.

Brendan hit some of the rats so hard that it drained his energy. He watched them die before being set upon by others, their evilness to get him making him think they knew he was tiring.

Louise saw a rat cling to the top of his helmet, its teeth

grinding against it as it tried to bite, so reached out a leg to kick it, but sighed after not being able to reach it.

"...I'm coming down, so steer them away from the float."

Brendan gulped as he found his second wind to run away, raising a smile as the hungry vermin chased him before Louise carefully climbed down. But a rat sprung from one of the crates to sink teeth into her thigh. She winced but didn't yell, knowing that would attract more of them, so slapped a hand against its head until it fell to the ground. She hobbled and removed her baton, ready to strike it, but the rat slipped underneath the float and ran away. She looked at Brendan swinging like a madman, as his arms and legs lashed out at the rodents, knowing just how lucky he was to be wearing the protective suit. But the pain in her leg exacerbated the nightmare as more rats raced from the field. She knew the blood from her wound was the reason, but she was struggling to stop it from pouring out. She closed her eyes as they aimed for her; her heart beating fast as thoughts of them reaching her made her shiver.

But Adam arrived, tasering two before they could.

Louise opened her eyes again as the rats lay stunned on the ground, the sound of their heads splitting beneath Adam's boots convincing her to get back to the house. He watched her near it before racing off to help Brendan, but he was unable to avoid some of the rats from racing past him. Louise grimaced as she reached the door, the rats gaining on her, ready to pounce, but it opened just in time and she was rescued before closing swiftly to the sound of squeals making everyone's hairs stand on end.

Adam reached Brendan and gripped his shoulder. "Let's get you inside."

Everyone from inside the house watched on in hope before banging on windows to stifle the rats, as the men kicked out at the creatures trying to grab onto them. Some became confused about which direction to take, but the others remained attacking, clinging on to slow the men down with their weight. It took an increased amount of effort to reach the house, but more rats blocked their path as they neared the door.

"We have to charge them!" Adam shouted, pulling a few off Brendan.

"They're pissing me off!" Brendan yelled, doing the same before throwing a rat to the ground.

They raced at the ones by the door, causing them to scatter towards the field, but Adam wasn't convinced they had given up as he banged on the door. Brendan lashed out as it opened before falling exhausted on the floor, witnessing Marie patch up Louise's wound as Harvey and Jack replaced the table.

CHAPTER SEVENTEEN

Peter and John staggered from the store to be smothered by worried helpers, the bloodstains on their bodies the centre of conversation as the bystanders tried to work out what had happened. No one had been brave enough to go inside the store during the ordeal, but the pleading screams coming from the customer *did* attract a few to press their faces against the window. John looked awkwardly around him, cursing as the blood still seeped from his leg before a lump rose in his throat to make him cough after Peter tearfully collapsed to the pavement to cry. But the crowd opened to let Cortney through, as her arms wrapped around him to stop the tears.

"Daddy," she said, now crying herself. "What's happened?"

Peter grabbed her and hugged her back. "Why aren't you with your mother?" he asked, sniffing.

"I needed to go home to fetch something," she replied, as Peter wiped her tears away.

John looked past the crowd at unidentified police officers walking towards him before making out two police cars parked at the side of the road. But he was still in the dark over who the officers were. He knew they weren't local police but was glad they were police, all the same, so waited impatiently for the first officer to approach.

His name was *Steve Johnson*, the acting sergeant at Wellbridge Police Station. He'd only been in Wellbridge for two days covering but had now been thrown into the deep end with probably the scariest mission he was ever going to face.

Accompanying him was *Carl Thomas*, a twenty-two-year-old constable, *Ray Turner*, a thirty-year-old who'd spent the last ten years at the same police station, and *Alice Price*, a pretty, twenty-seven-year-old, slim brunette.

"What's been going on here?" Steve asked, approaching John.

"Our friend was attacked by rampaging rats."

John's voice seemed to amplify through the crowd. But most were on edge and didn't believe his words even after a witness had said they thought they'd seen something furry jump on the dead woman's head. He felt claustrophobic as they grew closer, their eyes wide with curiosity, eager for more information. But he mentioned the word 'rats' again to spook them into backing away. It worked, as Steve watched on with mystery in his eyes. He also still wasn't convinced, even though Harvey had mentioned them to him, so would only believe it if he saw them for himself.

"Go on," he said with hope. "What happened?"

Peter returned to his feet, bringing Cortney from the ground with him.

"The rats happened! That's what fuckin' happened!" he said, staring at Steve before realising Cortney was still next to him. He apologised to her, but she just smiled.

"Where's your friend?" Alice asked.

Peter never replied. He just pointed towards the store entrance until Carl and Ray confidently walked towards it, but their actions worried John. He shouted out, so they would prepare themselves for an ambush, but his words were ignored as they disappeared inside.

Peter became curious as to why Cortney knew he was in trouble. But, after the reply came that she'd spotted a commotion taking place outside John's store and that he was meant to be helping John, she put two and two together.

"And you came to rescue me?" he asked her.

"Of course," Cortney replied. "You didn't think I'd let you come to harm with my birthday coming up, did you?"

"Oh! That's the reason." Peter tried to smile, but visions of his tortured friend crashed into his mind. "And here's me thinking that you wanted to rescue me because you loved me."

"That too!" Cortney said, laughing.

Peter hugged her again before turning his attention to the store, noticing everyone eagerly watching it as they waited for Carl and Ray to appear. But they never arrived, so Steve moved closer to the entrance.

"Hey! You two! Have you found anything?" he shouted.

He sighed as Alice joined him. "If you're trying to be funny, it's not working!" she cried out.

She jumped back after a loud burst of screaming sent tremors through her, the sound causing the bystanders to shudder as the store door opened to reveal Ray holding a rat attached to his neck.

"Help me! It's trying to bite my throat!" he bellowed, staggering towards the crowd to see most of them turn away in shock to almost faint.

But Steve raced over and slapped him around the head, as the dead rat dropped to the ground.

"What are you doing?" he hollered, pushing Ray. "This is serious! Just do your job!"

"Sorry, Sergeant. It won't happen again," Ray replied, smirking. "There's a pile of dead rats and two bodies inside. Not a pretty sight."

Ray winked at Alice, but his attitude towards the situation made her wish he had been fired from the police force years ago.

He has no remorse, she thought, shaking her head at him.

Tears flowed from within the remaining crowd as John bowed his head to say that Mrs Spencer, the local teacher, was one of the victims. And the other was an old friend from the neighbourhood. He didn't need to say who that friend was because any victim was upsetting to the people listening in. Children that were still watching the scene unfold appeared nervous, so their parents escorted them away.

All eyes now watched Carl leave the store; his face twisting like he was about to vomit as the vision of Ted's charred and chewed face, with his eyes seemingly staring right at him shook his legs.

"You don't want to go in there," he said to Steve, coughing from breathing in the stench.

"I won't. But we need to cordon it off." Steve scrunched his lips as he looked over at Alice. "I want you – "

"Don't even go there!" she replied. "You heard Carl. It's not a pretty sight." She hugged Carl before adding, "What about you Sarge? What are you doing?"

"I need to speak to our good friend Mr Nickels." Steve looked at the dead rat and sighed. "Just stay inside the doorway. That's all."

Alice grunted, letting Carl go before nervously walking towards the store. "As long as it's just that."

"Thanks," Steve said, reaching for his phone. "I need to find out what the fuck's goin' on around here!"

Carl moved over to Ray before following him towards John and Peter, both curious to work out why rats, that weren't meant to be living in the wild anymore were now running very wild in Aaronsville and killing people inside the store.

"Did you illegally keep them?" Ray asked John.

"No. I don't know why they were in my store," the reply came, as John kept his emotions in check.

But Peter moved in to pull him away, fearing Ray's questions may flip him over the edge as the sound of Steve talking on the phone received their attention.

"Yeah. We are here now." Steve glanced at the others. "But there's a problem. Two people have been killed by those rats you told me about."

"Damn!" Harvey cursed under his breath. "So, you have your hands full there and can't get here?"

"Not yet. Unless you want us to abandon the town."

Harvey looked at the others in the room with him as his emotions quickly changed, but the thought of kicking himself for his lack of leadership was pushed aside after fearing the others wanted to kick him first.

"No. You stay where you are. We're safe here for now."

"Okay," said Steve, surveying the area. "Is there anywhere specific, apart from the store that you want us to patrol?"

"Just spread out and keep watch. And don't forget us." Harvey looked over at Jack and Louise, noticing their batons stained with blood. "Oh! One more thing. What weapons have you got?"

Steve nearly laughed. "Weapons?"

"Yeah. What firearms did you bring with you?"

"None." Steve gulped. "No one said anything about firearms."

"Sorry. My fault. I should've said something."

Steve knew Harvey had become agitated because the sound of his breathing seemed heavy as he spoke.

"Hey! We could get some nets to catch the rats?"

"Mate, those little fuckers will chew through the nets to get to you. You need to sharpen up and use more force on them."

"But aren't rats useful to our hospitals? Don't we need them alive so doctors can use their blood for the sick?" Steve was confused. He knew how useful the rats were to the town, but, as he stared at the one on the ground again figured Harvey had recently seen something horrific. "So, do you want them dead now?"

"Look! Listen to me and listen well." Steve did. "You've got dead people there because a bunch of crazy rats killed them, and we're stuck in a farmhouse because there's more of them here. There's been a report of a dead dog and a missing farmer, and two pest control men were slaughtered before my eyes. So please, have you got a fuckin' weapon with you!?" Harvey shouted.

"We only have the usual equipment: batons and handcuffs."

Harvey's temper boiled over. "Are you thinking of handcuffing a rat?"

But Steve went silent, not knowing how to respond.

"...Forget about the handcuffs, but the batons will be useful." Harvey looked out the window. "As for wanting them dead, there may not *be* another choice, so just be careful."

"Okay. Will do." Steve ended the call by saying, "You be careful also."

———

Chris paced up and down in his living room as the time reached half-three in the afternoon. He was still worried about Sean, the man who had given him a job when no one else would. He'd often reminded Rachael of it, even when she was in one of her moods. Sean was the reason why they were able to provide for Rose, the reason he was a good friend. And right now, Chris wasn't coping.

He entered the bedroom as Rachael woke up.

"How's the baby?" she asked, sitting up in bed.

"Rose is fine."

Rachael knew the drained look on Chris' face wasn't down to him looking after a newborn for ninety minutes.

"It's Sean, isn't it?" she said, walking over to comfort him. "Have you heard from him?"

Chris pinched his nose. "Nope. And no one's seen or heard from him either. This is weird."

"I see you have your - 'I need to go and look for him' face on," Rachael said, trying to lighten the mood. But she knew it was a lost cause.

"I can't relax until I know where he is."

"Then go," Rachael said, releasing him. "I'll be fine...That short nap did me good."

"Thanks, love. I won't be long," Chris said, smiling before grabbing her face to passionately kiss her.

He walked away from the bedroom, touching Rose's head as she lay on the living room sofa, leaving the house as Rachael watched from a window; both waving as Chris got into his car.

CHAPTER EIGHTEEN

Alice appeared on the doorstep of the store with her arms folded, stamping her feet as she paced back and forth.

"What's wrong now?" Steve asked, fearing the reply.

"I can't say while people are listening." Alice smiled at the bystanders before adding, "Come here. Please."

Steve did. Followed by Ray and Carl.

Alice whispered that she was upset about the dead woman lying on the floor by the counter, shaking her head like she was demanding for the body to be removed before even thinking about stepping inside.

"What a typical female," Ray said, laughing.

"Shut up!" Alice snapped, nudging him as he passed her.

Ray and Carl entered the store, taking deep breaths as they picked up the body, but Alice couldn't look at it as they carried it into the kitchen.

"Happy now?" Ray said, shutting the door.

"Ray, you can stay here with a dead body in the same room as you if you want, but I can't do it."

Carl pushed Ray back towards the store door before he

annoyed Alice even more.

"Whatever!" Ray said, grinning for having the last word as he left.

He returned to Steve, laughing as orders were given out to patrol the town, but Alice smiled as she watched from the doorstep, happy that her plan had worked. She knew how easy it was to get the horny men doing virtually anything she wanted. A wink or a smile mostly worked, but when they didn't, she would unbutton her top to show just enough skin to make them act like dogs on heat.

Everyone watched Peter and Cortney slowly walk away but no one shouted at them, not even John. Peter held her close as they walked back home, knowing she was upset about the deaths. He didn't want more gruesome memories soaking up her fragile mind, especially if she was made to witness the bodies being carried out of the store, so, to protect her he needed to get her home. But he knew he would receive some serious verbal from his ex-wife when she found out that Cortney was at the crime scene.

John stood next to the officers, staring hard at his store. It was also his home, but right now it didn't feel like it. He knew he could've gone with Peter, but somehow thought he was being blamed for the rats being here and for Ted's untimely death. Maybe he wasn't, but John had a feeling he was.

"Do you have any weapons in your store?" Steve asked him.

John looked quizzical for a second. "Unless you want to fight off the rats with plastic light sabres or swords, then no, I don't have any weapons in my store."

Ray spat on the ground. "Are you taking the piss!" he shouted.

"No! I'm just telling you what weapons I have." John edged closer to Ray, hearing him breathe angrily to feel intimidated. "I sell food items, household products, gifts, and toys. That's it!" John snapped, showing some anger of his own. "Does it look like I sell weapons? Can you see any guns in my window?"

Steve pushed his way in between the pair before fists were thrown.

"Hey! Calm down, guys. This isn't helping." He looked down at John's leg. "You need to get that looked at."

"I know. And I will," John replied.

Steve knew that the recent trauma was the reason why John was losing control, but Ray didn't need a reason. He was always a dick, so it wasn't unlike him to want to get involved in a fistfight.

"Sorry for losing it," John said, pointing at the store. "It's just that a good friend of mine was killed inside there..."

He didn't want to tell Steve that Ted wasn't a good friend, but right now wished he was. His eyes watered as another vision of Ted whizzed through his mind.

"...I just can't get it out of my head."

Steve patted John on the shoulder as Ray's smirk faded. He grunted and walked away, leaving Carl to slowly follow.

"Sorry about your friend," Steve politely said. "But I need you to be strong right now and help me."

"With what?" John curiously asked.

"In finding some form of weaponry to fight off the rats." Steve looked at the other officers. "In case they attack again."

"Have you tried the police station?"

"Not yet. I was hoping for another way to keep the rats at bay. And anyway, the armoury cabinet only has two keys. And the people with those are stuck at the farmhouse."

"So, why don't you smash it open?" John asked.

Steve smiled at him. "Mate, I can't just smash it open. This isn't my town. I've no authority to do that."

John didn't want to get into the politics of the police force but was still lost as to why Steve wouldn't just break into the cabinet.

"Are you saying you could be in trouble for doing the right thing?"

"Yep...It may be the right thing, but if I shot up the town for no reason and the news got out about it then I could lose my stripes."

"It's not maybe the right thing, it *is* the right thing."

"But still, let's avoid using guns for now and try to catch the rats." Steve nodded.

"Whatever you say. But remember, I've seen what they can do."

"I know. I feel you but firing a gun at them could end up being more dangerous for us than using hand-held weapons. Trust me." Steve glared at Ray. "Would you trust him with a gun? He'll use the rats as an excuse to just keep firing."

John also glared at Ray. "Right now, I have no choice. But you can explain it to the families of the dead if you want to leave it."

"Fuck!" Steve shouted, blinking rapidly. "You're right. I'll speak to Harvey again; see if he'll permit me to open the cabinet."

"You're making the right call."

Carl walked away to gather himself but soon stopped after hearing a woman scream. He heard the word 'parents' as she raced towards him, so knew something was wrong, but it wasn't until she was right up close that he got the full story.

"Your parents aren't answering their phone?" he asked.

"That's right. I've been calling them all day."

Mandy Palmer felt embarrassed for telling him about the phone calls when all she had to do was drive to her parents to find out the reason. She was meant to take her children to visit hours ago but had phoned to explain that their father hadn't brought them home yet. That was the first time she called, and the first time the answering machine took her message. But six phone calls later, and six more messages left her worried.

"Where do they live?" Carl asked.

"Only down the road, at Millmoor Cottage. It's the local vegetable farm."

Carl scratched his head. "So why didn't you go?"

"I was all set to drive there after my boys came home, but, after hearing about the rats in the store I couldn't do it."

"Oh! I see! So, you phoned them instead."

"Yes, but no one answered." Mandy shook as she stared at the store before shaking even more after seeing the dead rat on the road.

But Carl entered her eye-line, forcing her to concentrate on him. "It's okay. It's dead..."

He turned to the others, waiting for some support, but they just spoke amongst themselves and left him to deal with it.

"...But you do know that not picking up a phone doesn't mean anything, right?" he asked Mandy.

"You don't know my parents. My father always sits next to the phone when he's not working. He would've heard the messages." Mandy paused, almost crying. "I was meant to help out today and get the vegetables ready for market. He would've been in touch by now to see where I was."

"Are you worried that the mysterious rats may also be there?"

"Yeah! I have a phobia of them." Mandy held back the tears. "Could you come with me to see if they're okay?"

Carl looked at the others again, knowing they were

listening in. John confirmed Mandy's fear of rodents and what she said needed to be taken seriously.

"I think we can handle it here for a while without you," Steve said, shrugging his shoulders. "So go with the lady."

"Are you sure?" Carl replied.

"Go on! It'll be your big test." Steve laughed, knowing Carl was nervous. "You can brag about your first solo mission when you get back."

"Okay. Will do," Carl replied, laughing back before looking at Mandy again. "Right! I'm all yours."

"Hey! Mandy! Do you want me to watch your *boys* for you?" John asked.

"Would you," she replied, feeling drained from negative thoughts. "They're just next door. But I think they wouldn't mind spending some time with you."

"I'm sure I can find something for them to do."

Mandy smiled, thanking him before walking Carl back to her house.

"You sure you want to look after some kids after what's just happened?" Steve asked John.

"I need to occupy my mind for a while, and Mandy's crazy kids will do that."

"If you're sure?" Steve nudged Ray. "Right! I think we'll keep Alice company for a while. Work out a plan."

He tapped John on the arm as he aimed for the store, but Ray grimaced like he still wanted to fight.

John looked away as he was left alone. He walked over to sit in a rocking chair standing on the store porch, breathing deeply as he rocked it back and forth upon wiping a tear from his face, but Mandy's shouting stopped him from crying. He looked at her closing in again, followed by her two boys, both racing towards him to jump at him like he was some form of a human bouncy castle. He caught them in mid-air to smile at their infectious energy.

"Hey! Kids! Did your mother tell you I was looking after you for a while?" he said, putting the boys down.

"Yes!" *Trey*, the seven-year-old shouted.

He loved spending time with John because he was like a cool father figure who would give him and his older brother, *Nathan*, loads of sweets from the store.

"Did you have a birthday recently?" John asked Nathan, as he stood up again.

"Yep! I was eight." Nathan ruffled Trey's hair. "But he's upset with me because he can't tell people we're twins now."

"Oh." John laughed as Nathan jumped on the chair to rock it violently.

He was more of a handful than Trey, but John knew how to handle him. He watched Trey climb up next to Nathan before Mandy said, "I want you both to be good for John. Do exactly as he says and when he says it."

The boys nodded as they used the chair like a climbing frame, but John knew Mandy was worried about the dead bodies being only a stone's throw away. She'd kept her boys in the dark about the people lying on the cold floor of the store, so hoped John wouldn't let slip, but, as he slowly walked her away he said, "I'll keep them out of the store. You have my word."

Mandy smiled nervously as she waved at her boys. "Thanks," she said before walking towards Carl.

John watched her close in on the young officer before the words, "What can we do for fun?" reminded him of what he was meant to be doing.

"We could go to Peter's?" John asked, looking over at Nathan, who was close to tilting the chair over from his crazy rocking. "He's got the new games console."

"But I want to go to your place!" Nathan cried out.

"We can't go to mine," John replied, scrambling for a reason until seeing Steve appear on the doorstep. "Because the policemen are using the store."

Nathan stared hard at Steve. "Why are they using it?"

This kid is a tough cookie to break, John thought.

Steve smiled after seeing John struggle to convince Nathan to avoid the store.

"We're keeping an eye on it because a rare bird sighting was seen inside," he said, shrugging at John before wincing for not using a better excuse.

"I want to see it! I want to see it!" Trey shouted in excitement.

John watched Steve, hoping he could come back with an answer to prevent the boys from just walking into the store.

"You can't," Steve quickly said. "It's so rare that we have to be very, *very* quiet, so as not to scare it off."

"I can be quiet," Trey whispered.

John laughed before stepping in to help Steve. "Trey! If you let the officer do his job, maybe he'll let you see the bird later?"

Steve mimed the word "no", but John smirked at him.

"Can you?" Trey asked, his eyes shining as he excitedly jumped up and down.

"Why not," Steve replied, cursing under his breath towards John as he turned to walk back inside. "Once we've captured it."

But Nathan huffed. "Captured it? Yeah, right..."

He wasn't as easily pleased, so sensed something was off. He huffed again as he jumped off the chair.

"...Come on, Trey, let's go to Peter's, see Cortney and play on the games console."

John winked at Steve as the brothers walked away from the store. And Steve sighed before going back inside.

"Wait for me!" John shouted towards the boys.

"Catch us up, old man!" Nathan shouted back.

John did, but the thought of Peter blaming him for Ted's death entered his mind again. And, as the steps followed and the distance became closer, the thought increased, leaving John to bow his head in shame upon reaching Peter's front door. He watched the boys near it, but it opened before they could ring the bell.

"Bring the little rascals inside," Peter said, standing on his doorstep.

John raised a smile, but the negative thoughts about Ted's death still floated inside his mind. He assumed Peter was just being nice because the boys were there, but that notion was shrugged off once entering the house. Peter hugged him to leave the boys confused, but, as they entered the living room, Cortney did the same to them. She was like a big sister to them, so, as soon as they pointed towards the games console she was plugging it in. She watched them spread out on the sofa acting as if nothing had happened, her heart in pieces upon feeling glad they were unwise to it all as she sat next to them.

Peter and John headed for the kitchen, but neither spoke as the kettle was switched on. But, as John watched him reach for some cups the moment got to him.

"Are you blaming me for Ted's death," he said, catching his breath.

"Blaming you? Why would I blame you?" Peter replied, calmly placing the cups by the kettle.

"Because it was my idea to bring him back here." John almost choked from feeling guilty again. "If I never had the stupid vermin then I wouldn't have asked you to call Ted. I thought you were blaming me for his death."

Peter hugged him again. "Don't be daft," he said, making the tea to feel a sharp pain of guilt. "What happened to Ted was terrible, but you couldn't have known it...He saved us, you know."

"I know. He killed himself to save us."

"Dad! Are you alright in there?" Cortney shouted.

"Yep! You just entertain the boys. I'm good here," Peter shouted back. "Oh yeah! Who wants chocolate biscuits?"

Three voices fought with each other as the men heard the 'Yes' word before Cortney shouted, "And drinks!"

Peter puffed out his cheeks before reaching into a cupboard to pull out a packet of biscuits, smiling weakly as John fetched cans of lemonade from the fridge. He grabbed the biscuits from Peter before carrying the items into the living room, placing them on a coffee table as the boys played a football game.

CHAPTER NINETEEN

Mandy shivered as she drove through the farmhouse gates, parking the car next to her father's to notice the silence.

Where the hell are they? she thought as Carl exited the passenger side.

She puffed out her cheeks and opened the car door to slowly walk towards the house, but stalled after seeing lines of blood on the ground.

"It is blood, but it doesn't mean it's their blood," Carl said, fearing she could lose it before shaking his head at unconvincing his words felt.

Mandy cried into his shoulder, but Carl needed her to be brave.

"...I'm going around the back," he said. "You go to the front door."

He let go of her as fear and adrenaline rushed through him, knowing she was watching him like a hawk as he slowly walked away. Mandy quivered as he disappeared from view before gulping hard as she stared at the house, but her breathing became erratic after finding the courage to walk to the door.

"Mum! Dad!" she shouted, seeing it slightly ajar.

She opened it fully and walked inside, but her legs felt like jelly as she moved past the hallway to enter the living room. She looked around but saw no one, just the flashing of the answering machine to remind her of how many calls she'd made. She entered the kitchen, close to crying because the house was too quiet, the room looking like no one had been there for a while.

But, where are they? she thought, spotting a box of eggs and a packet of bacon on the counter.

"Mum! Dad!" she shouted again, as Carl appeared at the back door.

"Any luck?" he said after being let inside the house. But, from the unhappy stare he received knew the answer was 'no'.

"This doesn't make any sense," Mandy said. "There's blood outside. Bacon and eggs have been taken out of the fridge, but not used, and my parents aren't to be seen."

She walked over and picked up the house keys hanging from a hook, shaking them upon spotting car keys in a bowl underneath before sweating fast and collapsing into a chair. Carl watched her, feeling lost with what to do or say. But knew he had to steer her mind away from her parents being hurt.

"Do you think they're working outside?" he asked.

"We would've spotted them, or they would've spotted my car. This doesn't add up. They have to be hurt."

I wasn't expecting this for my first solo mission, Carl thought, trying to stay positive.

He moved close to Mandy and rubbed her shoulder. "I'm just gonna check outside again."

He opened the kitchen door and walked towards the vegetable patch, spotting bite marks on the leaves to make him shudder.

"Looks like your parents had a visitor," he nervously said, as Mandy appeared on the doorstep.

"The rats got them!" she screamed, freezing on the spot.

All thoughts from earlier about rats being there resurfaced, convincing Mandy she was right. How *many* was another story? but just a single sighting would scare her to want to hide.

"I don't know if it was a rat, but the bite marks on the leaves are small," Carl said.

Mandy was losing her nerve, becoming more anxious. And it troubled Carl because he didn't know how to break her free. There was nothing in his police training involving something like this, something as traumatic, so was struggling to calm her down.

"...I'm sure they're fine," he soothingly said. "Just wait here while I take a look around."

Mandy stared at him, not answering as he disappeared around the side of the house.

Carl followed the path again but almost vomited after seeing something horrific on the ground. He took a closer inspection as his mind tried desperately to not believe it before gently picking up the bloody fingers to place inside an evidence bag. He heard a creepy noise behind him as he pocketed them but saw nothing as he carried on walking. But Mandy shouted out to him, worrying him to do a U-turn and head back to her. He faked a smile after seeing her in the garden, keeping a hand inside his pocket, hoping she didn't notice he was hiding something.

"...Let's get back to your car," he said, pointing at the vehicle.

But Mandy didn't flinch. She was just staring at him suspiciously.

Carl quivered as he felt the fingers, his heart racing upon knowing all wasn't right as Mandy remained where she was. He reached out to grab her but the rats came out of hiding to surround them in seconds.

"...Get back inside the house!" he shouted.

But fear was racing through Mandy faster now and she couldn't do it. She glared at the rats to feel a tug on her arm, but, even though Carl was desperately tugging and shouting, she still wouldn't budge. He pulled harder as the rats closed in, but Mandy kept pulling back.

"...You have to get inside. Now!" Carl shouted as he let her go before running past.

He aimed for the house to stand in the doorway, sweating fast upon glancing at Mandy; her fear scaring him into entering the building. He shut the door and watched her through the window, seeing her sob as the rats covered her body before swiftly turning away as they bit into her face, neck, arms, and legs. But her sobbing made him feel guilty to look again. He saw her fall to the ground, shaking violently as the rats ravaged her. He knew she was dead.

He kicked himself after realising his police radio was still inside Mandy's car, but after seeing the rats take more bites from her knew he wasn't going back outside for a while. He raced around the living room, looking for the phone number of John's store, but the sound of the rats tearing at the door sent shivers down his spine.

"Fuck! fuckin'! fuck!" he screamed, removing things like he was trashing the place.

He stopped and sighed as the noises coming from outside the door crushed his confidence. He couldn't see any books with phone numbers or any on pieces of paper, so searched the room for a mobile phone.

Everything is stored on those things, so the number will be there.

His hands were sweaty as he kept searching, but he still couldn't find anything to help send a message to Steve. *Come on, even old people must have a mobile?*

But the noises forced him to leave the room and head for the kitchen. He pulled a carving knife out of the knife block and held it in the air, thinking only about survival upon releasing his baton to glare at the living room.

"Right, you little bastards. If you want to play, then I'll play with ya'."

He felt nervous to the point of fainting, his legs just about holding his weight, feeling lost with what to do; swearing under his breath for not remembering anyone's phone number. He slowly moved back towards the noise, staying as focused as he could as thoughts of finding a way to warn the others drilled into him, but, after each deep breath, shed tears after seeing a flashback of Mandy being slaughtered. He closed in on the door as the scratching and biting irritated him, gulping after a hole appeared at the bottom.

"Come on you bastards!" he screamed, holding both weapons out in front. "Fuck! I haven't signed up for this shit!"

He was losing it, just like Mandy did, his body tightening as the hole enlarged. He shook his head and moved closer to the door, raising the baton like he was hitting something invisible.

"Come on then!" he shouted. But his actions were more like a football hooligan chanting at a rival football fan than a police officer protecting himself from a rodent attack.

But right now, he was ready for them.

He saw the first rat head appear through the hole to send his anger into a spin, but the rat never came into the house. It just remained half in and half out like it was waiting for something to happen, twitching its whiskers like it was smiling.

"I'll rip you to shreds!" Carl ranted, slamming the baton against a wall.

He went to charge the rat, but another sneaked up behind him, pouncing on his back to bite into his shoulder.

"Fuck!" he bellowed, trying in vain to reach it.

But he couldn't get to it, so reversed to slam his back against a wall. He was inches away from squashing it but another rat tripped him over, forcing him to crash to the ground. He lashed out with his baton upon rolling back onto his knees, connecting it against the rat to send it spiralling through the air until it smacked loudly against a wall, not getting up as the room echoed with the sound of squeaking. Carl thought it sounded like the rats were crying over a friend after seeing them glare at him like they wanted him to pay for what he did. He fought with them as they raced at him from the kitchen, lashing out with the knife to tearful yelps after being bitten on the legs before connecting with the weapon to see a rat's guts drop to the floor.

He tried to get up again, but two of the rodents jumped on his head and bit into his scalp. He felt the warm blood slide down his face to block his vision as he crashed the baton to the floor before frantically wiping the blood away to cringe after his hand was bitten. He squealed in agony as more rats jumped him, snapping his teeth down on one as it bit his tongue, its screech freaking him out as it dropped to die. He shouted as he returned to his feet, but the rats kept coming as he wiped his eyes again. He saw the dead ones and ran for the stairs, but the rat resting inside the door ran up his body and bit his throat. Carl stared at it through blurry eyes, choking to fall against the stairs, as blood sprayed the nearest wall.

CHAPTER TWENTY

C hris drove around the outskirts of Sean's farm as the time reached *4:00 pm*, but so far there had been no success for him.

Sean's not in the farmhouse and he's not out here, so where could he have gone to?

He parked his car next to a large, wooden gate, attached to a fence covering a field on the other side, with a dirt track leading towards the farmhouse. But Chris had a plan that didn't include the vehicle going any further. He wanted to walk through the field, knowing the corn filling it could hide anyone entering. He wasn't expecting Sean to be hiding but did fear the possibility that he could've collapsed after walking through it. The only way for him to find out was to walk through it himself.

He exited the car and stared across the farm, realising now how large it was and how much work Sean needed to do on it before looking at the farmhouse to smile at how tiny it looked in the distance. He drew a map inside his mind of where Sean was working and where Marie had spotted the dog before concluding that maybe Sean had lost it because of the sudden death of Trigger.

He made a move towards the cornfield, stepping inside to brush stalks away from his face, but field mice ran across his shoes to send shivers down his spine. He waited for them to appear, but nothing happened.

Come on Sean! Where are you? he thought; carrying on with his walk.

He and everyone else who knew Sean knew this was out of character for him. Even after seeing his dead dog, Sean would've gone back home to get himself together before doing something about his pet.

Maybe he took Trigger away to be buried? That's why he's taking so long.

Chris snapped off a piece of corn to notice blood on his fingers before seeing more blood appear on other pieces, leaving him worried. He bent down to pull the corn away but gulped after finding Trigger's body covered in insects and flies, Chris' eyes bulging as his mouth dropped open like he was about to puke. He glanced towards the farmhouse but couldn't move as fear held him tight around the throat; his mouth dry from the horror of seeing the insects scuttle in and out of the dog's body.

"*Sean! Sean!*" he bellowed.

Chris snapped from staring and ran through the field, stepping over the dog to see a path of blood-spattered corn stalks. It was like he was following it, but all he wanted was to get out of there. He became drawn to the trail as a moment of excitement raced over him, now needing to see where it ended.

"Sean!" he shouted again.

He heard noises in front of him, feeling spooked as pieces of corn swayed from side to side, so knew he was not alone.

He stopped as more pieces swayed, feeling agitated and sweaty as the noises closed in; shivering as the stalks moved by his feet. But a happy sigh escaped him after a few mice suddenly appeared.

"Nice to see you," he said before almost collapsing after a filthy rat pounced to bite into one.

He watched on in horror as a second rat attacked the back legs of the squealing mouse, biting his lip and gulping as it ripped the legs off with ease to fight over the carcass. Chris tried to avoid the hissing rodents but his trembling legs and heavy heartbeat got their attention. He squirmed as he raced back to his car, hearing them squeak behind him to scare him even more, opening the door and diving inside before slamming it shut to turn the key. But he froze after seeing more rats in front of him ripping into a piece of bloody clothing.

Fuckin' hell! That's Sean's work jacket!

He opened the door and bellowed at the rats, charging them to force them to scamper back into the field.

"Where the fuck are you?!" he screamed again, picking up the jacket. "Get back here!"

Chris looked to his left and saw a boot, shaking his head upon feeling confused because it wasn't spotted before. He thought the rats were playing tricks on him, sucking him in so they could attack him, so moved with more caution as he reached the boot. But the sounds were back, bringing more fear to make him spin around. He choked at every faint sound but couldn't see anything, staring at his car as the sounds increased to make him believe it was coming from behind it. Sweat fell from him at speed as he checked the ground around his feet, each step almost causing him to cry as he approached the rear of the car. But a sad frown escaped him after seeing a figure on the ground; a body with just a skull.

Chris knew it was Sean after glancing at the watch on the chewed wrist; a gift he'd given him on his recent birthday.

He leapt onto the bonnet to slide over to the driver's side, but a rat shot from underneath the car and clung to his leg. He punched it in the head until it let go, but others appeared, looking hungry and mad to see him. He stared into the eyes of the nearest one, his mind capturing a vision of torment and sadness as thoughts about the rats being man-haters confused him.

We saved you from extinction!

He swiftly avoided another attack upon sliding off the car, kicking out as he returned to his seat before diving back into it to slam the door shut, but the rats pounced onto the bonnet, covering it in seconds. Chris reversed the car sharply, steering it away as the rats held on before spinning it around to smash into the gate, closing his eyes briefly as the gate tore to pieces to send wood crashing into the rodents. They were knocked from the car as it sped down the dirt track, a cloud of dust and dirt spotted by Jack as he watched from the kitchen window.

"Harvey, we have a visitor!" he shouted, noticing the car wasn't slowing down.

Harvey rushed over to him. "Who is it?"

Jack studied the vehicle as it closed in. "Looks like the milkman."

"The milkman?"

"Yeah...He's the guy you spoke to on the phone. Chris, who works for Sean."

Marie appeared. "Did you say Chris was here?"

They watched the car screech to a halt outside the house, cringing from thoughts of the rats showing up to attack Chris as he nervously exited before eagerly watching him stumble to the door to slam his fists against it.

"Yep! It's Chris alright," Jack calmly answered.

Harvey and Marie removed the table to let him inside, but words babbled from his mouth faster than they could understand.

"Sit down," Marie said, grabbing a blanket.

She wrapped it around Chris as he sat, watching him stare at the door.

"What are you doing here?" Harvey asked, putting the table back.

"There's fuckin' rats out there!" Chris shouted, shivering beneath the blanket. "They killed Sean."

"How do you know?" Jack said, closing in.

Chris glared at him. "How do I know they killed Sean?"

"Yeah...How do you know they killed him?" Jack asked again, wishing now he hadn't.

"Because the body was wearing the same clothes Sean was wearing this morning." Chris shot up and raced to a window. "Go to the top of the cornfield, take a look at the body if you don't believe me," he said, glaring outside.

"Okay...Calm down...We believe you," Harvey interrupted.

"Now we know where he is," Brendan said as everyone frowned at him. "Sorry, Chris, I didn't mean it like that. I just meant we don't have to keep looking for him now."

Chris kicked the wall in rage. "No! We don't because he's fuckin' out there in the field torn to pieces," he said, rushing to the kitchen sink. "His face is missing." Chris choked upon filling a glass with water to take a sip as everyone grasped what he said.

"How many of those things did you spot?" Harvey asked.

"Ten or so," Chris said before swallowing more water.

"That's probably why we haven't seen any for a while."

Louise, still frantic as ever for being stuck in a confined space, ran towards the window Chris was recently at, bouncing up and down like a child to see if any rats were nearby.

"If they're at the field then we should get the hell out of here," she said, staring at everyone. "Like *now*!"

Harvey and Jack knew she was talking sense but, without knowing the exact number of rats on the farm still meant it was a risk to leave.

"Can you see any?" he asked.

"Nope..." Louise replied.

But Marie burst into tears again after Chris' words about Sean suddenly hit her.

"I agree with Louise. We can't remain stuck here. We need to help the people out there," Harvey said, now using Marie's sobs as a sign to finally get everyone out of the house. "No more hiding like scared sheep. It's time to go."

"We can all pile into Chris' car," Adam said.

Chris placed the glass down and almost laughed. "I only have a mini, mate. I can't fit seven people into it."

"You've got no choice. You have to," Brendan anxiously replied. "We all need to get to safety...I'm not risking running for another vehicle after what I've faced today."

Marie sighed and buried her head into his chest.

"I suppose we could squeeze three in the front and four in the back."

"There's no suppose about it, Chris, it needs to be done," Harvey snapped.

Louise dragged the table away from the door to pant from exhaustion as a daunting screech frightened Marie to cling onto Brendan like he was priceless.

"Is someone going to help me shift this or are you just going to stand there and watch?" Louise asked, huffing.

"We're just goin' to stand here and watch," Brendan replied.

But Louise's glare convinced him to help.

"I might've known you'd be a smart arse."

Brendan smiled at her, glad to see her back to her usual self of trying to pick a fight.

"You know me, Lou, always ready to take the piss out of ya'."

Louise smiled as he helped pull the table away.

"So...Who's going first?" she asked anxiously.

But Harvey moved in front of her. "Woah! Calm down, young lady. Remember what's likely to be out there before opening this door." He snapped his fingers to gain her attention. "Always remember! Always!"

Louise nodded as Marie, and Chris closed in.

"I've got the keys. I'll go first and get the doors open," Chris said.

"But did you lock them before coming in here?" Jack asked, smirking.

"No...Shit!" Chris shrugged his shoulders. "For fuck's sake, no. Course I never." He breathed deeply before saying, "Shall we go then?"

Harvey stepped in, putting everyone into a single file as the door was opened, with no one arguing over it as the order for complete silence during the walk drilled into them.

Chris led the way, closely followed by Harvey, Marie, Adam, Brendan, Jack, and Louise; their vision racing from left to right as Chris returned to the driver's seat while Louise and Marie squeezed into the passenger one. Harvey swiftly opened the back door to let Brendan and Jack slip inside before hurrying in himself, feeling his heart pump faster after squeezing in before almost being shoved out again after Adam entered from the other side. Brendan laughed as he sat on Adam's lap upon smiling at Marie glancing at him through the rearview mirror, hearing the sound of Harvey shutting the door as Chris drove off. But the car juddered to leave Chris fighting with the steering.

"I think the tyres have been popped," he said, exhausted to find another problem to deal with. "The fuckin' rats must have bitten through them!"

Everyone nervously looked for the rodents as Chris tried his best to steer, but, as the vehicle bounced its way over to Harvey's car the rats followed.

"Chris, can you make it up to my car?" Adam asked, as one of the tyres shredded to leave it hanging off the wheel.

Marie screamed after seeing rats race from the cowshed as Chris fought even more with the steering; his driving becoming worse as the car stalled.

"Brace yourself!" Harvey yelled as a flurry of voices bounced around inside the car to outshout each other before the rats swarmed all over it.

But Harvey raised his arm, shutting everyone up to listen to the rodents slapping their feet against the roof.

"Fuckin' hell! What do we do?" Brendan shouted.

"We fight our way through. What else *can* we do?" Harvey replied, steadying himself to do battle. "Adam! Brendan! Put your helmets on and get out there to clear a path. We need you."

Both men stared glumly at the rats upon mapping out a plan to get everyone to safety, knowing they needed to think fast on their feet and hope it worked.

"Okay, Brendan. You ready?" Adam ordered as Brendan lifted off his lap.

"Yep. Let's do this," Brendan replied, slapping down the visor on his helmet.

He crashed the door open onto two rats to knock them on their backs, but could only watch as they rolled back to their feet to glare at him. But Marie shrieked at the sight of the open door, leaving Louise in an awkward situation of having to calm her down.

Adam and Brendan exited the car to swing batons at the rats approaching, as Jack swiftly pulled the door shut, while Harvey used his finger and thumb as a make-believe gun to shoot the rats away from the bonnet. He poured with sweat as they made him more nervous until jumping at the sound of Brendan crashing his baton on the roof; seeing angry rats slide down the windscreen to avoid more swings. But he finally smiled as the last one jumped off the car.

Jack and Louise raced around in their seats to see the rats disappearing back into hiding, but they weren't convinced that they'd given up. Harvey and Chris did the same from their side as the last of the rats ran into a field before Harvey banged on his window to gain Adam's attention. He smiled at Adam for freeing the car but his smile faded quickly after seeing many rats reappear.

"Where are they going?!" he shouted, winding down the window to see the rats race off into two groups. But Adam never heard him. "I said, where are they going?!"

Adam looked around to lose focus, allowing a rat to pounce at the window to miss Harvey's face by inches, shocking him to fall into Jack to leave the others in the car shivering. But, as the rat pounced again, Adam's baton smashed its head against the glass.

Harvey quickly wound the window back up as more rodents attacked the car, cringing as Adam and Brendan fought them away again.

"Right! Is everyone ready to get the hell out of here?" Harvey snapped.

But no one was ready for this, ready to leave one vehicle to act like an Olympic sprinter in their pursuit to reach another, but this wasn't the time to think too much. This was the time to grit teeth and just go for it, not looking anywhere except at Adam's car.

"Let's do this!" Louise said, grabbing Marie upon trying her best to make her feel confident.

Door handles were gripped as Harvey bit his lip.

"Go!" he yelled, as the doors thrust open in synchronicity before five frantic people raced out of the car.

Chris kept the pace alongside Louise and Marie, but Adam and Brendan had to act like bodyguards to block the path of any rats nearing Harvey and Jack. Their visors steamed up again as their breathing became erratic, but Jack was struggling to keep up.

"Go on without me. Save yourselves!" he shouted.

"What the fuck are you talking about?" Harvey replied, closing in to point angrily at Adam's car. "Get your arse in there now." He pulled on Jack's arm. "I'm not letting you sacrifice yourself."

Louise stopped running to stare at the struggling men.

"Catch up with Chris," she said to Marie. "I'm going back to help."

Marie quivered as Louise left her, but the words made an impact. She shouted out to Chris as she carried on running.

Adam and Brendan felt the weight of their shields increase with each rat attack, feeling tired after a few were killed, as Louise closed in to flinch after Brendan stood on a rat's head.

Chris and Marie did what they were told: not looking back until reaching Adam's car. They hugged each other as they arrived, both scared for the others still trying to catch up.

"What do we do about them?" Marie asked.

"What *can* we do? We can't go back down there." Chris

hugged her tighter upon trying a handle on the car, pleased to see the door open to leave him praying to the heavens.

Marie climbed inside, rushing him to do the same. But he just stared at the others.

"Chris!" she shouted.

It worked. Chris snapped back into the moment.

He smiled before sitting beside her and shutting the door; both glued to the activity happening ahead of them; both hoping that the others would be with them soon, safe and sound.

Louise fought with the rats trying to reach Jack, as Adam and Brendan backed into them to give them more cover, but Harvey was finding it hard to zap a rat with his taser. He tried and tried as they moved swiftly, but eventually, the noise the taser made forced them to flee again. Jack looked at his protectors, pleased to be able to still move as Louise helped him to the car, while the others kept guard in case the rats came back. They closed into around twenty feet of the car before the rats reappeared to circle them, but none attacked as Chris and Marie huddled in the backseat.

"Get those doors open!" Harvey shouted, holding the taser out in front.

He stared at the rodents upon pushing Jack towards the car, but the circle wasn't closing in. It scared him more not knowing what the rats were going to do, fearing they would break away and charge, but they let everyone reach the vehicle. Harvey didn't know why this happened? but was happy it did.

"Okay, let's get the fuck out of here!" he hollered at Adam.

Everyone piled into the car to listen to Chris cry, as Adam turned the key to the words, "What about Sean's body?"

But everyone just bowed their heads, not knowing how to react.

"What can we do?" Harvey replied. "We can't go into the field to get him *now*. But we'll get him."

Chris sniffed as Adam backed the car away from the farm, picking up speed to drive along the muddy, farm road as the people in the backseat saw the rats race off again into the field.

CHAPTER TWENTY-ONE

I t was late afternoon when the car reached the police station with Harvey wasting no time in finding out more about the crazy rodents. He fumed as he entered Adam's office, turning on the computer before sitting in his chair.

"What are you looking for exactly?" Adam asked, approaching.

"I know nothing about those rats because I was trapped inside that house," Harvey replied, still mad. "So, I'm looking for an explanation."

"Explanation?"

"Yeah! As to why they're roaming around biting people when they should be inside a laboratory?"

"Sorry...I forgot to mention it before, but I visited the lab early this morning with Brendan." Adam watched Harvey almost lose it, but thankfully he never. "A security guard said the rats disappeared, so I assumed they were stolen because of how important they are."

"They're extremely important, but we've just eliminated what keeps our sick from dying."

LEE ANDREW TAYLOR

"I know," Adam shyly replied, feeling embarrassed. "But what was the other option? Let them bite us?"

Harvey wasn't going to start a fight over this. He knew, that to keep healing sick people they needed to stop killing the rats and just catch them, but somehow it wasn't going to be easy.

"We need to talk to the people at the lab. Find out what makes the rats tick." Harvey exited the chair. "Hopefully we'll work out how to catch them before they cause more damage."

"So, who's going to the lab?" Jack asked, entering the room.

"I'm going with Adam, but I need you to stop all access to Sean's farm." Harvey turned to Adam again. "Do you remember who you spoke to earlier? We'll find the guy and get to the truth."

"Yeah, I'll remember him."

"So, what do *we* do?" Louise asked, standing in the doorway.

"Come on guys! This isn't a mother's meeting you know," Harvey shouted.

"Sorry. I was only seeing what you wanted." Louise sighed, as Jack smiled at her.

"The truth is, I don't know," Harvey said, shaking his head as he tried to solve the situation. "I mean, it's not like we've ever dealt with anything like this before, or will again, so I'm lost right now."

They heard whimpers closing in followed by the words - "I'm not staying here, I'm off home," coming from Chris.

Harvey looked over at him and nodded. "Yeah. You do that. And take Marie with you." He waited for Chris to reply, but he never did. "That's okay--right?"

"Sure," Chris said, gulping as he wiped a hand over his face. "But do we keep this to ourselves?"

152

"No way, man. You can't keep this a secret." Harvey closed in on him. "Just be careful. Don't go overboard when you tell someone. I don't want them freaking out. We need to keep this problem in the confines of this town."

Chris turned and walked away, happy to see Marie next to the reception desk. "I'm taking you to mine," he said, holding her shaking hand before leaving the station.

Harvey gathered the rest of the survivors from Sean's farm, knowing none seemed up for what was to come. "I need you alert," he said, feeling drained. "We know that rats are on the farm and maybe some are still in the local store, but no more reports on possible sightings have come in." He moved around the room, keeping visual contact with everyone, his focus determined on putting things right. "So, we keep an eye on the store and find those freaks."

Jack, Louise, and Brendan waited for more to come from him, but Harvey seemed lost inside his mind. But Louise said, "Will do," to bring him around.

"I think we need to open the armoury cabinet. Don't you?" he said, staring at Adam.

Adam nodded. "Fuck yeah!"

"But we only shoot them if it's necessary. You got that?"

"Got it," Adam replied.

They closed in on the cabinet, leaving the others to wish and hope that a gun would come their way. They saw Harvey open it, nodding as he reached inside.

"Looks like Steve found the spare key that I told him about," Harvey said.

"I didn't know we had a spare key," Adam replied, scrunching his mouth.

"I don't tell you everything." Harvey sniggered, tapping him on the arm, as the others drooled over the guns on show.

"You all know that you're not qualified yet to carry a firearm, so put your tongues away."

"But what if we're attacked?" Brendan nervously asked.

"You do what you did before." Harvey winked at him. "Did the rats penetrate your suit?"

"No."

"Then you'll be fine. Only Adam and I can use a firearm from this force. I do not want to fuck this up, so please, no arguing over it."

He grabbed a box of ammunition to go with the gun he'd recently taken but noticed Adam was not so keen now.

"...You okay?"

"Not really. I've just remembered what happened the last time I held a gun." Adam froze after staring at the cabinet. "I'll be fine without one." He breathed deeply before saying, "Like you said: the protective suits are good enough to keep the rats at bay."

"You sure?"

Adam nodded, feeling sad that the unfortunate accident that happened a few years earlier was still locked inside his mind.

"If he doesn't want one then I'll gladly step in," Louise said, smiling.

Harvey laughed at her. "You know the rules, Lou." He saw her sigh. "Don't give me that look. It won't work."

"But how hard can it be?" Louise asked. "You point and shoot, right?"

"Yes! But knowing you, you'll point and shoot at a civilian." Harvey placed his gun in its holster. "I'm not risking it."

Jack and Brendan watched on, close to laughing as Harvey locked the cabinet before smirking at Louise as he walked away. But she just grunted as he left the room with Adam.

"What are we doing now?" Brendan asked.

"I'm off to the staff room. I need a break," Louise replied.

She left Adam's office and aimed for the room, still annoyed for not being able to have a gun, the others closely following as she opened the staff room door. But shock hit her after finding strangers sitting at the table. Ray and Steve were resting after recently patrolling the town, but their heartbeats picked up pace after Louise scared them.

"Who are you?" she said, bluntly.

"I'm Steve, and this is Ray," Steve replied, watching Jack and Brendan arrive. "I'm the acting sergeant at Wellbridge Station. We were asked to help you guys out."

"Oh yeah," Louise replied, thinking back to Harvey's conversation with Steve when they were stuck in the farmhouse. "So, have you come across any trouble while you've been here?"

"Not really. Just the murders inside the store."

"It's sad news," replied Louise.

"I hear you guys have been at war with some fuckin' rats," Ray said, closing in on Jack.

"Something like that. It's been a dreadful day so far," Jack replied.

They sat for a while, passing on stories about what they'd recently seen, knowing it was only a temporary time-out before searching for the rats again.

———

Adam and Harvey entered the university grounds not long before five, but the security guard from earlier wasn't on duty yet. They spoke to another guard, who told them that Troy was due around six, so decided to stick around in the hope of finding out more about what went on inside.

"Is there anyone here we can speak to? Someone more involved with the rats' project?" Harvey asked the guard.

"Yeah, sure. I'll pass on a message."

He moved over to a phone on the wall before picking up the receiver and pressing a number, staring at the officers as someone spoke on the other end.

"Got visitors. The law," he said.

Harvey watched the guard closely to see if his body language gave anything away.

"Any progress?" he asked, as the phone was replaced.

"Yeah, someone's on their way," the guard answered. "Please. Take a seat."

Harvey sat down but was up again within thirty seconds after a pretty lab technician appeared. She was a distraction both men needed right now. *Victoria Hodgson* was thirty-four years old, with brown hair, hazel eyes, and curves in all the right places. Her sparkling eyes sucked the officers in, leaving them confused as to why they were there. And she smiled because of it. She didn't mind the attention from two excited men drooling over her because it kept her away from what she was doing. And right now, she needed a break.

Adam was the first to pull away from staring at her face and, instead looked at a pound-sign tattoo on the side of her right hand.

"Cool tatt," he said quietly.

Victoria's smile widened and her eyes lit up. "Thanks," she replied, happy that he noticed.

"Would it be okay to have a guided tour?" Harvey interrupted.

Victoria saw him glancing at the door she'd just appeared from, her smile shortening after the question sunk in. She had a feeling this was going to happen, so never questioned it. The stories about where the rats had gone had been floating around inside her mind all day, with most of the lab team watching out for news reports on the TV to find out if they were safe.

"Sure," she replied, leading the way towards the door.

Adam was mesmerised by her; her lab coat swinging from side to side as she moved, hooking his attention, so Harvey nudged him to keep focus.

Victoria took them into a room consisting of many cages, with some with rats only a few days old inside. She watched Adam admire the babies but knew Harvey was waiting for a reason as to why they were on their own.

"We have to keep them in here to stop their parents from attacking them." Victoria paused, watching their reaction. "It's been happening for a few months," she said, moving closer to the cages. "I don't know how it started. One minute all was fine, but the next, all hell broke loose."

"And the parents attacked them. But how do you know they did?" Adam asked.

"Because there were dead babies in the cages." Victoria gulped. "Ripped to pieces."

"Ripped to pieces?" Harvey butted in, rubbing his chin.

"Yes. They were torn apart. It was awful."

"When was the last time this happened?" Harvey asked, walking around the room.

"About three weeks ago." Victoria cringed. "Since then we've been monitoring the pregnant ones, and, as soon as they give birth we take the babies away."

"But isn't that dangerous? Shouldn't they be with their parents at such an early age?" Harvey asked, carrying on with his walk.

"Are you not listening to me?" Victoria questioned nervously. "They can't stay with their parents."

"Hey, I'm sorry." Harvey held out a hand, hoping she'd calm down.

Adam looked on in shock. He figured something had triggered Victoria's courage to defend her decision about the babies and it had nothing to do with Harvey not listening to her.

"It's fine," Victoria said. "I'm sorry too. I should never have questioned you."

Harvey winked at her. "Okay. Now shall we get back to it?"

Adam smiled at Victoria and she, in turn, sent one back to make him blush.

"We monitor the babies at all times, taking extreme care until they're old enough to go back in with their parents."

"So why aren't they attacked when they're put back in the cages?" Harvey questioned.

Victoria shrugged her shoulders. "I don't know the answer to that one, but maybe the professor will?" She turned to look at another door. "He's in his office. Do you want to speak to him?"

"After you've shown us around is fine with me," Harvey finished.

Victoria nodded, calm again as she moved along the room, answering questions as they arrived.

"Over here is where we mix the food for them," she said, nearing a container.

Adam stared at it, taking a closer look at the contents. "Meat? Why do you feed the rats meat?" he said.

"Again, you'll have to ask the professor," she said, passing a few empty cages. "He has strange ideas that no one here can work out, so I'm sure you'll be in the dark over this too."

Adam took a sniff inside the container. "Whoosh! Smells rotten."

Victoria became amused by him. "I know! It does stink a bit," she said, moving a cage out of her way. "But the professor assures us that the meat helps to increase the strength of the blood to help heal the sick."

"What kind of meat is it?" Adam interrupted.

"I don't know. I'm vegetarian," she replied, laughing.

"Oh...Cool."

"Do you have any enemies? Any outside threats aimed at the rats?" Harvey asked, switching the conversation back to why he was there.

"Why'd you say that?" Victoria seemed stunned.

She'd worked at the lab for years, with not a single threat being aimed at anyone, so Harvey's words worried her.

"Because the rats escaped. So, how did they?" Harvey bombarded her with more questions before she had time to respond. "Did you have any problems with animal rights? Is anyone against using rats to heal people? Anything we can work on?"

"We had no problems, as far as *I* was aware." Victoria stared at the baby rats. "But maybe the professor knows something?"

"I hope so because those rats were caged up, with no escape, but they are now roaming around causing havoc and biting people."

Harvey's tone deepened with each word, leaving Victoria struggling.

"Biting people?" she replied quickly.

Adam and Harvey looked at each other, feeling lost as to why she was so in the dark about what the rats had done.

"You're not joking, are you," Harvey responded. "They're attacking anyone who gets in their way."

"Then people shouldn't try to hurt them," Victoria

replied, smiling at the babies. "That's probably why they bit. They got scared."

Adam almost hugged her for being so innocent, and so naive, but knew she would probably kick him in the balls for doing it. Victoria looked like a pretty, sweet woman, but Adam felt there was another side to her, a side he could see in a bar, drinking pints of beer and out shouting any man who challenged her, and it freakishly turned him on.

"You're not listening to me," Harvey said, eager to finally get to the bottom of it. "No one is trying to hurt them. It's *them* that's doing the hurting. Running around and attacking people for no reason."

Victoria became light-headed so sat down to take it in, her heart racing as the words confused her. She thought about her years of studying, of looking after the rats that were to be the saviour of mankind and the cure for illnesses, but right now, it all seemed for nothing.

"How can it be true? I've worked with them ever since they were placed here, ever since the virus. It can't be true, just can't." Victoria truly believed in her words.

She looked at the officers, hoping for some sympathy, but knew they didn't care as their faces fumed every time the word 'rat' was mentioned. It was enough to stop her from trying to make them appear fluffy and harmless.

"It doesn't matter if you think it's true or not. What matters is how we can catch them?" Harvey said.

They turned to the sound of the professor appearing in the doorway. His name was *Walter Toade*; a fifty-five-year-old, small, bulky man who wore thick glasses. He had a round face that gave him the resemblance of a real-life toad. It freaked his staff out but none would say what they thought to his face because Walter had a way of frightening them. There was something about the way he stared at people. It was hypnotising and creepy.

"Hello, officers. Can I help you?" he said. "Thought I'd heard unfamiliar voices in here, so had to check it out."

"Yes," Harvey replied. "We've come to speak to the security guard who was on duty early this morning."

"Oh, you're talking about Troy Bentner." Walter moved closer to the others. "Do you think he's to blame for this?"

Adam moved past Victoria, brushing her shoulder. "I don't think he was," he interrupted. "I saw him this morning and he seemed so cut up that they'd escaped." He closed in on the food container again, picking up a piece of meat. "He claimed they disappeared while he did his checks at around five, but there was no sign of a break-in."

"No sign of a break-in because he did it!" Walter barked.

Harvey butted in. "What makes you so sure?"

Walter reached out, taking the meat from Adam's hand before throwing it back in the container. "It's obvious," he replied. "He's a fucking nightmare! That's what he is. He's always in trouble."

"In trouble, how?" Harvey asked.

Walter walked over to the baby rats. "For starters, he's been caught drunk on duty on more than one occasion."

"More than one occasion? He's only been drunk on duty once and that was on my birthday," Victoria said, angry that Walter was so keen to blame Troy.

"Vic! He's been drunk more than once, so let's leave it at that."

Walter scrunched his eyebrows, waiting for a comeback, but Victoria refused to get involved in an argument to prove Troy was not a drunkard. She knew Walter was lying. He had a habit of doing it. She knew the real reason was that he was jealous of

Troy, jealous because he fancied her too. She had turned down his advances several times, with the most recent one being only yesterday, so knew his pride was still sore. She bit her lip, cursing under her breath as she listened to Walter's excuses.

"...He's been late on numerous times, neglectful towards the rats, even obnoxious to the students, so I know he's to blame for their disappearance."

"But they haven't disappeared. They're everywhere!" Harvey shouted at Walter. "They've been attacking people all over town." His face reddened. "Surely you've seen the news reports?"

"I have," Walter replied, slightly embarrassed now. "But my rats aren't killers. Someone's making it up."

Adam pulled Harvey back before he took a swing at Walter.

"Cool it, chief."

But Harvey's rage brewed after a vision of the vermin catchers lying between the vehicles almost caused him to kick something.

"I saw what they did!" he shouted, glaring at Walter. "I saw them tear two guys to pieces. They didn't stand a chance of escape." He turned away to compose himself. "They were innocent men just trying to do their job..."

Walter backed down after realising Harvey wasn't lying about what he saw.

"...I need to know how we can catch them?" Harvey asked, calm again.

But Walter became silent.

"You need to set up a net to capture them," Victoria said, taking over.

"A net?" Adam asked, not sure if it was the right answer.

"Yeah, a net. We use wire ones, not the usual sort. Those

will be ruined within seconds if the rats bite them. But they can't bite through the wire ones."

Adam smiled at her, believing everything she said. If she told him the rats could dance, act and sing, he'd agree.

"So, let's get the net," he replied.

Walter stared at the others, hearing everything being told. "I'll have to make a call to the city. They're kept there."

"Okay, but do it now," Harvey said.

CHAPTER TWENTY-TWO

J ack and Louise sat in the police car as it moved along the road leading to the Palmers' farmhouse. Jack's concentration on the road allowed Louise full control of what was appearing in front of them, but nothing unusual was sighted. He drove close to Mandy's car, parking next to it before staring nervously at the house, turning to Louise to sigh as he exited. She did the same as they both closed the car doors as quietly as possible, but the silence worried them.

"Why would Steve say one of his men was here when it's so quiet?"

"I don't know, Lou, but Mandy's car is here, so maybe they're out the back?"

"Remind me again why we had to come here and not one of his officers?"

"They don't know how to get here." Jack huffed, knowing Louise was whining again. "Steve said no one had reported in, so we need to check it out."

"Don't they have Satnavs in their town?" Louise replied angrily, looking inside Mandy's car to see a police radio. "No wonder he never got in touch or heard Steve," she said, reaching in to grab it. "He left this in the car."

"Shit! I hope they're in the back, chilling out with a nice cup of tea." Jack looked hard at the front door. "Just keep your wits about you. I don't want to see one of those rats again today."

They moved closer to the house but jumped at the sounds made by the birds. And Jack almost laughed when Louise nearly dropped her baton.

"Not funny," she said. "I hate this shit."

"But it's excitement and adventure. You love all that, you said."

"Okay! Just forget what I said. I freakin' hate this right now."

Louise knew Jack's attempt at trying to be funny was just his way of coping with the pressure of another heart-pounding moment, and, just like earlier, when they were trapped inside the Riley farmhouse, the situation was getting to them, making them scared. The silence sent them cowering back towards the police car, but Jack wasn't going to let his nerves win.

"Stop! Why are we backing off like scaredy cats?" he said.

"I know. It's strange. We haven't seen anything yet and look at us."

Jack puffed out his cheeks as he neared the front door, but his face turned pale after a bird landed nearby. He shook himself to refocus before seeing a blood trail leading off into the field like a newly painted canvas; shaking his head as Louise spotted it also.

"This doesn't feel right," she whispered.

"I know."

"You go around the back," Louise said as her courage faded fast.

But Jack's face drained of blood. He stared at her for a few seconds before agreeing with what she asked, knowing there was no other choice for him. 'No' wasn't a word he could bring into this situation. 'No' would mean no end to the nightmare but possibly an end to his life so had to go and check it out like he had the heart of a hero. He raised his baton and looked up at the sky before disappearing from view as Louise looked down at the blood again. She followed the trail in her mind, deciding whether to follow it for real or just enter the house, but the house won. She squirmed as she closed in on it, as the hole in the door caught her eye. She reached for the handle to open it, seeing the blood trail continue inside before entering the house to shut the door to search the living room. But more blood patches were seen on the floor.

Jack's breathing became rushed as he reached the back door, but he was happy to have made it so easy. In his mind, the rats were blocking his path, so to find it obstacle-free was a bonus. He tried the handle and the door opened, allowing him access to the kitchen. His breathing slowed as the door closed, his eyes straining to see if something was moving around him.

"Did you find anything?" Louise asked as he neared her.

"Nothing...No indication of where the family has gone to. But it doesn't look good if there's blood everywhere."

"What about the constable? Carl. Do you think he got them out?"

Jack neared the stairs, accidentally standing in a puddle of blood. "Damn!" he shouted, almost breaking down in front of Louise. "If he did then he would've grabbed his radio to contact Steve." Jack wiped the congealed blood off on the base of the stairs. "But no one's contacted us to confirm any news." He looked up the stairs before saying, "Get in touch with Steve and ask him if he's heard anything. I'm going to check up there."

"Will do," was all Louise said.

Jack tapped his baton against the bannister, hoping the sound would encourage anything upstairs to appear but saw nothing as he gripped the baton tight to stand on step one. Louise looked on, concerned as he reached step four, but, by the time he'd reached the final step she was making the call. It was very short, so probably too short to be good news, but Jack remained hopeful.

"He's heard nothing!" she shouted up to him.

There was no reply, so Louise followed him up the stairs, but, as she reached the top became nervous because she couldn't see him.

"...I said, there's been no news!" she shouted again, holding her baton out in front after the silence spooked her even more.

She tightened her grip until her knuckles went pale, turning her head from left to right after Jack appeared from one of the bedrooms looking terrified like he'd witnessed something as bad as the sightings from the Riley farm.

"Don't go in there," he said, nervously wiping his mouth.

But this was Louise, the rebellious one, so the words - Don't go in there - were brushed aside.

She rushed past him to accidentally kick a human head that was on the bedroom floor, becoming dazed to almost falling over as Jack's eyes watered up. He wiped them to stare at her but the fear rose to leave him crying before spotting droplets of blood on the carpet that led down the stairs.

"I'm getting out of here!" Louise screamed, running from the bedroom to knock him against a wall.

"Hey! You must call this in and tell Harvey. He needs to

know what's happened!" Jack screamed back, turning to follow her.

"*You* phone it in!" Louise shouted, flinging herself at the stairs. "I'm fuckin' leavin' this place."

Jack watched her race to the bottom as the sound of the front door opening proved she wasn't joking, but he needed to calm her down before everything spiralled out of control. He followed her outside to find her collapsed from shock, appearing startled by something she was watching near the police car.

"What's up?!" he shouted, grabbing her to get her attention.

His vision was obscured so he nudged her out of the way, but he froze at the sight of a headless body on the ground, fully coated with sticky, coagulated blood; the police uniform giving away the person's identity.

"Carl," Louise said, feeling sick as she looked away.

"I think the rats are playing with us. They must've dragged the body here," Jack said, shaking Louise to stop her from losing it.

He pushed her until she jumped over Carl's body, but a voice came from his radio to spook her even more. She went to answer it but a rat raced at her to put her off, leaving Jack to strike out at it to miss as it slipped under the two cars.

"Just answer it. I'll deal with this!" he ordered.

Louise fumbled nervously as she dropped the radio to the ground, hearing Jack grunt as she bent down to retrieve it, but she froze again after witnessing a hand by the back wheel of one of the cars. She looked awkwardly up at Jack as he chased the rat away before cringing after bending some more, as the hand guided her to the rest of the body. She shot up again to freak out after agreeing that the rats were taunting her, knowing they were watching her from a hiding place.

"...Just answer that call!" Jack hollered.

Louise saw him swing at the escaping rat as fear gripped her, with the voice on the radio becoming nothing more than white noise.

"...Louise! Answer it!" Jack yelled, approaching her after the rat escaped. "There will be more."

They heard the voice blast from the radio again, and this time Louise answered. "Hello," she said, her voice shaking.

"Is that you, Louise?" Steve asked, curious as to why she sounded weird.

"Yeah, it is." She fell silent for a few seconds, allowing him to do all the talking as the hand holding the radio quivered before breathing deeply to say, "The rats are here, and they've killed two people."

She listened with Jack to other sounds coming from the radio so knew Steve wasn't alone; twitching her ears as it went silent to make her think she'd startled the others.

"And Carl. Is he also dead?" Steve slowly asked.

"Yes," Louise replied, as someone sniffled. "We can't stay here..."

But Jack grabbed her arm, yanking her towards him.

"...What?!" she shouted, gulping after spotting a mass of vermin approaching at speed.

"Get inside the house!" Jack yelled.

"Why the house? Why not the car?"

"We'll have no chance of driving out of here. They'll smother it before the ignition starts."

"Then we squash them under the wheels."

"Do you want to take that risk? That we squash them all before we crash?"

Louise had no time to answer because the rats were attacking. She threw the radio at the closest one to receive a disgusted glare from Jack, cursing under her breath as Steve's voice was still heard. But, as the rats ran over the radio, the batons knocked them on their backs.

Jack was tiring fast as he moved towards the house, calling out to Louise to do the same, but, as he reached the door noticed she wasn't behind him. He yelled at her as she fought with the rats before yelling again after seeing she was also tiring, his words grabbing her attention to catch him up. They kicked out as they reached the door before quickly opening it to race inside, slamming it shut as Jack took a rest against a wall. But Louise was now slamming down her baton at every rat head that appeared through the hole. It reminded her of a game she used to play but the rats were harder to hit.

Jack watched her closely as a shuddering pain shot through him, the sound of the baton crashing against the base of the door becoming torturous to him. He shook his head and yelled before moving past her to push the TV off its stand, bending down to squirm as he pushed it towards the door.

"Get the back one shut down!" he shouted, sweating as he shoved it against the hole.

Louise ran towards the other door.

———

Steve remained with the handset in his hand as Brendan, Alice, and Ray stood beside him. Alice was unable to hold back the tears as she allowed Steve to hug her.

"I need you to show me where your colleagues are," he said to Brendan.

"But what about me?" Ray spluttered.

"What about you, Ray?!" Steve shouted, still hurting after finding out Carl was dead. "It's not always about *you*."

He glared at Ray to force him into submission, seeing him bite his bottom lip as Alice blew her nose and wiped her eyes. But her emotions changed quicker than lights at a road crossing.

"Right! Let's fuck up these bastards!" she cried out, feeling fearless.

The others came close to laughing at the foul words coming from her but knew it was wrong. She was very close to Carl, so the moment was tougher for her. Ray and Steve knew that, so they just nodded.

"I want you both to stay here for when Harvey and Adam arrive," Steve said. "And patrol the town, in case the rats show up."

"But Sarge, I need to go!" Alice yelled as her eyes welled up again. "Please!"

Steve puffed out his cheeks as more words arrived. He knew why she wanted this so badly, but her tears failed to convince him to change his mind. He reached out to hug her again, but this time she pushed him away.

"...But I need to go!" she cried out.

"I know," was all Steve said as he reached out to hug her again. And Alice let him comfort her.

Ray and Brendan watched on as the moment became hard to deal with.

"Are you taking your car?" Brendan asked Steve, changing the conversation to avoid falling into sadness.

He waited for an answer, and Steve raised his thumb to confirm. Brendan smiled at Alice and walked towards the door, as Steve un-glued himself from her to catch him up.

"It's your turn to comfort her," he said to Ray, laughing because Ray hated all the emotional stuff.

Steve watched him slowly walk towards Alice, winking as

he attempted a hug, but Ray's face was priceless as he tutted to himself.

"...Put some effort into it," Steve said, as Alice pushed Ray away.

"Get off me, you animal," she said, slapping him on the chest. Ray sighed and left her alone.

———

Jack stared nervously at a cuckoo clock hanging on a wall in the front room, noticing the time was now *5:30 pm*. He heard the constant crashing against the TV unit so knew the rats were biting into the wood, as he turned to see an angry-faced Louise enter the room.

"Is the back door secure?"

"Yep!" she replied, snarling towards the noise. "I've just spoken to the station. Backup is on its way."

"Let's hope they get here soon," Jack said, producing the best smile he could.

———

Steve drove away from the station, but within minutes was parking up on the side of the road. Brendan thought it was weird but never questioned it as Steve exited the car to walk towards the back. He opened the boot to retrieve a protective suit, putting it on as Brendan arrived to smile.

"What are you smiling at?"

"The suit, man, it's awesome. You have sharp points around the wrist and ankle areas." Brendan touched one of the points. "Wow! That's sharp."

"Yep...It *is* awesome," Steve replied chuckling before

reaching for his helmet and closing the boot. "My town gets a little rowdy sometimes, especially at night." He walked back to the driver's side door. "And it's getting worse."

"What do you mean, worse?"

"We don't have enough officers to keep the town safe when it all kicks off. That's why I got a few of these made... One kick or slap from this baby and someone's goin' to cry in pain." Steve placed the helmet on the backseat before sitting back in his. "They don't pester my town again after that."

"Damn right they don't," Brendan replied, sitting back in the passenger seat to place his helmet on his lap.

Steve winked at him as he put on his seatbelt before starting the engine to drive along the lane, heading towards the farmhouse, but rats came out of nowhere to run across their path. Steve panicked and swerved the car, squashing some before coming to a halt.

"Get your fuckin' helmet on!" he shouted. "It's time to get busy."

Brendan was just about to do it when two rats leapt onto the windscreen to spook him, glaring at him like they were possessed. They opened their mouths to reveal bits of flesh still embedded between their sharp teeth, scaring the men as they ground them against the glass, the sound excruciating, forcing the men to place hands over their ears.

"Why don't they just shut the fuck up!" Brendan hollered, as the rats used their teeth like can openers to get inside the car.

"Woah! Hey! You need to keep calm," Steve shouted back. "I don't know why? Or how? those furry things out there have turned out like this, but losing it won't make the situation better."

"You wanna bet!"

Brendan jumped in his seat after more rats appeared on the bonnet.

"Those aren't normal," Steve said, flinching at how evil the rats looked.

"You think?" Brendan sarcastically replied, but Steve let it pass.

He hadn't forgotten his orders of trying to catch the rats, but right now was only thinking of getting them off the car.

"What do we do?" Brendan asked, shaking.

"Get on the phone and tell Jack we're close. And that we're clearing a path so they can get out."

The rats somersaulted at the windscreen to produce tiny cracks in the glass, forcing Brendan to lose his head before Steve could take control.

"They're truly pissing me off!" Brendan cried out, placing on his helmet. "I'll shift em'."

He opened the door to surprise Steve, leaving him too late to stop him as a baton swung through the air. But it missed the rats to crash against the bonnet.

"Come on, man!" Steve yelled. "Stop hitting my car and just get those rats away."

Brendan muttered something but Steve was too busy shutting the door to catch what it was. He was about to yell but his phone rang, catching him off guard to creep him out.

"Where are you?" Jack frantically asked as it was answered.

"Not far away. But we have a problem with a few rats."

"How many have you got with you?" Jack asked.

"Just five for now. Brendan's trying to scare them off."

"He won't scare them off," Jack tiredly replied.

He looked over at Louise squinting like she'd heard something, jerking his head as she raced towards the back door until hearing -"They're trying to get in from here now!"

Steve overheard the shouts to send his mind racing, as his concentration switched from Brendan still lashing out to trying to work out what was going on inside the house. He made out the words: "I can't stand this" coming from Louise before: "I want out of here" caused him to struggle with the tension.

"What's happening?!" he shouted down the phone. But Jack was gone to leave him thinking the worst.

He had left the conversation to catch up with Louise, hoping to stop her from doing what she did the last time she flipped out. Jack knew she could've been killed then if it wasn't for the heroics of young Brendan, so needed to calm her down. But how could he when he too was losing his nerve?

"Louise! Fight the fear! You must fight it!" he shouted, unaware that the wood from the TV unit was coming away.

———

Brendan looked tired again as his suit became heavy, as Steve saw the rats taunt him. They ran across the bonnet squeaking like they were talking to each other, making Brendan chase them to annoy Steve to want to leave the car, but a spurt of anxiety washed over him to make him feel cold and afraid. He saw the rats nearing the edge of the bonnet like they were ready to pounce on Brendan, as he just stared pleadingly waiting for help.

"I'm on my way," Steve said, slowly opening his door.

———

Jack and Louise flipped the kitchen table over but were too late to push it against the back door before two rats got inside, as the hole created appeared quickly to surprise them. The rats scurried past Louise to race towards Jack, but he avoided them as they sprung at his face.

"Get away from him!" Louise screamed, charging at them.

She seemed desperate to impress him now, knowing her wild tantrum from earlier was still hanging in the air between them; hoping that being courageous would put her a step closer to him forgiving her for pushing him.

———

Steve still felt the burn of anxiety as he stood outside the car to shout, but nothing was coming out. He knew he was lucky that the rats were still focused on Brendan as he was in no position to fight them, but suddenly a loud bang caused Brendan to shrink to his knees. He looked at Steve's shaking hand after firing off a bullet, shocked as the rats ran off before rising to re-enter the car.

"Damn! Fuck! My car!" Steve shouted, feeling annoyed at shooting it.

"Forget about your car. You could've shot me!" Brendan shouted back. He waited for a reply, but Steve was turning the ignition. "You took your time to help."

"Sorry," Steve grunted, as the car started again.

He drove towards the farmhouse before parking the car, exiting quickly to the sound of Louise screaming after a rat had jumped off the stairs, landing on her head before scratching at her scalp. Jack slapped a hand at it, connecting firmly to send it crashing into a wall, as Louise held her head to feel blood against her hand.

"You okay?" he asked, seeing the redness as she held it up.

"What do you think?"

They shuddered after two more gunshots were heard

close by before noises arrived outside the front door, Louise racing to the window to see Brendan and Steve kick out at the rats.

"Are you in there?" Brendan said, banging on the door.

Louise wiped the blood away from her face as Jack searched for the rats.

"Yeah, we're here," he replied, aiming for the door.

But a rat pounced on his right arm, biting it to make him scream.

"What's going on!" Brendan shouted, slamming his shoulder against the splintered door.

Louise ran to remove the TV cabinet as Jack grimaced before clenching his teeth to grip the rat in his left hand, but it snapped at his fingers to make him angrier.

"Let them in!" he shouted, holding the rat tight as the wound bled onto the floor. But he cringed in pain as it bit deeper. "I've got this."

Louise pushed the cabinet away and opened the door but shrieked as another bullet was fired. She moved back to let the officers enter but Steve glared at Jack.

"We need that rat alive!" he shouted, rushing towards him.

But Jack tried to ignore him. He pulled at the rat as it bit him again, swearing as he yanked it away to see blood dripping down its face, its squeals making his teeth hurt as it wriggled to escape.

"If you want them alive then you go ahead, but I'm not going to," he raged as he violently threw the rat against a wall, splitting its face on impact as it fell lifeless to the floor.

"You shoot at them then preach to me to save them." Jack searched the room to find a towel before wrapping it around the wound. "You've got a nerve."

"You had one in your hands. You could've kept it," Steve

replied, annoyed at Jack for his outburst. "I'll pretend I never saw it, but it's on you if Harvey finds out."

The second rat escaped out the door to be closely followed by Brendan and a reddened face Louise, but no matter how fast they ran, they couldn't get near it.

"How many did you have in here?" Steve asked Jack.

"Only two."

"Good. Now let's get you out of here before they all turn up."

They left the house as the smell of death lingered behind them.

CHAPTER TWENTY-THREE

Troy Bentner turned up for his shift at the university dead on time but was a sight for sore eyes due to the air of indifference about him. Harvey watched him walk towards the reception desk, his uniform shirt-tail hanging below his jacket as he casually neared the others before spotting Adam to acknowledge him, but Adam's energy was drained. And not even the lovely Victoria could keep him from almost nodding off.

"Hello again," Troy said, placing his lunch box on the desk. "How come you're back? You find out who stole the rats?"

For some crazy and unexplainable reason, Troy hadn't seen the news report smothering all local TV stations recently. He'd been fishing peacefully with his brother at a lake thirty miles away. Troy loved peace, especially today, after being on duty when one hundred rats mysteriously went missing, but he knew he was in for some serious questioning once the Toad man caught up with him. After turning his phone off for most of the day and only putting it on again thirty minutes before his shift, Troy had seen fifteen missed calls from the one and only Mr Toade. And from those missed calls were seven left messages. Troy never listened to any of them because he knew what was going to be said; all having some reference to him being a lazy bum who slacked off from work all day and who was now the prime suspect in why the rats disappeared.

"They weren't stolen. They somehow escaped," Adam replied, wiping his eyes.

"Fuck off, did they! You being serious?!"

Harvey seemed astonished that Troy was so far in the dark over this, but from the way he dressed, grew to think that Troy was just plain old stupid.

Maybe this was why he only got a security job. A dumbass nitwit is what he is.

Troy removed his jacket and placed it on the comfy chair he spent most of his shift. "How could they escape? Why would they escape? And why didn't I notice?"

Harvey sniggered as he covered his mouth with a hand, but

Troy looked at him worried.

"...What's so funny to you?"

Harvey moved past Adam until he was in Troy's face, leaving him thinking he was about to be arrested for something he had no idea about.

"What's so funny to me, you ask?" Harvey disapprovingly looked him up and down before cursing under his breath. "You're a mess. Look at you..."

But his approach shocked Adam. He couldn't believe how Harvey crushed the other man but had a feeling he was also drained and stressed. The farmhouse fiasco would linger in their minds for quite a while, sucking all positive memories into a vortex before unleashing the horrifying ones back out again. The deaths of the pest control men, the news of Sean's body being found on the farm, and the fact that Harvey crashed his car, circled emotions that Adam didn't want to think about.

"...You come in here looking like a right scruff. You're not professional in your work, so it makes me think you're not professional in the way you handled the rats." Harvey breathed as if he'd just finished a marathon. "Convince me otherwise and I'll back off."

Adam ushered him away before he collapsed.

"I do my job. I..."

"You do nothing of the sort!" Walter yelled out, arriving next to the others.

Troy felt ambushed. He wanted to retrieve his jacket and run home but was cornered by two, angry men, both angry for different reasons, but both angry all the same.

"I'm not taking this crap. The pay isn't all that, so you can stick the job."

Troy's fury over the accusation was enough for him to reach for his jacket, but it was Adam who stopped him, not the other two, as they were too busy playing the 'who's the scarier, me or him?' game.

"Mate...Stay," Adam said, reaching out to calm Troy down. "I'll talk to you if you want." He looked at the other men, waiting for a response, but all they did was nod.

He took Troy to a corner of the room as the man still felt on edge, but Adam reassured him that he wasn't going to give him a lecture before asking him about the rats. He wanted to know if there'd been any strange occurrences happening with them recently, but Troy seemed lost to the question.

"I dunno. I dunno anything about the bloody rats," he anxiously replied, shrugging his shoulders. "I'm a security guard, not an animal lover."

"Okay, mate, calm down," Adam said.

Victoria seemed concerned as she watched on, now interested to know more about the outcome with the rats, but she kept looking at Adam. She didn't know why she liked looking at him but she'd been glued to him ever since he brushed past her, stuck to his every move, every word, and his shiny, green eyes.

"...Where were you before they disappeared?" Adam asked, knowing it was a good enough question to impress Harvey.

Troy thought about his usual routine when coming into work upon calming down. "Well, I usually patrol the grounds at around four-thirty in the morning."

"You patrol the grounds?!" Walter yelled, interrupting him. Get away do you? All you patrol is the staff room or the fuckin' toilet."

Troy tried to ignore him but only managed a few seconds.

"How do you fuckin' know what I do? You're not even here at night!"

It was Walter's turn to want to get up close to Troy, but, as he moved towards him, Harvey reached out to force him back.

"Because I view the tapes every day. That's why!" Walter replied.

Troy gulped hard. He hadn't thought of that.

"And what's on those tapes?" Adam asked, trying to pacify the situation.

"Are you sure you want to know what's on the tapes?" Walter said, smirking.

"Yeah...Really," Adam replied, holding Troy back.

"He comes to work, sits down, and eats God knows how much junk food before wandering over to look at the rats for a second. He then does, guess what? Yep! You got it, sits fucking down again..."

Everyone turned to stare at Walter as he almost lost control.

"...And he goes to the bathroom around a dozen times. I'm glad there are no cameras in there because God only knows what he's doing." He pointed at Troy in anger. "Then he falls asleep in his chair for a few hours."

Harvey noticed Troy was on the verge of charging Walter like a raging bull, so stepped in to say, "Can I see the tapes from last night?"

"Yeah, sure." Walter glared at Troy before adding, "Follow me." He walked back towards his office, as Harvey followed.

Victoria shook her head as she watched them disappear before staring at Troy.

"I've stuck up for you on many occasions, but if he's got evidence that you've been sleeping on the job then I won't be helping you again."

"Don't worry about it," Troy said, smirking. "He's talking out his anus again."

"How is he? He has the proof."

Adam was glad to keep out of it but knew he would be needed to speak again soon. That moment was about to arrive.

"Would you like coffee?" Victoria asked him, now ignoring Troy's attempt at a reply.

Adam shook himself before saying, "Yeah, sure. Why not. Harvey may be some time in there."

"Some time? Have you heard Walter go on? When he's on a mission, he's on one," Victoria said, laughing.

It became infectious, causing Adam to do the same as Troy lowered his guard and smiled.

"Don't listen to the toad man," he said, as Adam became curious. "He's lying about me sleeping, well, sleeping at that time." He laughed, but Victoria wasn't impressed. "I know where I was at four-thirty this morning and that was walking around the university."

"How long do these walks last?" Adam asked.

"About thirty minutes..."

Adam nodded, knowing that would make it *5:00 am*, the time when Troy noticed the rats missing.

"...When I got back to the room, they were gone. You know the rest."

Adam did know the rest, the rest of how they escaped or were stolen from their cages that had one with smashed glass.

"Can you tell me more about the large rat from the broken cage?"

"That rat is probably the most intelligent one I've ever seen," Victoria said, knowing it was her cue to butt in.

"Why?" Adam asked, writing everything down in his notepad.

"Walter tried many experiments on it. However, it didn't matter to that rat because it brushed them off like they were nothing."

"What kind of experiments?" Adam sternly asked.

Troy seemed concerned. He didn't know about half of what happened in the lab, but Victoria changed the subject, knowing she'd said too much.

"How many sugars do you take?"

"Forget about the coffee," Adam replied, almost chuckling. "What experiments did Walter do on the rats?"

"Nothing outrageous, so stop looking at me like I'm a rat bully."

"So, tell me?"

Victoria tried using her charm to sway Adam away from questioning her more about the large rat, but his mood was way too serious and that's where it was staying for a while. She had no chance, so had to admit defeat. She explained, to the best of her knowledge, the experiments she'd witnessed over the past few months. Experiments that had not been tried before, like electrocution therapy, and dunking the rats in water for long periods. In some cases, the periods were too long, and the rats died. But Victoria seriously didn't know why the professor did it.

"You just told me the experiments were nothing outrageous, but now you're saying Walter drowned some of the rats deliberately."

"I don't think it was deliberate, just some were stronger than others," she replied.

"But the blood of a rat is our saviour, so why risking killing them off?"

Victoria became nervous about being in this situation.

"All I'm saying is the professor was trying to find a way to increase the potency of the blood so it healed quicker. So, by trying to find the most powerful rats there was bound to be a few casualties."

"And the large rat, with the piece of ear missing, is that the most powerful one?"

"Yes," she replied sheepishly.

Victoria walked away to make the drinks, teary-eyed after remembering seeing the dead rats floating in the water tank. And Troy followed her to leave Adam writing more notes on his pad.

———

Harvey sat in Walter's office, skimming through the CCTV recording from the night before; his main concern aiming at *'Why there were no cameras located inside the room where the rats were kept?'*. But Adam had already filled him in on that one long before they arrived at the university.

He slowed down the recording as the counter clock on-screen registered *4:30 am.*

"Yep. There goes Troy to do his rounds."

Walter nodded, but he still didn't believe it was real, that Troy was there. However, he was, and he was getting up from his seat to do his rounds.

"Maybe he did his job properly that time, but he's still a lazy sack of...."

"That's not the point," Harvey swiftly said, interrupting him. "He was doing his job at that moment in time. That's all I needed to know."

————

Adam entered the room of the empty cages, hoping to find evidence he had overlooked the last time he was there. He moved towards a table resting against a wall, the legs only six inches tall. It confused him as it was different from the other tables in the room. He knelt in front of it and removed a torch from his police belt, shining light underneath it to see fragments of glass before spotting a piece of paper slightly moving from a faint breeze blowing it. Adam felt the breeze against his fingers, smiling after working out where it came from, but Victoria appeared, holding a cup of coffee before he could investigate.

"Here you go," she said, feeling lost as to why he was sprawled out on the floor.

Adam almost hit his head on the edge of the table from the surprise visit, his torch off again as he awkwardly smiled at her.

"...You want it down there?"

"No..." Adam laughed as he got back to his feet to take the cup. "Thanks."

"What were you doing down there?"

Adam sipped the coffee before taking a pen from Victoria's breast pocket, smiling as he stirred the drink and sipped it again.

"That's better," he said, sucking the end of the pen before replacing it.

"But you have a pen," Victoria snapped, feeling a touch annoyed.

Adam laughed. "But mine's not a crappy BIC pen like yours."

Victoria shook her head and smiled back.

"...What's behind this table?" Adam asked, feeling like it could be a clue.

Victoria wasn't sure at first, but, as her mind worked overtime to remember, a vision of what was behind the table entered her mind.

"Why do you want to know what's behind there?"

"Because air is blowing underneath it. That's why."

"The air vent."

"Yeah...I kind of worked it out," Adam replied, sticking out his tongue.

"Then why ask?"

"To be certain."

Victoria did it again. She probably did it without even noticing, but she did it. She smiled in a certain way, the way you would smile at someone if you wanted to see them again, or even kiss them. And Adam noticed it. He also felt her eyes on him, like they were stripping away his uniform to reveal his naked body. He felt the urge to pounce on her to give her a deep, lustful kiss, but two things stopped him: One was the cup of coffee, as he didn't want to spill it over her, and two was the sound of Harvey and Walter walking back into the room.

"I've just seen the CCTV footage and can confirm that Troy was doing his rounds at four-thirty, so missed what went on in here." Harvey stared at Adam like he'd interrupted something between him and Victoria. "You okay? You look very red."

Adam was indeed blushing, as he glanced at Victoria sucking her lips before faintly giggling as she left the room.

"There's something you need to see," he said to Harvey.

"I hope it's not your erection," Harvey bluntly replied.

"No!" Adam stuttered as his face burned with embarrassment. "I need a hand removing this table." He touched it. "I think I may know how the rats escaped."

"How?" Walter asked, getting involved.

"If you help, then you'll find out."

They each grabbed hold to pull the table away from the wall, revealing a two-foot by one-foot air vent cover at the bottom. And in it was a hole big enough for the rats to slip through, the teeth marks encased in the plastic giving away their method of escape.

"Bloody hell!" Walter shouted. "What happened to my vent cover?"

Harvey looked at him, baffled that he didn't know the answer. He grunted before explaining that the hole was made by the rats.

"It was probably planned," Harvey said, removing the cover from the wall.

"Planned? By whom?"

"Not whom. What!" Adam said, now annoyed because Walter still found it hard to believe that his rats could plan an escape.

"But they're just rats," Walter replied.

But Adam shushed him up by passing on his theory of events. The fact that the glass was only broken in one cage, the one that belonged to the clever, stubborn, large rat.

"You see, I have a feeling that the mentioned rat pressed the button to release all the others from their cages while Troy was on walkabout. Then, they snuck under the table, biting through the cover, and escaping down there." Adam pointed beyond the hole and into the darkness.

"There are pipes down there. Where do they end up?" Harvey asked.

Walter stood lost, with no sign of an answer arriving soon. But Victoria overheard the question as she arrived with more coffee.

"They end up at the Palmer farm. Why?" she asked, feeling like she was going to be told something she didn't want to know the answer to.

"Because that's where most of them have been sighted today. The pipes must've led them there."

Harvey finally knew the answer as to why the rats were on the Palmer and the Riley farm. No one had transported them to those locations, meaning no one was involved in their disappearance. And no one involved meant Troy wasn't guilty.

CHAPTER TWENTY-FOUR

The atmosphere inside Chris' house was uncomfortable for him, as he watched Rachael stare blankly at a still-shaken Marie.

"And you brought her here because?" she said, her eyes boring holes into him.

"Don't start! Not now! Not after what's been going on today."

Rachael knew Chris was annoyed with her. He never usually said anything when she snapped at him, but this time he did, and the anger in his tone worried her. She sensed he was frightened by something, but so far, wasn't letting her in on it. She tutted, staring at Marie again, but her distressed state proved that something major had happened recently.

"So! Which one of you is going to fill me in on why you both look like you're about to cry?" Rachael said.

Just then Marie did; the tears falling fast as she collapsed into a chair. Rachael noticed she looked shocked like someone witnessing the devil in a horror movie.

"Are you happy now!" Chris snapped at her. "Can't you see she's upset?"

"Keep your voice down. I've only just put Rose in her cot." Rachael stood at the foot of the stairs listening out for her baby, but all was quiet. "If you wake her, I'll beat you to an inch of your life."

Chris looked at her differently for a second. "Yesterday, or even first thing this morning, I would've been worried by what you just said, even slightly frightened, but not now, not after what I've seen today," he angrily replied.

"And what did you see?" Rachael whispered, moving away from the stairs to hold him. But she stopped after Chris' stare was unrecognizable. "What is it, Chris? Tell me what's on your mind?"

He shed a tear, breaking down to let her hug him; holding her tight like she was a priceless jewel he didn't want to let go of.

"Sean's dead," he whispered, as another tear slid down his face.

"How do you know he's dead?"

Chris knew he couldn't tell her too much about what he saw, and to be honest he wasn't one-hundred-per cent sure of how Sean died, but seeing those crazed rats at the farm with Sean's body was enough to convince him that they were behind it.

He stopped hugging her and wiped his eyes before explaining the edited version of what he saw at the farm. He told her that Sean's body was in one of the fields but didn't go into detail about how badly mutilated it was and wasn't likely to either before saying he panicked and drove to the farm. The trapped officers let him in.

"Why were they trapped?" Rachael asked.

"Because the rats wouldn't let them out."

"So, was Marie there as well?"

"Yeah," Chris raspily replied.

Rachael looked at Marie differently now; her smile caring as she sat down to comfort her. It was her way of saying sorry for giving Marie a hard time. Chris smiled as he watched on.

"So, why were there loads of police in the house?" Rachael asked.

Chris sat opposite, prepared for the downpour of more questions to arrive.

"I don't know the full story. All I can gather is that two of them went to the farm then a third one arrived. But that person was set upon by the rats, so everyone had to barricade themselves inside. Backup was called but the rats pounced on them, so they too had to hide inside the house."

"So, Marie was working today. That's why she was still there," Rachael suddenly guessed.

"Yeah, I was," Marie answered, crying the last of the tears.

"I'm sorry, Marie, really I am," Rachael said, motioning to Chris to put the kettle on. "It must've been awful for you."

Marie froze after a flashback of the rat she stabbed entered her mind. "It was."

Chris entered the kitchen to a faint burst of scratching at the back door, stopping him in his tracks as he listened. But it faded quickly to make him believe he was imagining it. He rubbed his head and stared at the door before switching on the kettle, turning to look at the door again as he grabbed three cups from a high cupboard.

"You take sugar, Marie? I can't remember!" he shouted.

"The baby!" Rachael shouted back. "She's asleep."

"Then you should also stop shouting," Chris said as he popped his head back into the living room to wink at her.

Marie relaxed slightly to giggle.

"I'm not shouting, you're shouting," Rachael replied, seeing the funny side after Marie's little laugh.

Chris smiled at her before saying to Marie, "Sugar?"

"None thanks."

But the scratching sound was back as Chris re-entered the kitchen. And this time it was louder. He became worried as he cautiously approached the back door, checking the room for any sign of a rat, freaking out from the sound of the door being attacked by the rats who'd visited Tess. And with them was the large one.

Chris never moved after a small hole appeared at the bottom of the door, but did when a rat's head came through it; his insides quivering as it squeezed into the kitchen. But he wasn't going to let it get past him. He grabbed the kettle and threw its boiling contents over the rat, hearing it squeal as it shuddered. But it wasn't dying. It just glared at Chris before running along the floor, ready to pounce, but he quickly reached for a chair to block it off, breathing heavily as the legs scraped across the floor tiles to alert the women.

"What's going on in there!" Rachael shouted, more worried about waking Rose.

"Get upstairs. *Fast!*" Chris yelled back.

"Why?" But within a second Rachael knew the answer.

She grabbed Marie and ran for the stairs, with neither looking back as they reached the top to enter the bedroom. Rachael nervously shut the door as her ears tingled to catch Chris' footsteps closing in, but nothing was heard, as she ran to the bedroom phone, picking it up to dial out as a buzzing sound was heard.

"Someone's cut the line," she said.

"Not someone," Marie replied, knowing the rats did it.

"Shit! My mobile is downstairs," Rachael shouted, throwing the cordless phone at the wall.

Marie watched her almost break like a China doll, but Rachael regrouped. "Sorry...I hope I didn't frighten you." She looked down at Rose still sleeping, wondering how she did it with all the noise in the room. "I can't stay here." Rachael panicked, thinking only of Chris. "I have to help him..."

She listened out for him again, hoping for a positive sign, but still, there was nothing.

"...Keep Rose safe," she said, looking at the baby again before reaching for the door handle.

Marie just stared at her, too frightened to reply; shaking as the door was opened to nod as Rachael left the room. But the sound of it closing made her gulp.

Rachael quietly made her way towards the bottom of the stairs, but her eyes watered the closer she got to the living room. She searched for her mobile phone whilst glancing at the kitchen door, wanting to enter the room to check on Chris because the silence freaked her out. But awful thoughts of him being attacked sent a shiver down her spine. She picked up the pace to carry on searching but her hopes faded fast after she couldn't find her phone, her heart melting from fear as she crept over to stand by the kitchen door.

Chris glared at the scolded rat he'd kicked as it lay stunned on the floor, but the sound of the others forcing their way into the room grabbed his attention. He panicked, even more, knowing he couldn't fight them all, holding the chair as the door was opened.

"Get back!" he shouted at Rachael, racing towards a drawer.

She watched him swing the chair like a lion tamer keeping a lion at bay, slowing the rats as the drawer slid open, but one raced for him as he searched for a knife.

"Behind you!" Rachael yelled.

Chris turned swiftly, depositing the knife into the rat as it jumped onto the kitchen surface, but could only watch on as the rest closed in. He stared at the large one, probably because it was more noticeable, as the others helped the stunned one back to its feet.

"...What can I do?" Rachael asked, shaking. "You need my help."

"No! Please!" Chris replied, pulling the knife out of the rat with a trembling hand. "Just get back upstairs!"

The large rat slowly reached him, sitting to twitch its whiskers as the others glared, but Chris knew he couldn't fall for whatever this was. Even though the large rat's presence had him almost hypnotised. Rachael shouted at him again, and again, but Chris wasn't acknowledging her. He was just watching the large rat lick dried blood away from its paws.

But Rachael wasn't going back upstairs. Whether it was fear to move? or she was fighting back? but either way, she'd got Chris' attention and he was glad she was still there. This was the Rachael he'd fallen in love with, the strong, protective woman he'd met all those years ago, and right now, her protective instinct was kicking in. But Chris didn't want her to get too comfortable. He knew she was in grave danger, but also knew she was very stubborn when annoyed.

"I'm not going anywhere until those freaks leave you alone." Rachael grabbed the broom from the corner of the kitchen and swung it at the rats. "Shoo! Just fuckin' leave why don't you!" she screamed at them.

She swung the broom at speed to see most of the rats jump over it, but the stunned albino one took a hit to the head to sprawl across the floor.

"...Why don't you just kill that thing!" she shouted, pointing the broom head at the large rat.

It glared at her, arching its back as if about to attack, hissing and showing teeth as its eye colour changed to a devil red.

"Be careful," she said as the other rats ran towards her.

Chris cringed, dreading the worst as they closed in, but was soon smiling after Rachael avoided being bitten. He attempted to help but the large rat sprang through the air to land on his leg, leaving him trying to shake it off as Rachael swung the broom again. But this time couldn't connect with the mouth-snapping rodents. They chased her away from the kitchen, circling her inside the living room as Chris was bitten, but he gritted his teeth and whacked the chair against the large rat's back. It winced, squealed, and dropped to the floor as the chair was aimed again, but the albino rat pounced onto it, snapping teeth at Chris to force him back against a wall. He shook the chair vigorously until the rat dropped to the floor before slamming it down on the rat's head to crush its skull.

Rachael tired after more failed swings with the broom but was glad to have not been scratched, or worse *bit* by a rat. She freaked when one pounced onto the broom handle to embed its claws into it, her hands letting go to give the tiny beasts an advantage as Chris arrived with a handful of plates. She looked at him with more shock etched on her face as he threw the plates like discs, but each throw missed the rats as they raced around the room. Chris held up the last plate and frowned. He knew Rachael could hate him for smashing up her best crockery, but all he wanted was to get her to safety. He watched her shiver, so reached out to grab her, tossing the last plate over his shoulder as he gripped her hand, hearing a squeal as it landed on a rat's back.

Typical! he thought.

"Did you kill the big one," Rachael rushed from her mouth.

"Never mind that one. Just keep hold of my hand. I'm getting you out of here."

Rachael was loving this side of Chris; his change in demeanour was turning her on. But she wasn't going to let him know when the rats were planning to charge again. They turned to the sound of Rose crying, fearing for her life as the rats halted to pay attention before seeing Marie stand on the stairs holding her in her arms.

"Take my baby back upstairs!" Rachael barked. "*Now!*"

"But she's crying for you," Marie tiredly replied.

Chris saw a rat aim for Rachael, so pushed her out of the way to take the hit, cringing as it clawed at his leg.

"Go! Now!" he screamed at her.

She watched on nervously as he fought the rat off before shaking her head and running for the stairs, yelling at Marie to hand Rose over as they returned to the bedroom. She was furious with herself now for leaving Rose with someone who was pretty much a stranger to her, glaring at Marie cowering on the bed like someone about to be hit. It shocked Rachael into backing down.

Chris picked up the broom to swing it as snapping teeth came close to connecting, but he was clawed at again as a rat clung to him. He lashed out a hand to knock it off as it stood next to the others before he frantically scanned the room to find an escape route, but the large rat ran at him from the kitchen, looking even angrier than before. Chris felt the fear rush over him harder now as the rats sniffed the blood from his wounds, knowing they would soon jump him again if he didn't find a way out.

"Rach, you stay where you are and look after the others!" he shouted. "Don't come out of that room, no matter what you hear down here." He waited for a reply, but nothing arrived. "You hear me, Rachael?"

Chris held the broom handle close to his chest, but his

sweat made the grip harder to maintain. He gulped as he stared at the large rat before wincing from the pain, briefly closing his eyes to smile as Rachael replied.

CHAPTER TWENTY-FIVE

W alter looked at his watch as the phone rang in his office. It was the driver of the van delivering the special net, telling him he was outside. He sighed, knowing that within an hour the sun would set, and, so catching the rats would likely be impossible, but he had to try and save some for future breeding.

"The net is here!" he shouted to the officers, leaving his office.

"Good. But it needs to go to the Riley farm!" Harvey shouted back. "I figure that's where most of the rats are."

"Okay. I'll get Troy to have a word."

Walter dialled the front desk, knowing Troy spent most of his shift there. But, even though he only mentioned that Troy needed to tell the driver to take the net to the Riley farm, and to give him directions if needed, Troy still felt like more was to come from him, like more bad words aimed at his ability at being a security guard. But Walter said nothing else.

Troy looked outside as he replaced the phone, smiling as he left the building. He caught up with the driver sitting in the van before checking out the words – *Kelvin's rodent services*

— written on the side, nodding after remembering the experienced company from before the virus outbreak. Troy's father used to talk about *Kelvin* the rat catcher but, even though Troy's job was to only talk to the guy, he still didn't want to fuck it up. He explained everything to Kelvin about where to go and that the police would be there when he arrived but didn't disclose information on how deadly the rats were.

He waved Kelvin off as the van drove away, but was almost knocked over by Walter, Harvey, and Adam rushing towards him.

"Stop that van!" Walter shouted.

"He's off to the farm," Troy replied. "Like you asked."

"We're heading there now, so just wanted him to wait for us."

Walter walked towards Adam's car, looking at the ground as if thinking of a plan, as Harvey and Adam followed, but Troy wouldn't return inside until the car drove away. He saw Victoria standing in the doorway, staring out into the street like she was indecisive about leaving.

"Your shift is over, so why are you so fidgety?"

"No reason," she replied. "Just seeing if they've gone."

"Why? Do you feel lonely now Mr sexy policeman isn't here?"

"Shut up!"

But Troy sensed she was on edge as if afraid to leave. "You not going home then?"

"Nah," she replied, still looking at the street. "Thought I'd stay and keep you company for a while."

Troy was about to say something comical but changed his mind after seeing how nervous she was. "Yes, they've gone."

He felt a sense of relief not having the eagle eyes of Walter watching his every move, and Victoria smiled because of it.

She chuckled before saying, "Wouldn't it be funny if Walter had a secret webcam in here and was watching you right now?"

"Nope, it wouldn't." Troy stared at every corner of the room just to make sure. "He'd best not be watching me."

Victoria chuckled again. "I know. It would be so freaky."

Troy moved back into his seat before lifting his legs to spread them on his desk. "Do you think they'll catch the rats?"

"If you'd asked me this a few hours ago then I would've said yes, but, after hearing that they've gone crazy, I truly doubt it."

———

Ray and Alice were the first to arrive at the farm after Harvey's call to the station led to them feeling unused. But now they felt involved. They sat inside the car, waiting nervously for the others, as Ray's macho side faded as quickly as the daylight. Alice nudged him to step out of the car, almost laughing to see him so freaked out by the rats as he quickly shook his head.

Ray flashed the car's lights after seeing other vehicles approach as Adam's car did the same.

"Who's that in the backseat?"

"I don't know, Ray, but I'm sure you'll find out if you *ever* leave this car."

They saw Adam exit, waving his hands like he was doing sign language, but Ray was confused.

"What's he going on about?" he asked anxiously, as Adam pointed at Kelvin's van before drawing an invisible square.

"I don't know," Alice replied, nodding. "So just nod like me."

Ray smirked at her. "You nod if you want to, but I'm not. I'll just tell him he's fuckin' mental."

"Ray! And you wonder why you have no friends." Alice punched his arm. "I think he's telling us the net is in the van."

"And you got all that from his crappy drawing?"

"Yep," Alice said, still nodding towards Adam as Harvey exited the car to put on a riot suit.

"Looks like we need to do the same," Ray said, reaching over the backseat to pull two suits towards him.

He tossed one to Alice, but she'd gone shy to put it on while he was sitting next to her. She sighed and climbed over the back, but a swaying hand clipped him around the head.

"Come on! Watch the hair."

"Just keep your eyes on the front," Alice quickly said, squinting.

Ray did, but Alice wasn't fooled. She knew he was sneaking a view from the rear-view mirror, so leaned over to turn it.

"Are you two ready?!" a voice shouted from outside the car.

They looked up to witness Adam wearing protective gloves as he placed on his helmet.

"Almost!" Alice shouted back.

Ray did the same and exited the car, adjusting his helmet as Alice followed, but she shook from thoughts of not seeing any of the live rats. Adam pointed at her hands to remind her to put her gloves on, leaving her sighing as she reached into the car to grab them. Ray laughed as they headed towards the van, where Harvey and Kelvin were waiting.

"Are you sure they can't escape from it?" Harvey asked.

"Don't you worry about a thing," Kelvin replied winking. "The rats won't get out of this net." He walked towards the side door as the others followed. "Did Walter tell you about the sticky residue on the net?" he said, opening it.

"No," Harvey replied, looking lost.

Kelvin smiled. "Yeah. It's what keeps them inside; the glue stuff."

"Walter just said that the net was strong enough to stop them from biting through."

"That too. But the glue makes sure they can't run back out again."

Adam and Harvey took it all in, but Ray still had doubts about any of it working. He was a tough cookie to please. He stood back with Alice while the others dragged the net off the van, watching them try to work out the best place to set it up.

"Should we place it near the house?" Harvey asked.

"It's wise to do that because the rats will go there to look for food," Kelvin replied.

"Sounds good to me," Adam said.

But Harvey grabbed Ray before telling him to help carry the net. Alice watched him move towards it before reaching out to grip a piece, not wanting to be left out as it was taken towards the farmhouse.

CHAPTER TWENTY-SIX

The police station received a phone call, with the person on the other end sounding frightened to the point of screaming. Jack was talking to Chris, and, just from the background noises could tell all wasn't well.

"Where are you?" he asked.

"I'm in a cupboard under my stairs," Chris replied, kicking at the door. "The fuckin' rats are tryin' to chew their way in and I've nothing to fight them off with."

"Is there anyone with you?"

"Yeah, my girlfriend's upstairs with the baby, and Marie's here..."

Jack heard Chris gulp before loud bangs shook his eardrums.

"...I can't protect them, and I don't know if they're okay," Chris finished.

Jack frowned as he clicked his fingers to get Louise's attention.

"We need to get suited up and get to Chris' house. And we need to do it now," he whispered before returning to the call. "I'm on my way."

The phone went silent in Chris' hand as the scratching intensified. He stared at the door, knowing soon the rats would get in to attack him, shaking as he'd never shaken before. But a tiny smile escaped him because the rodents had stayed downstairs.

"You fuckin' won't get me!" he hollered, making sure they heard so they didn't go towards the bedroom.

His voice pushed its way through the tiny ceiling above his head to reach the room where two frightened adults sat, as Rose lay in her cot gurgling, feeling comforted by the familiar sound.

Marie was lost in a pool of tears as Rachael, who had become indecisive as to stay or venture back downstairs, got up and walked towards the door, staring worryingly at Marie as she placed an ear against it.

"He's okay," she whispered.

"Shouldn't we help him?" Marie asked.

"You heard what he said. He said to stay in here."

"Earlier you were a bitch to him, so taking orders was the last thing on your mind, but you've changed. Why?"

The 'bitch' word annoyed Rachael, but it wasn't the time to fuss over it.

"Earlier, I didn't believe there was a gang of crazy rats out there. Plus, I thought he was fucking you behind my back, but I got them both wrong." Rachael bowed her head. "So now I need to do what I'm told and keep you and Rose safe."

"And Chris? Who's keeping him safe?"

Rachael felt like screaming but couldn't risk raising her voice again. She glanced over at Rose to smile at how innocent everything around her felt, her calmness to the situation making Rachael more positive.

Chris sat with his back firmly against a wall, sweating in a panic as his feet pushed against the bottom of the now breaking up into small holes door, kicking out at each rat head that appeared in hope of at least injuring one or breaking its teeth. He cringed from the pain as the squealing caused his eardrums to burn, so knew he'd hurt one.

"You're not getting in here," he whispered, staring at the door.

———

The sound of a speeding police car, with its siren blaring, caught the attention of most of the people in town as the church bell rang. It was now *7:00 pm*. Steve drove like a maniac as Louise, and Jack sat in the backseat, but their riot-suited bodies bounced from side to side before colliding against their shields.

"Right, you guys ready!" Steve hollered, feeling electric.

"I'll be ready once my head stops spinning," Louise queasily replied.

"Sorry," Steve said, glancing at her through the rear-view mirror.

"How do you know where Chris lives?"

"Jack told me."

"Oh," Louise replied, smiling as Jack hit his head on the roof.

They saw Marie leaning out of an upstairs window as the car screeched to a halt outside the house.

"Chris is trapped downstairs. Help him! Please!" she shouted, watching them exit.

Helmets were placed on as Steve and Jack charged the front door. It was released from most of its hinges as they entered the house, but Jack gulped after spotting rats running in and out of the downstairs cupboard.

"It's too late!" he cried out. "They've got him."

Louise pushed past him to race towards the cupboard but slowed down after a rat pounced to miss her by inches. She freaked out as it ran off, feeling on edge as she looked inside, but smiled to surprise the others.

"He's not here!" she shouted, swinging her baton at the rat as it came back.

Steve stayed by the door, acting as a security guard who was prepared to stop the rats from escaping but had a feeling it wouldn't be easy. He focused hard with a sternness in his eyes, gripping his baton ready to strike, as thoughts of keeping the rats alive were quashed. He knew it was too risky trying to save them. He braced himself and held his shield, waiting for them to strike.

But something crashed against a wall in the kitchen to spook everyone. Steve watched on as Jack and Louise charged into the room until the sound of a third person made him think Chris was alive. He was, and he was swinging a vacuum cleaner pipe, crashing it against the wall after missing the rats. He turned the cleaner on to spook the rodents before sucking one onto the end of the pipe, nervously laughing as it failed to break free from the immense suction; his face red with rage as blood spilt from the bites and scratches.

The others shouted at Chris, but he was too far gone to notice. He slammed the struggling rat to the floor, pushing the pipe down hard against its belly, as its squeals echoed around the room, but a gun fired and a bullet ripped through its head.

"Jesus! Louise! That nearly hit me," Chris shouted, freaking out even more.

"Can you turn that thing off!" she shouted back, waving a finger towards the cleaner.

Chris did it and backed away, but he couldn't stop staring at the gun.

"...Why were you hoovering the house?"

"I wasn't," Chris replied, nervously laughing at her. "This was the only thing I could find inside the cupboard to keep the rats at bay." He almost collapsed but used the pipe to stay upright. "They charged in so fast...If it wasn't for my trusty cleaner I would've been dead."

"Before today I didn't rate those cleaners," Jack said, laughing. "But, after seeing the suction pull that rat in, I think I may buy one..."

He cautiously stared at Louise as she held the gun like a wild west heroine, shaking his head as she aimed it at the retreating rats.

"...I thought you couldn't have one?"

"I couldn't," she said blushing.

Jack sighed as the rats ran beneath his feet, but he was more scared of Louise firing the gun at them like she was at a shooting gallery. He froze as bullets ripped apart the floor, missing the rats as they ran towards Steve.

"For fuck sake Lou, put that gun away before you shoot one of us!" Steve yelled, grimacing at the rats closing in.

He desperately attempted to re-stand the door in the hope of blocking off the escape route but struggled to hold it in position and keep his guard up.

"...Are you lot going to help me or just watch?!" he yelled as

everyone raced from the kitchen.

Chris arrived with the pipe still in his hand to see Steve kick out at the rats, as the door came close to falling off its hinges.

"...Get them away from me!" Steve shouted as fear raced through him.

But the sound of batons slamming against the floor caused the rats to run around the living room.

Jack and Louise chased them but tired quickly, as the large rat watched from a corner of the room. It focused on Jack as he stopped to cough like a man who smoked forty cigarettes a day before squeaking out a command for the others to jump him; moving swiftly as some squeezed inside his protective suit to claw at his back.

"Can someone get these fucks off me!" he bellowed, seething as he tried to reach them.

Louise tried to help but was worried to swing her baton at the clawing rats.

"...Just do it!" Jack cried out, glaring at her. "And do it now!"

She gulped and smacked her baton against his back as Chris winded him with a swing from the pipe against his stomach.

"...Sssshit!" Jack screamed, toppling over as the rats jumped off him.

Chris turned on the cleaner again to startle them, including the large one to see them race away from Jack and aim for Steve, as Louise came close to crying over what she'd done.

"Would you fuckin' believe it, they're scared of my cleaner," Chris said, laughing nervously.

But no one laughed with him as Louise helped Jack off the floor. They saw the rats swerve away from Steve to aim for the stairs, running up them to disappear into the shadows.

"You can turn it off now!" Steve said sternly.

Chris winked at him and did it, but his mouth dropped after remembering who was upstairs. He raced for the staircase to push Steve as he tried to stop him, reaching it to climb them as Steve shouted, but it made no difference as Chris aimed for the top.

"Get back down here!" Steve shouted again.

"Not until my family are safe."

Marie opened the bedroom door after hearing Chris' voice, feeling excited at finally being rescued, but the rats rushed her to leave her flopping to the floor in fear. They bit into her arms and legs as a petrified Rachael watched on, as Chris stood nearby unable to help, his head spinning from the horror as he was pushed to one side by the officers. They attempted to save Marie, but the large rat tore at her face and jugular, leaving her whimpering on the blood-soaked floor. But seconds later she was dead.

"Rachael! Grab the baby," Chris screamed.

She was just about to when one of the rats pounced on the cot. Her legs trembled after a terrible thought of her daughter dying in a sick way almost caused her to faint, but, as the rat sprang for Rose, it landed on an arm appearing swiftly above her head, hanging lifeless after being stabbed. Steve moved his arm away after blood landed an inch from Rose, but she just gurgled and smiled.

Chris raced into the room to hug Rachael, but she just stared awkwardly at Jack standing by the door. She followed his vision switch from her to Rose and back again as she mimed the words - 'I'm sorry," but Jack gulped as he stared at the baby again.

Louise grabbed the duvet from the bed and placed it over Marie's body, feeling emotions she wasn't used to upon seeing Jack's weird behaviour. She was lost as to why he was still watching Rose. His injuries suddenly became the least of his worries as memories of his life before the police force crashed into his mind. Memories of a time when he worked for the hospital and worked with a certain lady who'd recently given birth. He'd left that job after getting too involved with her, feeling it wasn't right to see someone from work, especially when they were with someone else, but Jack didn't know until now that the other person was Chris. This was the first time in over eight months that he'd seen Rachael.

A tear fell on Chris' back after Rachael guessed what Jack was thinking. She knew she couldn't deny it if he asked her but prayed he wouldn't, especially seeing as Chris was in the room, but Chris was too busy shedding tears after what just happened to Marie.

Steve removed the rat from his wrist and tossed it into a corner, becoming alert again after wondering where the others were.

"Can anyone see the others!" he yelled, wiping the rat's blood from his arm.

But Rachael glared at him before picking Rose up and cradling her in her arms.

"I think they headed downstairs again," Louise replied.

"Right! I want you both to grab some clothes. You're coming back to the station where it's safe," Steve said to Chris and Rachael. "Until this town's rid of those pesky critters."

Neither of them argued about the decision. They just grabbed what they needed and followed the officers outside.

CHAPTER TWENTY-SEVEN

Everyone remained quiet at the farmhouse as they waited for the rats, but Ray found it annoying, his patience running out before the net was even in position. If he had his way, then he would blast them all and get it over with.

Walter had just taken a call from *Clive Finchley*, a professor ranked higher than him. He knew it would happen eventually. Clive sounded infuriated after hearing that some of the rats had been killed, so had pleaded with Walter to convince the police to trap the rest inside the net. He was reassured after Walter told him the plan.

Ray smiled sadistically after overhearing Walter talk to Harvey about the conversation, hoping Harvey would tell him to go fuck himself and that the rats were going to be wiped out. But that didn't happen, so Ray was left even more annoyed. He watched Adam and Harvey leave Walter to walk towards the back of the house, having no idea what their plan was, but in truth, he didn't care. He just wanted out of this.

"Do you want to help me look for them inside the house?" Walter creepily asked Alice.

She said 'yes' even though his voice scared her, but Ray sighed

as they entered the house, feeling left out for not having any orders. He got bored fast, so re-entered his car and switched on the radio to sing along to the song that was heard. He was enjoying himself until a hand reached inside to turn the radio off.

"Why don't you just fuck off! And do one," he screamed at Kelvin. "I'm taking a break…"

Kelvin nervously retreated as he tried reasoning with Ray, but he was too pumped up to listen.

"…I said, I'm taking a fuckin' break!" he yelled, turning the radio back on.

He waited to see if Kelvin would attempt to turn it off again, becoming angrier when the man ignored him to reach back inside the car, but this time Ray exited to throw him to the ground.

"Noise will make them scatter. Can't you see that?" Kelvin questioned.

"Make them scatter? Let me tell you something, there are no fuckin' rats here so how can they scatter?"

Harvey overheard Ray's violent shouts so raced back to witness Kelvin get to his feet.

"What's going on?" he asked, moving in between the pair.

"Nothing!" Ray answered sharply. "I wanted to listen to some tunes but this prick tried to stop me."

"You wanted to listen to some tunes, did you?" Harvey became annoyed upon smiling sarcastically. "Who'd you think you are? You're not the bloody pied piper you know."

Ray was lost for words to fight back after trying to get his head around the pied piper bit, so spat on the ground to see Alice arrive.

"What have you done?" she asked him, knowing he'd been acting like a child again.

"I've done nothing," he replied, standing next to her. "Why do you always assume I'm to blame for everything?"

"I've heard all about you," Harvey said. "And none of it's any good."

Ray lost it again, so Alice tried calming him down.

"What you mean, none of it's any good?" he angrily asked.

"I mean, I can't work out why you were accepted into the force." Harvey walked closer to him. "You're an imbecile. You're always in trouble with your superiors. You don't obey orders, and you think you know more than everyone else." He was right in Ray's face. "Have I missed anything?"

Ray smirked at him. "Yeah! You missed out the bit about me fuckin' your wife."

Harvey snapped and punched him in the jaw. And Adam saw it as he arrived.

"Calm down, chief. You don't want to lower yourself to his standards."

"You all saw that. That's an assault that is!" Ray hollered, gripping his chin.

"I saw nothing," Adam replied.

Everyone agreed with him, even Alice. It wasn't what Ray expected from her, but she'd had enough of his trouble-making when bored and he needed to grow up.

Ray cursed under his breath before walking at speed towards the back of the house.

"Don't be long. You have a job to do!" Harvey shouted out to him.

But Ray kept on walking. He never spoke, just walked.

Alice felt sorry for him but knew he couldn't keep doing what he did and get away with it. This time he didn't.

"...Right, let's get back to work," Harvey told the others. "If no rats turn up soon then we'll need another place to set up the net."

He stared at the house, knowing Walter was still inside searching for his beloved rats.

CHAPTER TWENTY-EIGHT

Everyone inside Peter's house settled down to watch a movie, with Trey, Nathan, and Cortney all sitting on the sofa as *Ratatouille* played on the television. Peter and John sat in armchairs on either side, seemingly lost in bad thoughts about what had happened in John's store as the sound of a plate crashing to the floor in the kitchen interrupted them. John comforted the children as Peter slowly left the room.

Hmm, it must've fallen from the plate rack, he thought, feeling confused.

"Is everything okay in there?" John shouted out.

"Yeah! Everything's fine." Peter bent down to pick up the broken pieces. "One of the plates fell from the rack."

"How come?"

"I don't know..."

But the cat flap swung to frighten Peter.

He looked around for Twinkle (Cortney's cat), but couldn't see it anywhere, scratching his head because he could've sworn Twinkle had just entered the room. *But where was it?*

"...It's all sorted!" he shouted out before placing the broken pieces in the bin. "I hope you pressed pause on the movie."

He re-entered the room to see a smiling John holding the DVD remote.

"Of course, I pressed pause," he said, pressing the play button. "Didn't want you missing out on what the rat in the movie is doing."

They both laughed, knowing the moment was only temporary; an escape from what was happening outside.

———

Two cars filled with emotional people came to a halt outside the police station, as Jack drove the police car containing Rachael, Louise, and Rose, while Steve drove an emotional Chris. He had wept all the way to leave Steve stuck for something to say. He stared at Chris through the rearview mirror, but Chris wasn't looking back.

Jack glanced to his left and shivered after seeing many rats run across the street. "Look over there."

"I spotted them," Louise replied. "But let's get you cleaned up before going after them."

She knew he had struggled to drive, especially after his back hurt every time he leaned against the seat, but Jack was just being Jack. And sometimes that worried Louise. She exited the car to check where the rats had gone, pleased they weren't in sight before opening the back door, but she became a nervous wreck after Rachael handed Rose over to her.

"It's okay, she's not a piece of fragile china," Rachael said, smiling as Louise cradled Rose in her arms.

"I know," the reply came as Rachael left the car to take Rose back.

She carried her into the station as Jack opened his door, but his wincing grabbed Louise's attention.

"Don't you move...I'm coming to get you!" she shouted at him, holding the car door as he gripped onto her arm.

"Stop your fussin'," he said, rising from his seat. "I'll be fine."

Louise pretended not to hear him as she helped him towards the station, but the pain ripped through him with every step he took. Steve smiled at them as he closed in, happy to see Louise take control as he walked Chris closer to the main entrance.

"You got this?" Steve asked her as he reached for his phone. "I'll be in soon..."

Louise nodded as she escorted Jack into the building before Chris slowly followed.

"...Did you catch any rats?" Steve asked Adam, as the phone was quickly answered.

"Not yet. Why?"

"Because there's been a sighting in town."

Adam swore under his breath. "You don't think they've left here and gone to you, do you?"

"I don't know, but there are loads here." Steve glanced at more rats running down the street. "It looks like they're planning another attack. I doubt we'll be able to maintain them if they do."

"What do you mean? You had trouble that you've not told me about?"

Steve knew he should've kept Adam in the loop over what was happening at Chris' house, but everything happened so fast that there wasn't time to stop, pause, and phone in a report.

"There was a death of a female in a recent house we had to go to...I've brought the survivors back to the station."

"Shit! Sorry to hear that. Just keep everyone safe."

Just then a nosey Harvey turned up to listen in on the conversation.

"What's going on?" he asked.

Steve overheard Adam telling Harvey what was said before his voice returned to the phone.

"You're in charge over there, so keep order until we arrive." Adam looked in front of him. "If no rats turn up soon then we'll head back to town."

Steve shook himself as the phone call ended, as thoughts of clearing the people off the streets became a priority. He looked for the rats but they were gone, so slowly entered the station.

"I need everyone fit and able to help get the locals safe," he said, clapping his hands before seeing Louise clean Jack's wounds. "You okay?"

Jack looked at him and gulped from the pain, but he wasn't going to say 'No' when the town needed his help. "I'm fine. It's just a flesh wound."

"Good," Steve said, thankful for the answer. "I want you and Louise to come with me."

"But what about us?" Chris asked, fearing for his life more than before.

"I want you and your family to stay here to block the windows and secure the doors." Steve walked over to Jack to hand him the key to the armoury cabinet. "Here's your chance to grab a gun before Harvey finds out."

"I don't think so, but thanks," Jack replied, cringing again, as Louise wrapped a bandage around his chest.

"Surely there's something you want apart from what you've got already?"

Jack smiled as he walked over to the cabinet. "I've always wanted to try one of these," he said, opening it to grab a taser gun.

Steve and Louise laughed.

"Keep it with you," Steve ordered, as Jack closed the cabinet. "Because we're not coming back until those things are caught or destroyed."

———

The clock above the TV ticked to half-past seven as another loud crash emerged from Peter's house. A mug stand had fallen over, smashing all the mugs to smithereens. John and Peter rushed to the kitchen feeling confused as to why it had happened. But suddenly, John's face turned pale as if something had scared him.

"They're here," he whispered.

Peter knew exactly what he meant. "What do we do?" he whispered back.

"We get the kids to safety."

But Cortney appeared in the doorway, surprised to see the mess on the floor.

"Are you okay, dad?" she asked, seeing him stare at the smashed mugs.

"Yeah, love, I'm fine." Peter touched her shoulder before hinting for her to go back to the living room. "There must've been an earth tremor or something."

"A tremor?" she replied, feeling lost. "Wouldn't other things have fallen if it was a tremor?"

"Maybe," he said, now physically turning her around to walk her back to the boys. "A plate fell also, so there's your 'other things' theory sorted."

Cortney pulled a face as they arrived back in the living

room, but the boys were now fidgeting instead of watching the movie.

"Can we see! Can we see!" shouted Trey, feeling excited and eager to investigate the mystery of why things had fallen in the kitchen.

But Peter panicked as the thought of three, energetic children running loose suddenly hit him.

"Do you want to play hide and seek?" he asked Trey, hoping the change in subject worked.

"Hide and seek?" Nathan asked, not feeling the excitement as his brother was.

"Yeah," Peter replied, smiling.

Nathan looked him up and down, still unsure of the idea, but soon agreed after Trey pulled on his arm.

John watched on from the kitchen with a brush and pan in his hands. He was nervous but tried to hide it as he picked up the broken mugs, smiling weakly as Peter organised the rules on his version of hide and seek.

"...You can only hide upstairs," he said to the children, knowing there would be a 'why?' to come from at least one of them.

It was Cortney who asked it, but Peter explained it was because he and John were too old to run around the whole house looking for them. Cortney giggled.

"Right, off you go!" Peter said, puffing out his cheeks as the children ran up the stairs.

"What you up to?" John asked as Peter closed in on him.

"This is our chance to search the house for those fuckin' rats."

They rushed around the kitchen to open cupboard doors, searching for evidence that rats had been or were still there. But, after a minute, the sound of a bored Cortney shouting, "Are you coming to find us or what?!" spooked them.

"Just a minute!" Peter shouted back. "You keep hiding!"

They paused, thinking she was about to come down again, but, after hearing nothing resumed the search. This time at a more frantic speed. John checked inside cereal boxes before pouring the contents onto the floor, knowing from previous experiences that rodents would go for the cereal, but nothing out of the ordinary was seen. Peter grabbed a broom in case a rat closed in but shrieked after remembering how useless he was at hitting things back at school. He just hoped his swing had improved since the days of having been picked last for tennis, baseball, and cricket.

"You okay?" John asked, seeing Peter shaking.

"I will be once this is over with." Peter sweated as he gripped the broom handle tight. "You do remember how good I was with a stick at school?"

John laughed nervously "How good you were? You were very, very good. Not!"

"I know, that's why I'm nervous as hell." Peter looked at the cereal on the floor. "What if a rat jumps out at me, but I swing like a pussy and miss it? It'll get me."

"Peter! Mate! Just concentrate and think of the kids. They need us to win."

"I'm getting bored now!" Cortney shouted again.

"Okay! We're coming to find you!" Peter scarily replied.

"Why are you trying to sound like Dracula?"

"I wasn't, was I?"

John nudged him as the cat-flap swung again, but this time it sounded like a crazy man swinging an axe. Never before today had they been petrified by the bloody cat flap, but here they were holding onto each other like Scooby-Doo and Shaggy after they'd seen a phantom.

"Fuckin' flap!" John shouted.

"Shush! Don't shout because the kids will come down."

"Dad! Are we playing this game or what?" said Cortney, clearly frustrated.

John poked Peter. "How come only your daughter is speaking? The boys are very quiet."

"Maybe they've fallen asleep?" Peter giggled, rushing to the bottom of the stairs. "Cortney! love! Can you find out where the boys are? They seem very quiet."

"Duh! You dummy! They're quiet because we're playing hide and seek."

Peter shook his head, feeling stung by her swift reply. "I know we are, you, clever clogs, but just check to see if they're okay."

Cortney could tell from the tone of his voice that he wasn't as chilled as before but thought it was because he was looking after someone else's children.

"Okay, will do. Then will we play the game?"

"Yep! Then we'll play the game."

Peter brushed the cereal into a pile before scooping some back into a box, cursing after realising it was Cortney's favourite.

"What's got into you?" John asked.

"I have to salvage some. Cortney will expect it for breakfast."

"Get a grip!" John replied, slapping the box out of his hand.

Peter lost his nerve after seeing something rush towards him from the corner of his eye but sighed with relief when the cat appeared, as John shook his head at how freaked out he was getting.

"Hey, girl," John whispered to the cat. "You want some food?"

Twinkle purred and rubbed against his leg as Peter breathed deeply before reaching into a cupboard.

"Here you go, get this down ya," he said, emptying some cat biscuits into the cat bowl.

But, as he placed it on the floor, Cortney rushed into the kitchen.

"I can't find them anywhere!"

"What do you mean you can't find them?" Peter asked.

"The boys have disappeared."

John's jaw dropped as Peter turned pale.

They ran past Cortney, climbing the stairs as she stroked Twinkle, but the cat arched its back and hissed at something she couldn't see. She became curious by its rage as it growled like a deranged monster, seeing it run back through the catflap before shaking her head to see the mess on the floor.

"What's happened to my cereal?"

Peter and John searched the upstairs rooms to find them empty, as an open window in Cortney's room left them petrified. Peter rushed to it, leaning out to stare at the conservatory roof as thoughts of the boys leaving the house left him shaken.

"Bloody hell! John. They've gone outside," he yelled, staring anxiously at the slowly darkening sky.

John raced down the stairs, fearing the boys had come to harm, his heart crushed as he opened the front door to shout into the street.

Cortney heard him as she looked at the catflap swaying back and forth, but she wasn't scared, she was just curious. She walked closer to see Twinkle pop its head through the flap, smiling, waiting for the cat to come to her, but it didn't, it just remained where it was. She called Twinkle's name a few times but it never responded; its eyes were now motionless as Cortney reached out a hand to stroke it. But Twinkle felt stiff.

"Hey, girl, what's wrong?"

She placed her hands around the cat's neck to gently tease it through the flap, but only the front half of its body emerged. Cortney quickly let go, jumping out of her skin as a rat clung to the cat's stomach, biting into it to ignore her as she collapsed against a cupboard door. She whimpered as the rat carried on feeding before finally screaming to alert John.

"Go upstairs to your dad!" he hollered, closing in. "I'll take care of this..."

He nervously helped Cortney off the floor but she froze at the sound of the rat, her eyes the only thing to move as she followed its movements.

"...*Do it now!*" John blasted.

Peter overheard the shouting, so ran to the top of the stairs, but his legs trembled after seeing Cortney crying at the bottom.

"What's up?" he said, knowing the answer already.

But he received no reply as he rushed down the stairs to hug her like he was never letting go.

John eyed up the rat as he reached for the broom before taking a swing as the flap shook violently, but his worry increased as he stared silently at a dozen more rats entering the kitchen. He dropped the broom as they bit into the cat's face, ignoring him until he tripped over the handle before shrieking to scare him to run for the stairs.

CHAPTER TWENTY-NINE

Troy had fixed the broken glass on the cage and had swept up all the broken pieces to place in a bin as Victoria did other things. He had no idea what the other things were, but she was now snooping inside Walter's office. To others, it may have seemed like she got on with the crazy professor, but deep down, Victoria was just like the lab assistants, the security guards, and even the students in not liking him. He was by far the most arrogant of all males she'd come across, and she'd come across quite a few. Some were ex-lovers, ex-colleagues, or even ex-friends, but Walter Toade, AKA the Toad man, was top of her list.

Victoria didn't know why she was in his office, but something had drawn her there. That, plus the fact Walter wasn't at the university gave her the courage to take a sneak peek at what he had inside. It was always locked when he wasn't around, but she knew where he kept the spare key. How she knew was another story, but she knew.

She sat at his desk and unlocked a drawer, but something caught her eye to shock her. It was a pair of her underwear. One of her favourites.

I washed this the other day, so how did it get here? That little bastard must've stolen it from the washing line.

Victoria sometimes brought her laundry to work to wash during her dinner break, especially when working long hours, as it was easier than driving home to do it. Walter knew she did it. He let her, and now she knew why.

He's a pervert who likes sniffing my panties. But why sniff them when they're clean? She almost smiled but a vision of Walter made her angry.

She placed the underwear on the desk before searching the drawer again, stopping after spotting a bottle of K-Y-jelly before staring awkwardly at the bin; feeling sick after noticing many crumpled-up tissues.

He's a fucking pig! No wonder he kept the door locked.

She opened all the drawers but saw nothing else out of the ordinary, so walked over to a tall filing cabinet in the corner, lifting the shutter to glance inside to find nothing unusual or out of place. But, as she was about to give up and leave, curiosity overtook her. She opened compartments to flick through files, feeling fascinated after seeing a shoebox hidden at the back; removing it to place on the desk whilst listening out for Troy. She lifted the lid to find a neatly folded lab coat with the name *Edward Munsun* written on it, picking it up to cringe after spotting spattered bloodstains all over it before dropping it on the table to catch her breath, as the name reminded her of the man who Walter sacked recently.

But why is his lab coat inside a box? and why is it in Walter's office?

Victoria stared at the blood patches until convincing herself that Edward may have had one of his unexplained nosebleeds whilst on duty before shaking her head and checking the box again. She spotted a bloodied knife to feel emotional after remembering that one went missing from the university canteen around the same time as when Edward was presumably sacked, seeing it glisten in the light, making her wish she wasn't so nosey.

But Troy shouted out to grab her attention.

"I won't be long!" she shouted back as Troy said something about making a cup of coffee before his voice faded into the distance.

She was about to leave the room when something on the desk caught her eye. It wasn't a scary something. It was something that made her smile. It was a business card with Adam Sayer's details.

He must've left it for Walter.

She breathed deeply, wanting so badly to phone the man who'd made her smile earlier, and who'd made her feel less like a lab assistant and more like a woman.

———

Adam's phone rang three times before he answered it. He wasn't going to, but everyone was glaring and pointing at him to make him feel embarrassed.

"Hello! Who's this?" he asked, holding up a hand as the others returned to looking for rats.

"Victoria. Walter's assistant."

"This is a surprise!" Adam grinned. "What can I do for you?"

Harvey leaned in to listen, but this time Adam moved away from him. "It's the university," he whispered before returning to talk to Victoria. "So! Are you okay?"

"Can you come to the lab?"

Victoria found it hard to explain what she'd seen so just said she'd found something that he should look at, but Adam wasn't in the mood for playing mind games. He recognised her tone was off and shaky so promised he'd be there very soon, knowing that in minutes 'Operation Farmyard' would be abandoned because of no sighting of the rats.

The phones went dead, leaving Victoria pleased as she replaced the lab coat and shut the lid on the box.

CHAPTER THIRTY

Trey and Nathan closed in on the store, feeling excited and nervous. It was Nathan's idea for them to sneak out of the house during the fake game of hide-and-seek because he'd filled Trey's head with the wonders of seeing the rare bird that Steve had mentioned earlier that day. It left him curious, so Nathan wanted to please him.

"You sure it'll still be there?" Trey asked.

"Sure, why not?"

They reached the door as rodents scurried unnoticed nearby, staring at the boys as they kept their distance.

"But the store is closed," Trey sadly said.

"So!" Nathan clanked a bunch of keys in his hand. "I took these earlier when John was in the kitchen."

"You know that's stealing, don't ya?"

"Shut up, Trey. Do you want to see the bird or not?"

"Yeah, of course, but you can't steal things. That's what mum always said."

"It's not stealin', it's borrowin'. I'm borrowin' 'em so we

can see the bird, then I'll give 'em back." Nathan hugged Trey. "You okay with that?"

Trey smiled. "Cool! I'm okay with it."

The excitement of seeing the bird prevented the boys from noticing just how quiet the street was, as the sound of the rats communicating nearby was washed out by the jingling of the keys.

"You ready to see this amazing bird?" Nathan asked, putting a key in the door.

Trey jumped excitedly up and down as Nathan opened the door, but the light was fading inside. Nathan knew that turning the light on would attract attention, so he pulled out a mini-torch from his pocket.

"You're like a detective," Trey said, feeling more excited.

"A detective who is goin' to find that bird."

They laughed as the torch was turned on, but the laughter was short-lived after seeing blood patches on the floor; frightening them to the point of almost giving up. Nathan grabbed Trey tight as he shut the door.

"You okay?" he asked, pulling Trey tighter.

"Nope."

"So, shall we go back?"

Trey nervously looked at him, close to tears after staring at the blood again, so Nathan took it as a 'Yes'. But, as they headed back to the door, Trey said, "Nope."

Nathan smiled, hoping he'd say that.

He was just as scared as Trey but his scared was more of a fun one.

"Come on! Don't worry about the blood on the floor, we need to find that bird."

"But Nath, what if the blood belongs to the bird?"

"There's only one way to find out."

Nathan was loving this. Not that the bird may be injured or dead, but the thrill of the moment.

"Come on birdie, birdie! Where are you birdie, birdie!" he shouted.

"Shush! We need to keep our voices down or it'll fly away."

"Sorry," Nathan whispered. "That's if the blood isn't from the bird, right?..."

He nudged Trey, knowing the words were making him believe the bird could be in trouble.

"...You do know I'm joking, right?" Nathan walked over to the counter. "Everythin' will be okay."

Trey watched the torchlight circle it before smiling after spotting the comics next to the window; picking one up and opening it as the night sky sent a dark shadow inside the room to swallow his vision.

"Damn!" he said, feeling annoyed as he reached for the light switch.

"No lights, Trey!" Nathan swiftly replied, throwing a pen at him. "You don't want to frighten the bird."

"Sorry, but Nathan. Nathan," Trey whispered, as Nathan moved to the other side of the counter.

But he disappeared behind it to leave Trey guessing why?
"...Nath?"

Trey smiled to see him reappear with his hands behind his back, but the smile faded after Nathan moved to the front of the counter.

"What are you hiding?" Trey asked, squinting nervously.

"Nothing," Nathan replied, smiling again.

"You've got something behind your back. I can see it."

Nathan closed in, tossing a dead rat onto the comic, laughing as Trey tearfully freaked out to drop them on the floor.

"Shut up! You wuss! It's only a rat."

Trey cried as Nathan kicked the rat away.

"I'm sorry," he said, feeling bad for what he did. "I thought you'd think it was funny." He hugged Trey again before wiping a tear from his eye. "Don't cry, little bro. Please..."

He then pulled a silly face to make Trey laugh.

It always worked. And even now, as they stood in the darkening store with a blood-soaked floor and a dead rat nearby, it still did.

"...Let's find the bird."

"Okay," Trey replied, smiling again.

"Oh yeah! What was it you wanted before?"

"Nothing. I was just goin' to tell you that the latest edition of your favourite comic is in stock."

———

Brendan wanted so badly to find some action as he walked through town with Steve, Louise, and an injured, but still capable Jack.

"You sure you can carry on?" Brendan asked him, knowing the answer already.

"Stop your whining." Jack cringed. "You youngsters want time off for splitting a fingernail." He laughed, but Brendan knew he was just putting on a brave face.

"Jack, you're just a crazy old fool."

"Hey, less of the old."

"I think those rats are up to something," Louise said, butting in.

"Why?" both men replied.

"Because I've just seen some gathering over by the store."

"Okay...You and Steve can monitor those until Harvey gets

here while we head to the other end of town; see if we can spot more," Jack replied.

Steve was about to have his say, seeing as he was the authority figure, but decided not to after the plan made sense. He nodded as Jack and Brendan walked away before seeing Louise eagerly watch the rats.

————

Trey and Nathan plucked up the courage to walk past the counter, as each step brought them closer to the back of the store.

"You still scared, little bro?"

Trey reached out and held his hand. "Nah! Not scared no more."

"Good, 'cause there's a bird here that we need to find."

But a sharp bang stalled them as they reached the stockroom. Nathan puffed out his cheeks as he shone the torch at the door, his hand shaking as Trey hid behind him, with neither speaking as they walked into the room.

————

Jack and Brendan walked along the road, cautious and on edge, shining torches from left to right. They closed in on Peter's house as consistent shouts drew them in until seeing John leaning out of a bedroom window, his voice now hoarse.

"Quick! Hurry! Rats have gotten inside, and two boys are missing!" he called out.

"You find out where the boys are while I check the house," Brendan told Jack.

"I'll go with you," the reply came, but Brendan refused the help.

"Jack, you're injured. You should look for the boys. I'll sort this mess out."

Jack looked at Brendan and smiled. Of the eight months he'd known him, this was by far the proudest he'd been. Gone were the childish tantrums at work, the squabbling fights with Louise, and the name 'nephew of the sergeant', and in their place was a man who thought of others first, a brave man. He watched Brendan slap down his visor, feeling emotional as he raced towards the house.

"Do you know where the boys went!" Jack shouted to John.

"No! One minute they were here and the next had climbed out of this window."

Peter appeared alongside John, fuming and wanting out of the house, as thoughts of being trapped for a second time by the rats brought back sad memories of Ted, leaving him scared for his daughter.

"We're coming with you!" he shouted to Jack.

Cortney pleaded with him, tugging on his shirt to stop him from going. "Dad! Please! You can't go out there. Please!"

She cried, and her tears almost changed Peter's mind, but he held her until she stopped, fighting back the need to cry himself.

"I want you to hide inside the wardrobe." He kissed her on the forehead. "And don't come out until someone comes to get you. You hear?"

"No! Please! Daddy! You can't go."

Peter winked at her as John braved himself to go outside, climbing out of the window and onto the conservatory roof as Jack looked on with admiration.

"You got anything to fight them off with!" he cried out to John.

"Just my faith in the Lord," the saddened reply came.

Peter hugged Cortney tighter before whispering, "I need you to be strong for me."

Her tears faded as she slowly walked towards the wardrobe, but the fear of the moment strangled her emotions as she climbed inside. Peter blew out his cheeks as he looked out the window, seeing John reach the ground before turning back to the wardrobe to close his eyes; sighing as he opened them to go outside. Cortney stayed silent as he disappeared, thinking only of - *What would happen if the rats got inside?*

She cringed at how tight the wardrobe was after a vision of trying out a coffin made her nervous before gulping at the sound of squeaks entering the room; staring at a thin beam of light appearing at the bottom to see dark shadows rush past.

———

Jack slapped both men around the arm as Peter courageously arrived. But he was just as nervous as John, and Jack noticed.

"You two are brave," he said, as they suddenly shied away.

"We're not brave. We're just trying to do the right thing," John replied.

———

The brothers huddled inside the stockroom, as the sound of rats scurrying close by frightened them. Trey choked from the feel of one brushing past him to sneeze like he had an animal allergy, as Nathan squeezed Trey's nose to soften the sound. But the rat heard as it stopped to twitch its whiskers. It stared at Trey, leaving him close to wetting himself as his heart bounced in his chest, but Nathan moved in front of him so the rat couldn't see.

"Shush!" Nathan whispered. "Don't make another sound."

Nathan held Trey tight after hearing more rats enter the room, but they scurried off back into the store. He wished he had chosen another spot to hide after realising the stockroom was the ideal place for the rats to look for food upon sighing to think of a way to get his brother out soon; glancing towards the rat as it remained twitching its whiskers. He knew they couldn't escape via the way they came in, so needed to escape out the back. He just hoped it was clear.

He saw the large rat appear in the doorway to feel shocked by its enormity as an effort to stop Trey from looking failed. He knew the rat would make Trey want to scream if he saw it, but, as he was about to, Nathan placed a finger on his lips. They followed the rat's movements but it wasn't going towards them, it was just staring at them to send a shuddering fear down their spines. Trey freaked out and ran as the large rat opened its mouth, leaving Nathan too slow to stop him as it followed him around the room. He saw Trey haul himself onto a shelf unit before the rat reached him, happy to see him now out of reach as the rat attempted to pounce, but he wasn't feeling excitedly scared anymore.

"Just stay up there!" he yelled. "It's too big to jump that far."

"But I'm scared." Trey pushed his knees up close to his chest. "I don't want to die."

Nathan felt like charging the rat, but the other one was moving towards him to worry him. He could hear Trey constantly shouting his name as the squeaking suffocated the words, leaving Nathan struggling as the other rat closed in. But, after more shouts, he plucked up the courage to haul himself onto the same unit, shaking it to almost toppling it over. The brothers quivered and cried as another five rats appeared in the doorway, all glaring in their direction.

———

Steve and Louise spotted more of the vermin gathering outside the store.

"This doesn't look right," Steve said.

"What do you mean?" Louise replied, feeling concerned.

"I mean, look at them. They aren't even attempting to go inside." Steve stared at the surrounding area. "It's like they're trying to stop us from getting in."

"Why? What can be the reason behind that?" Louise shone her torch at the rats. "And anyway, how do they know we're here?"

"Put that away!" Louise did. "If they didn't know before then they sure as hell know now." Steve was angry with her. "Look at them staring out into the street. It's like they can smell us." He spat on the ground. "I'm sick of this shit!"

Louise backed away from him, thinking he was about to lose it, but voices closed in to stop Steve from doing whatever it was he was about to do.

"It's Jack!" Louise shouted, watching him close in with John and Peter.

"Two kids have gone missing," Jack said, gasping for air.

"I hope your bandage is still on," Louise replied.

"Two kids, you say?" Steve interrupted.

Jack panted as his heart raced before slowly standing upright. "Yep! That's what I said."

"They escaped from my house after we were invaded by rats," John cried out.

"Not you as well," Louise replied, feeling tired.

"What have I missed?" Jack asked.

"See for yourself," replied Steve, pointing towards a horde of rodents sitting on the front porch of John's store.

The others followed the line of his finger until feeling curious as to why the rats were there.

"...It's like they're waiting on orders," Steve said.

"So why did you ask about the missing kids?" Jack asked, scrunching his eyebrows.

"Because I think they're inside that store." Steve gulped hard, feeling emotional as a reminder of the two boys he'd spoken to earlier washed over him. "Makes sense as to why the rats have gathered there. They're waiting to feed on something that's about to be killed." His words shook the others. "The boys don't have long. Once the rats enter they'll be dead."

"Then we need to save them," Louise said, springing back to life again.

"Any suggestions?" Steve asked.

"I don't know, but we can't let those freaks get 'em."

Steve saw the agony in her eyes so knew she was on edge, but, before being able to calm her down, John burst into tears; the moment bringing the reality of it all crashing down on him as Peter comforted him before slowly walking him away.

"We'll have to go around the back to find a way in, but someone needs to stay here to keep those rats occupied." Steve shrugged, knowing no one wanted to be left alone.

"There's a secret way in that most people don't know about," John said after overhearing the words.

"Really?" Jack asked as Peter almost laughed.

"Yeah!" he said, giving John another hug. "Many years ago, someone built an underground base. Maybe they thought the world was going to end or something?" He stared at the store again. "So, they built a tunnel leading from the back entrance to the field opposite."

"You're shittin' me?" Steve said, choking with nervous laughter.

"Nope!" replied John. "We can get inside the store via that base."

"But who's staying here?" seemed the most terrifying four words to come from Steve's mouth since arriving in town. He scanned everybody but stopped on one person. "How fast can you run?" he asked Peter.

"Why'd you pick me?" he replied, panicking. "I'm taking you to the tunnel." He sweated faster than he'd ever sweated before.

"I don't need both of you to take me to the tunnel. However, I *do* need the help of Jack and Louise." Steve smiled at Peter. "So, it looks like you're the chosen one."

John cringed, thankful it wasn't him. He waited for Peter to disagree, but was stunned at how easily he caved in.

"I can run when I need to."

"Good, because you need to make those rats chase you," Steve said, knowing deep down Peter may be sacrificed to save the boys.

Louise became lost in other thoughts as her mind drifted towards another person. She kicked herself for not noticing before but the missing boys had become a top priority. She looked over at Jack as he prepared himself to help find the boys, knowing he was still in a lot of pain.

"Hey! Jack! Where's Brendan?"

But Jack pretended to ignore her. He hoped she would back down, but his ignorance annoyed her to ask again.

"He ran into Peter's house to save his daughter," he said, looking at her, feeling guilty.

"And the prognosis is?" she asked, knowing Jack probably didn't know.

"Mmmm...Not sure...We came here to look for the boys." Jack looked at the ground. "No one knows how they are."

"Fuck me!" Louise yelled. "This is killin' me." She turned to leave. "I'm going to get him out of there."

"But what about the boys!" Steve hollered at her.

"You and Jack can get them out. You don't need me. Let me find Brendan and the girl."

Jack reached out and touched her shoulder. "You take them back to the station. We'll get the boys and meet you there."

"Will do!" was the last words Louise said before racing off through the now ghostly town; the empty streets becoming creepy as she aimed for the house.

"She'll find your daughter," Steve said, turning to Peter before glancing again at the still-waiting rats. "Are you ready for this?"

Peter shrugged his shoulders. He had no answer, so hoped his legs wouldn't let him down.

Steve's plan of sneaking off around the back of the store after Peter distracted the rats sounded easy inside his head but he knew the realistic version wouldn't be as simple.

It may not even work, meaning there could be more than two boys dead by the time it was over.

CHAPTER THIRTY-ONE

Adam arrived back at the university to be ambushed by Victoria, but her mouth spit-fired words so fast he couldn't keep up. He tried his best to catch some, but what she said wasn't making any sense to him. He knew nothing about a man called Edward Munsun, so found the reason for being there slightly worrying. Victoria didn't go into too much detail whilst Troy was around, but, as soon as he left to do his rounds, she was back talking about the missing man until Adam believed her. It was hard for him not to when her choice of words sounded so convincing.

"How do you know something happened to him?"

"Just look at his lab coat if you don't believe me. It's full of blood."

"Maybe he just had a nosebleed?"

"That's what I thought at first, but why was his coat stuffed inside a box with a blood-covered knife?" Victoria prodded him.

"Okay! Ease off, girlfriend." Adam gently grabbed her finger and moved it away.

"I know something's wrong, so please take a look?"

Adam smiled at her the same way he did when he first met her that day, so couldn't say 'No'.

"Lead the way."

They reached Walter's office, and so far, Troy wasn't to be seen. Adam stared at the box on the desk, thinking now it was all a joke, scrunching his lips to glance at Victoria before moving towards it.

I hope she's not playing games with me. Not today.

He studied the box as his heart raced, thinking either a bunch of rubber snakes would jump out at him or something so horrible that he would be violently sick.

"Go on then, take a look," Victoria said, pushing him towards it.

"Okay! Okay! Just stop pushing me..."

Adam didn't know how to act around her. He tried hard to keep up with the serious police sergeant look but she made him nervous. He smirked as Victoria pushed him again before putting on gloves to remove the lid, seeing Edward Munsun's name on the lab coat to freak out like it wanted him to find out what happened to the man himself.

"...Did you touch this?" he asked, lifting the coat.

"Yeah...Sorry," Victoria replied red-faced.

But Adam smirked again. "It's okay. I'm sure you won't get arrested."

"Arrested? Why?" Victoria rushed out, stepping back with worry.

"I said, you won't be, so stop panicking and tell me more about this Edward guy."

Victoria explained everything she knew about the man, from when he first started working there, to his personality, and when he was finally sacked by Walter, presumably for mocking his name and calling him a toad. Adam almost laughed after hearing that bit but remained focused as he laid the coat on the desk.

"He was only here for six months, but no one has seen him for at least the last two."

"Do you seriously think he was sacked because he mocked Walter?" Adam asked, examining the knife.

"No! I don't." Victoria watched him closely. "It's not true."

"But are you sure?" Adam said, removing a plastic bag from a shelf before placing the knife inside.

"Yes! Edward was just a nice guy. A bit geeky, but nice," she said, as her stare towards Adam became more lustful. "He was working on a breakthrough with the rats, but it was all top secret."

"A breakthrough?"

"Yeah!" Her body shook with excitement. "Stop looking at me like I'm making it up." She was close to laughing after Adam pulled a face.

"I believe you. It's just I can't work out why he was sacked after only six months, especially when he was working on something with the rats."

"I know, it's all a bit weird to me as well. This is why I called you. Why would his lab coat be in Walter's office? And why is it covered in blood?"

"And why is there a bloodied knife?" Adam added, feeling the urge to touch her. But he knew it was wrong. "Why are we asking each other questions when all you want to do is kiss me?" He smiled and moved closer to her.

"I don't," was all Victoria said before Adam planted a passionate, soft kiss on her lips.

The kissing intensified as he pushed her back against a wall, stopping briefly to smile before nibbling her ear to leave Victoria's knees quivering. She reached down, gripping his erect penis over his trousers before slowly unzipping them as he begged her to go faster.

"What are you doing?" Adam weakly asked, fighting the urge. "We can't do this."

"Just shut up and fuck my face," the reply came, as Victoria revealed his cock. "I need feeding."

She licked the end until he pleaded with her to take it all in, but a *bang! bang! bang*! on the door halted her progress. Victoria turned to glare at the door as Troy shouted, "Vic, are you in there?"

Adam gulped hard after staring at Troy's blurred image through the steamed glass window before closing his eyes as thoughts of Troy walking in to see Victoria giving him a blowjob like some cheap hooker crossed his mind. But seconds later, Troy gave up and walked away as Adam felt the urge to cum. But he didn't as he pushed Victoria's head away, seeing her stick out her tongue as she rose to kiss him again.

"Yuk!" Adam whispered, cringing after tasting his penis before checking to see if Troy was still lurking outside the door.

"Stop moaning," Victoria said, smiling.

They kissed again as they pushed each other against the wall before rolling across it at speed to lose their balance; colliding with the filing cabinet to rock it from side to side until it moved away from the wall. But the noise stopped them in their tracks.

"Phew! What just happened?" Adam said, zipping up his trousers.

"I think we were almost fucking," a frustrated reply came. "And I use the word 'almost' in a not-so-happy way."

"Sorry...But maybe the cabinet moving was a sign that we should stop?"

"Why?" Victoria felt annoyed for not getting bent over Walter's desk.

"Because there was a hole behind it," Adam said, staring at it.

Victoria gaped at the mystery hole whilst Adam inspected it. He knew it was man-made, but the reason for it being there confused him.

"...Did you know anything about this?" he asked.

But Victoria had no answer for him. She was just as lost as he was.

She saw him lift a torch from his belt to shine inside the hole, as a rotten stench wafted out of it.

"What's that smell!" Victoria yelled, covering her nose with a hand.

"Well it's not my dick," Adam replied, holding his hand up to apologise.

Victoria looked at him and giggled. She loved how his presence made her feel less agitated, his smile relaxing her when all around her chaos was unfolding.

Adam scrunched his nose before rolling up his sleeve to place a hand inside the hole, feeling around as the torchlight lit it up, his face performing many facial expressions until his last one shocked Victoria.

"You okay?"

Adam 'yelped' like a dog who had just had its foot stood on as he whipped his arm out of the hole; his body shuddering as she repeated the words.

"Yeah, I think so." He waved but his fingers seemed numb. "It felt like I was shaking the hand of a dead person."

"What?"

"It was a cold feeling, like the feeling of touching death..."

Victoria felt sick as she saw him glance at the hole again.

"...I want you to look away," he told her.

"Why?"

"Do I need to say why?"

She closed her eyes as the torchlight lit up the wall before Adam bent over to peer inside the hole. He saw something jammed between the bricks, so reached in and grabbed it, but sweat poured from his brow after pulling out a rotten and discoloured hand that had been hidden inside the wall unnoticed by anyone except the maggots squirming around within the palm.

Adam disgustingly dropped it and Victoria heard it fall.

She opened her eyes but quickly shut them again after the remains of a human head rolled to the front of the hole, crashing to the floor to frighten her as maggots reeled around all over it. One crawled out of the only eye still available to make her want to scream, as the stench escaping the head strangled her to cough up vomit.

She cried before screaming out loud, as her voice echoed out of the room to be heard by Troy. He raced towards the office as his heavy boots smacked against the floor before yelling as his shadow appeared in the steamed glass window again, but this time he didn't hesitate. He opened the door to find Victoria crying into Adam's shoulder.

"What's happened?" he asked, feeling lost.

They moved to the side, leaving him flabbergasted after seeing the head; almost dropping to the floor after the eye seemed to stare back at him.

"Is that Edward?" he asked, feeling sick to his stomach.

"I think so. Well, what's left of him," Adam replied, focusing again.

"But he was sacked, wasn't he?"

Victoria, still crying, rushed towards the door. "So, Walter said," she sheepishly replied, making sure not to look at the grotesque sight again.

"I need to know everything about this Edward guy? And everything you know about the relationship between him and Walter!" Adam was furious as he yelled at Troy like he was to blame.

"But can you please do it outside this room?" Victoria asked, gripping the door handle.

"Oh yeah, sure," Adam replied.

He gently pushed the others back outside the office as the stench lingered close by.

CHAPTER THIRTY-TWO

As Steve, Jack, and John waited patiently out of sight of the rats, with each edging closer to making their way towards the secret tunnel, Peter was plucking up the courage to distract the rodents and hopefully make them chase him. He hadn't sprinted since his college days, so hoped there was still some power in those legs of his.

He finally appeared in the open after watching his friend and the others sneak off behind the store but wasn't planning on getting too close to the rats that haunted his mind. He shouted at them, but they took no interest in him.

"I'm over here!" he shouted again, but still none looked at him.

So, he gave up shouting to pick up a large stone from near his feet. *That'll get your attention*, he thought, throwing it at the rats. But it missed and smashed a window, showering glass to stir the rats into action.

"Fuck! I'm still shit at throwing."

They hissed at him and ran at him, but Peter was off like a rocket, refusing to look back; his legs moving as fast as they could in any direction to get the rats further away from the store.

———

It didn't take long before the others made it to the tunnel, but they sighed after noticing the secret door was covered with overgrowing brambles. Steve and Jack looked awkwardly at John before reaching down to pull them away.

"Right! Peter should've gotten their attention by now and has led them away from the store, so we'll have less to deal with when we get inside. But I want you, John, to keep close to us," Steve said, looking at him. "You got that?"

"Yep! Sure thing," John replied, gripping a large padlock covering a thick bolt on the door. "Shit! I don't have my keys on me."

"Please don't say that," Steve said, feeling more stressed.

"I didn't know I'd need them. And anyway, if the boys are inside my store then they'll have 'em."

They frantically searched for something to break the lock, shining torches as Jack shouted, "Found something!" before picking up a piece of metal belonging to a gate and handing it to Steve.

"Cheers," was all Steve said as he thrust it behind the lock, pulling and pulling to splinter the door as the lock broke away.

Everyone puffed out cheeks, glad to see it fall as Steve pulled the bolt away, but, as he opened the door, a damp and musty stench hit everyone in the face. Steve released his gun as the foul smell wafted away before taking a deep breath as he entered the tunnel, but a large cobweb latched itself to his head before a spider ran over him. He didn't seem to notice as he walked down the three wooden, creaky steps, but the spider made John quiver as it dropped to the ground.

"Fuck me! It's dark down here," Steve said, reaching the tunnel's soiled surface to shine his torch from side to side.

He shivered from the coldness, as nervous thoughts of a rat jumping out at him freaked him out.

"Everything okay down there?" Jack shouted.

"Yeah, all good," Steve replied, staring at what was inside the tunnel.

It was almost bare, apart from the odd, wooden box, a few glass bottles, and spider webs that gave it a Halloween feel, but Steve still felt nervous. He gripped his gun tight, hoping that the next time he shot at a rat he would hit it.

John was next to reach the bottom of the steps after pulling a cobweb from his face. He looked at his hand as the web stuck to it like glue, wiping it off against his body before standing next to Steve to hear him laughing. They saw the light from Jack's torch blast into the tunnel, but, as he followed them down, one of the steps cracked to leave him falling headfirst to the floor.

"Fuck! When will this day end," Jack screamed, now aching from new injuries.

———

Louise made it to Peter's house without seeing a single rat before spotting Brendan helping a distressed Cortney out of an upstairs window.

"Hey, are you okay?" she asked.

Brendan looked battered, bruised, and exhausted. "Just help the girl," he replied.

Cortney climbed down off the same ledge, crying from fear as she buried her head into Louise's chest. It surprised her, leaving her unable to refuse, so she gently stroked Cortney's hair as she mumbled words about rats being inside the house.

"It's okay, you're safe," Louise said to her.

The touchy-feely stuff wasn't what she did, she knew that, but right now couldn't stop herself from hugging the distraught girl.

"I'm on my way down!" shouted Brendan.

Louise glanced up at him to almost smile, but terror shot through her body after seeing rats jump at him to be fended off by his baton.

"Hold on! I'm coming!..."

She let go of Cortney to tell her to find a hiding place, seeing her shake before racing towards the house.

"...Just hang in there!" were the last words aimed at Brendan, who'd just clobbered a rat so hard that it flew out of the window to die on the roof below.

No other thoughts, apart from saving him, the guy she'd always bickered with at work, were inside Louise's mind as she neared the door. She spotted the blood-smothered cat flap before seeing the back end of the cat at the side of the house; its insides scattered close by leaving her flinching as she opened the door to release her gun. She was alert and ready for anything to jump out at her as she approached the kitchen, moving quietly with caution until standing in a pile of 'Rice Krispies', but the sound was nothing like the 'snap' 'crackle' and 'pop' she remembered. A shiver whizzed down her spine as her tearful vision switched from the catflap to the hallway, fearing the rats knew where she was as she held her breath; her gun hand shaking as she prepared herself to be ambushed. But no rats arrived as she walked towards the hallway.

Loud bangs coming from upstairs alerted her to speed

things up, but, as she reached the bottom of the staircase, a rush of rodents stormed towards her. She fired the gun, but the bullet missed to crash into step nine as two rats leapt over her head.

"Move out of my *fuckin'* way!" she screamed, but the rats in front of her seemed undisturbed.

Louise nervously stood on the next step, about to shoot again, but was left confused as a rat rolled around in front of her. She aimed the gun at it as the rats behind her jumped on her back, digging their claws into any weaknesses not covered by the protective suit.

"Just fuck off and leave me alone!" she shouted, releasing her baton to try to pry them off. "Brendan! Brendan! Talk to me!"

She felt the stares from the rats in front of her burn her skin, as their statue-like appearance left her extremely afraid, but she knew she couldn't let them win. She felt blood seep down her back, but the pain was masked by her fury. She gritted her teeth and winced after feeling more claw marks before purposely leaning back to fall to the bottom of the stairs, crushing the rats with her body weight before prodding them with her baton to see if they moved. They didn't.

"That'll teach you to mess with me," she said, almost crying from the pain.

She looked up as a rat leapt at her, but her gun fired instantly as it closed in; the bullet exploding its head to leave blood stinging her eyes.

The remaining rats scurried back to the top, aiming for the room where a tired-out Brendan stood. He'd tried his best to keep them at bay the last time they attacked and felt lucky they hadn't penetrated his riot suit, but, after a violent battle that left another few rodents dead, he was exhausted. He sat on the open window sill to hear squeals as the rats aimed for him, but all he could do was watch them attack.

Louise shouted up to him again but the words were lost before they reached him. She raced up the stairs to stand by the bedroom doorway, seeing him fall out of the window.

"BRENDANNNN!!!!"

She screamed upon reaching it, but no matter how loud she shouted it couldn't prevent Brendan from bouncing off the conservatory roof to crack his head on the pavement. She climbed outside to rescue him but knew deep down it was too late.

Cortney trembled after witnessing Brendan's fate, crying fast tears as she stepped out of her hiding place to see his body twitch. She looked up to see Louise almost slip off the roof, her screams becoming more frantic, reaching the ground before moving aside to let her stand over Brendan's body. Louise stared at the puddle of blood that dripped from his head, still hoping he was okay, that he wasn't dead, but his head was crushed.

"Wake up," she whispered, kneeling to hold his hand.

Cortney looked away, crying even harder.

"...Why, oh *why*!" Louise shouted at Brendan as the clothing surrounding her knees got soaked in blood. "You should've called for backup." She turned to see his riot helmet on the ground. "I've told you time and time again to strap it up when wearing it, but you never listened." She punched his chest as her body became emotionally broken.

"Is he dead?" Cortney asked, whimpering as she placed a soft hand on Louise's shoulder. "I think we'd better go. They're coming!"

Louise glared at the rats bundling out of the house.

"Why can't you just go away!" she shouted at them, grabbing Cortney's hand. "I need you to run to the station..."

She wiped tears away from Cortney's face, but Cortney refused to go alone. She was too scared to.

"...Get to the station, *now*!" Louise screamed, pushing Cortney to start running.

"I can't! I need you to go with me."

Louise watched the rats spread out, knowing they were planning an attack.

"*Run*!" she screamed, getting to her feet to go with Cortney.

They turned to see how close the rats were, but none had chased after them; they'd stopped once reaching Brendan's body to feed on his face.

———

Steve walked in front to light up a path with his torch as the men neared the back entrance of the store. He was pleased to see no rats but knew it could change at any time.

"Are we nearly there?" he asked John.

"Not far now," John replied, coughing. "The ladder leading to the stockroom floor is just ahead."

"I've never seen a trapdoor in your stockroom before," Jack said.

John looked at him. "It's the old stockroom. It was too small, so I use it to store my rubbish bins."

"I see the ladder," Steve said.

"About time," Jack replied, shining his torch on it.

Everyone gathered to stare at the trapdoor.

"Who's going to open it?" John asked, wincing from even thinking about the idea.

"It's your store, *you* open it," Jack replied.

"Fuck that! I'm not doing it."

Steve and Jack laughed before realising he was being

serious. They looked at each other like they were having a stand-off, hoping that the other would man up and take charge, but neither did. They just acted like scared sheep.

John sighed as he pushed Steve out of the way before nervously grabbing the ladder to climb it, but, as he reached the top to grip the handle of the trapdoor, sweat fell off him like rain to make the others move to one side. He closed his eyes momentarily as he lifted the door, but the sound of it creaking spooked him even more as the others prepared themselves for rats falling on them. John raced down the ladder breathing like he was hyperventilating after the door landed on the old stockroom floor.

"I've done my bit," he said, breathing easier. "I'm not going to be the first to go up there."

The other men agreed before Steve whispered, "Are you ready?"

He received no reply, just nods, so started climbing the ladder, with John close behind as Jack watched on, shining his torch towards the stockroom's ceiling to see Steve disappear from view. And seconds later a trembling John followed.

Steve placed a finger on his lips as John reached him, but neither rose to their feet. They just remained with their bellies on the ground, waiting for Jack to appear. But the light from his torch disappeared as he climbed the ladder. It reappeared again as he reached the top to reveal rats inside the room, leaving Steve to curse under his breath as they squealed and scurried away back into the darkness. Steve and John quickly rose to their feet as Jack stayed half-in-and-half-out of the hole; his nerves on edge as his torch went off again.

"It's too late for that now!" Steve snapped, as the rats squealed even louder.

Jack sighed. He switched the torch back on as a rat ran

past his face, but its tail slapped him around the head, leaving him quivering to the point of almost dropping down the ladder. He raced out of the hole with a pale expression on his face before slamming the door shut to stop the rats from escaping, but the noise alerted more. He knew he'd fucked up again after Steve's glance made him feel small. He watched Steve aim his gun towards the sound of the rats, but his torchlight failed to catch one for him to shoot.

"It's too risky when we don't know where the boys are," Steve said, holstering the gun after the thought of shooting a child worried him.

He removed his baton and swung it through the darkness, skimming a rat's head to send it brushing past his leg, but, as Jack's torch lit it up, it quickly escaped before Steve could swing again.

"Fuck! Fuck! Fuck!" John shouted, frightened even more because he had no form of lighting to help him. "Why haven't I got a weapon?"

"Stop your whining!" Steve shouted back. "You wanted to help. You knew the risks."

"You told me you were leaving your faith in the lord. That was your weapon, you said." Jack tried not to laugh.

"Did he say that?" Steve asked, swinging his baton again. "And how's that going for you?"

"Okay! Okay! No need to take the piss." John lashed out with his feet to try to kick a rat, but to the other men, it looked more like he was trying to dance.

Jack produced a glowing smile after booting one against a wall. He was happy for connecting a perfect kick, but the smile faded quickly after the rat returned to its feet.

"You need to search for the boys!" Steve shouted towards John.

"But how do you know they're here?" he replied.

"I don't, but you still need to look, just in case." Steve felt exhausted as he carried on swinging. "We'll keep the rats at bay." He shone his torch towards a corner of the room to reveal a shovel. "Use that to keep them away."

John raced over to pick it up, but a rat pounced and bit his leg. He gritted his teeth and punched it away.

"I'm on my way to the front of the store," he said, cringing from the stinging pain.

"Help us! Please help us!" the brothers cried out.

John used the shovel as a shield as he rushed towards the sound, hearing the rats bounce off it as he closed in on the boys.

"Where are you?"

"On top of some shelving," Nathan replied, breathing erratically.

"I know where you are."

John stared at the door of the small kitchen as thoughts of Ted still being behind it flashed inside his mind, but Ted's death blocked out the cries from the boys to leave him unguarded.

Ted never committed suicide. He was murdered by the filthy rats.

John turned away as anger exploded inside him. He held the shovel like a tennis racket as he appeared in the doorway of the new stockroom, seeing the brothers huddled together as rats attempted to reach them. They were close to biting them as they ran across the shelving unit, but so far, every time they pounced, the brothers had kicked them off. John gaped at the recently fallen ones as they went through the motion of re-attempting to climb the unit.

"Are you hurt?" he asked, as the words gained the attention of the rats.

"Nope!" Nathan shouted back, kicking out at the nearest ones.

"Good!" John said, swinging the shovel.

He connected perfectly against a rat to snap its body against a wall but knew he couldn't prevent more attacks on him. He just hoped the shovel would take out a few more so the boys could climb down from the unit.

"...I'm going to make them follow me out of this room," he cried out before being bitten again. "When they leave..." He winced under his breath. "I want you to get down from there and head to the next room." He felt another bite but didn't want the boys to know. "There are policemen in there......They will get you....to safety."

John was almost in tears as he shouted at the rats to follow him before disappearing from view to take them with him. The brothers listened out for him, but the only sound heard was the shovel colliding against a wall.

"Don't be frightened, little brother. I'll keep you safe," Nathan whispered.

Trey smiled at him, truly believing he would be fine. Nathan waited for the crashing sound to reach the front of the store before plucking up the courage to climb down from the shelving unit, but Trey needed more reassurance. That came after he heard Steve shout his name.

"Are you ready?" Nathan said, grabbing Trey's hand to help him down.

"Yep."

But they froze on the spot as more rats raced towards the front of the store before seconds later, the sound of John screaming acted like a starter pistol in a race to send them running towards the officers.

"Get over here!" Steve shouted, spotting them close in. "We're taking you to the station."

Trey started crying. "Why are you arresting us? We've not been naughty."

Jack laughed as Steve replied, "I'm not arresting you. You're going there to be safe from those rats."

"Come on you wimp," Nathan said, hugging Trey tight. "Let's get you out of here."

But Trey jumped after another echoing crash made by the shovel frightened him. He moved away from Nathan as the shovel hit the wall again and gripped Steve.

"I can't stand this!" Steve yelled, shining his torch towards the sound. "He's in trouble."

Jack noticed him constantly staring like he was waiting for John to appear, so tapped him on the shoulder.

"You help him," Jack said, gathering the now silent boys. "I've got this covered." He then escorted them to the trapdoor. "Just *Go!*"

"Just get them to the station. I'll be right behind you."

Jack lifted the door to let the boys climb down into the tunnel but didn't follow. He just stared towards Steve's torchlight disappearing towards the front of the store, hoping it would guide both men out of the darkness. But, as he waited, saw no sign. He cursed under his breath and stepped onto the ladder, but a gun firing spooked him. He wanted to help, but the sad eyes of the boys as they looked up at him changed his mind. He smiled at them before climbing down and lowering the door.

CHAPTER THIRTY-THREE

The police station filled up with many people by the time it reached *8:00 pm*, as Chris and Rachael made drinks for the still-shivering boys, the injured Jack, a worried Cortney, and a tearful Louise. Jack hugged her as the news about Brendan's death spread like wildfire, as thoughts about the men inside the store tortured his mind. Chris shed a tear after seeing them console each other, as a vision of Marie's death made him shiver.

"We should go back to get them out," he said, trying to act like he wasn't scared anymore.

But Rachael shook her head. She knew from just looking at the wrecked officers that a rescue attempt right now would probably fail miserably, so moved in front of Chris to point at his head.

"What!" he snapped at her.

"Just think before you speak." Rachael wanted to swear at him but knew he was finding the moment also tough. "Can't you see they need a break?" She dragged him back to finishing the drinks, rubbing his arm before saying, "I'm sure Steve will get John out."

Chris smiled worryingly at her. He knew she wasn't fully sure of herself about any of the missing men returning, so pushing him away was just her keeping busy, but she was right about leaving the officers alone to give them some breathing space. He kissed her on the forehead before backing off from his macho approach to saving the men.

"What do you think will happen?" he asked, a now ageing in appearance, Jack.

"I don't know," he muttered; his energy drained as he slowly glanced at Chris. "But Harvey needs to know what's happening."

"Why haven't you told him?" Rachael asked, hugging a worried for her father, Cortney.

"I'm just lost as to what to say to him." Jack turned away to compose himself before turning back to say, "This is harder than telling family members that someone's died."

Rachael smiled at him, knowing exactly what he was talking about. She'd seen him tell people at the hospital, and every time had been tough for him. She watched him walk away but he collapsed, crying into his hands.

Louise rushed over and hugged him, almost crying herself. "Let's check you over before you make that call," she said, but Jack was reaching for his phone.

"I'm fine! Stop fussing child!" he cried out, shocking Louise.

So, she let go and backed away.

"You're not fine," she softly replied, hoping he'd calmed down.

"Look at you...You're pale because you're still bleeding."

Jack knew he was. He could feel the blood seeping through the bandage but he didn't want to trouble anyone. Now he'd no choice.

"Okay, okay, so I'm still bleeding." He watched Louise

fetch him a chair. "But at least I'm still alive, still breathing," he said, sitting down on it to grab her hand.

But just then, just for a split second, Louise thought only of Brendan.

Jack knew he'd triggered a memory so mimed the word "*sorry*", but Louise remained strong.

She smiled at him, shaking her head for having to play nurse again before grabbing the first-aid kit from a shelf, seeing him relax as he held the phone, ready to make the call. But, as she reached him, he raised a hand.

"I'm all yours," he said, wincing. "After I've spoken to Harvey."

"Sure," Louise said, keeping up the smile as she opened the kit before seeing him put the phone to his ear.

"Hi, Harvey. Are you nearby?" he said, coughing in pain.

"You okay?" Harvey replied, noticing all wasn't great.

"Yeah, I'm fine. Just a few cuts. Nothing to worry about."

"I'm closing in on the town..."

Harvey was unconvinced that Jack was fine, so wanted to say something. But he knew it wasn't the time to chat about war wounds, it was the time to get the job done.

"...Is Adam with you?" he anxiously asked.

"No...I thought he was with you?"

Harvey sighed. "No worries. I'm sure he'll be with you soon. He went to the lab first."

"Okay."

Jack wanted to say more, and Harvey knew it, but the silence lingered longer than expected.

"Anything else you want to tell me?" Harvey asked, eager to get the conversation started again.

Louise nudged Jack to remind him that she was there for him, making him feel thankful for her support.

"We have a man down and another is M.I.A," he

nervously told Harvey, as he waited for a quick reply or a scream in anger. But neither arrived as Harvey's heavy breathing left Jack sweating.

"Tell me everything when I reach you. We're bringing the net."

"Will do," Jack replied as he raised Louise's hand to kiss it.

He knew the knots in his stomach would stay for a while but having her by his side was helping him cope better with the sadness.

He jumped after a loud THUD crashed against the door before slowly letting go of her hand, moving towards the sound as everyone eagerly waited to know who was outside. But the THUD happened again to spook them before a voice cried out, "Let me in!"

"That's Steve!" Louise shouted.

Jack unbolted the door before opening it to see Steve crash to the floor, his energy drained as sweat poured out of him.

"What happened?!" Chris cried out, slamming the door in fear of seeing a rat as Louise and Rachael helped Steve to a chair.

"Water. I need water," he whispered.

Cortney raced off to fetch some, eager to get involved so she could find out what happened to her father's best friend. But, on her return, after handing the water over to Steve, no information was received. He weakly smiled at her before rushing the water down his throat like it was the best drink ever.

"Where's John?" she asked him.

But Steve's hand shook as he dropped the plastic cup. He was close to shutting down after hearing Cortney's words, leaving her feeling guilty as she tearfully picked the cup up to cry into Jack's chest, thinking only of her father and where he could be. She pushed herself away from Jack and headed for the kitchen but stopped after hearing Steve burst into tears; his reaction alerting the others as they waited for the verdict. But Jack pushed everyone back to give Steve space.

"I rushed to the front of the store," he said, gulping, puffing out his cheeks. "And saw John swinging a shovel at the rats." He gulped again and wiped tears from his eyes "But they were all over him, biting at his face."

"But he's okay, right?" Cortney asked, trembling, feeling unsure of her words.

Rachael noticed she was struggling, so comforted her as she waited impatiently for Steve to reply, but everyone's staring eyes made him feel nervous. He looked at the floor as the room fell silent before choking into his hand; his throat stinging as he tried to talk. Then suddenly he said: "No...He's not."

Louise placed a hand over her mouth as Jack said, "We need to know more."

Rachael placed an arm around Cortney and walked her away, knowing she needed to remove her from the conversation, so Steve waited until they left the room.

"He was down by the time I reached him," he agonisingly said, holding on to Jack as if about to faint. "The hand holding the shovel was only kept together by tendons...The wrist bone was chewed through." Steve shook his head. "He was gone before I could rescue him."

"But I heard a gunshot?" Jack questioned.

"Yeah, but it was only to scare the rats away from him. That's all I did." Steve angrily punched himself in the chest. "I fired my gun three times just to get the *fuck* out of there."

Jack never asked for any more. What Steve just said was enough to convince him that John had died a brave man.

He frantically searched for the boys, hoping they never

overheard, pleased to find them inside the canteen room munching on biscuits like it was their first meal of the day. He smiled at them before returning to the others, as the thought of a final question pressed against his mind. He saw Steve sink into the chair, fearing physical and emotional stress was holding him down, so knew it wasn't the right time to ask, but he couldn't keep it to himself.

"So how did you get out unscathed?"

Steve's face fumed a bright red as he rose from the chair. "I told you, I shot at them..."

But Jack sighed, feeling unconvinced that a few bullets would save Steve from being attacked. He had an inkling that Steve knew what he was thinking, but, as he approached him, the man lost it and punched a wall.

"...They didn't want me!" Steve shouted, cursing from the sharp pain in his hand. "The little bastards had their feed, so didn't want me...I shot at the ground to get them off John, but it didn't work. They just snapped at me and carried on biting." He kicked the chair and walked away. "I froze. That's what *I* fuckin' did."

Jack reached out and gripped him tight. "You're only human," he whispered.

"Are you happy now?" Steve said, shaking as he cried into Jack's shoulder. But Jack wasn't letting him go until he stopped.

Steve wasn't normally like this, a wreck, but today he couldn't help it. He was just like Jack said, only human. He felt scared, anxious, baffled, and helpless; the same as everyone else was feeling about everything that was going on outside.

"...I'm okay now," he softly said as Jack let go.

"Harvey's on his way back," Jack said, walking over to the

water cooler to fill a cup with water. "And I think Adam's coming back too."

"That means my officers will be here," Steve replied before briefly closing his eyes. "All except Carl".

"Sorry, mate," was all Jack said, as he raised the cup to his mouth.

"You don't look fit to carry on," Steve said, noticing him cringe after every gulp.

"He's not," said Louise. "I've told him zillions of times to rest, but he's like a stubborn old goat!"

"An old goat?" Jack was close to laughing, but the pain increased to stop him. "You've just called me an old *goat*."

"Now that was funny," Steve said, glad to be finally thinking about something else for a while.

"I wouldn't need to call you anything if you just listened to me." Louise closed in on Jack with the first-aid kit in her hand. "Steve's right, you don't look fit. You need to take it easy...Let me sort your wounds out."

"And let the others take over when they get back," Steve said.

Jack removed his protective suit as Rachael stood in the doorway; her sorrowful eyes staring into his after feeling bad he'd been attacked. But, after giving him another saddened look, she turned away and returned to her family.

"What was that all about?" Louise asked.

"What was what, all about?" Jack replied, surprised by the question.

"Jack, I'm a female. The look you two gave wasn't a look between strangers, so spill."

"Yeah! Spill," Steve said, feeling excited to be involved in the conversation.

But Jack turned a beetroot red. "There's nothing to spill, so leave it."

"Ooooohhhh...Jack's in love," Louise started singing as Chris overheard.

"What's goin' on?" he asked smiling before feeling like he wasn't meant to hear anything.

Jack glared at Louise to stop her from singing.

"Nothing," she said, scrunching her lips. "I'm just teasing Jack."

"Teasing him about what?"

"Just teasing him about Rachael. Nothing to lose your wig over."

Louise was either deliberately trying to cause a rift between Jack and Chris or was impersonating a dumb blonde again, but Jack knew, if she didn't stop soon, there could well be more than just rats to worry about.

"Rachael?" Chris asked, feeling uncomfortable now. "You mean my Rachael?"

"She's messin' with you, so just keep your cool, yeah!" Steve cried out, noticing Chris glaring at Jack as if he'd just fucked Rachael in the bathroom.

"I'm calm," was all Chris said before he slowly walked away.

"Thanks, Lou," Jack said with a sigh. "Now you've stirred a fuckin' hornet's nest."

Louise knew she'd hit a nerve.

She cleaned his wounds before preparing a bandage, but her mind spun in overdrive from the tension between Jack and Rachael. *Was there more to it?* she thought, watching him stare at the other room.

"But you don't love her, so why are you mad at me?"

"Just forget it," Jack said, placing up a hand before cursing under his breath.

But moments later Chris shouted his name.

It worried Louise to stare at him suspiciously, but Jack

wouldn't look her in the eye. She knew something wasn't right so waited for him to slip up, but Jack stayed strong, still avoiding her stare.

"What did you do?" she said, nudging him. "Did you screw her behind Chris' back?"

"No! I did not screw her," Jack replied, huffing. "We used to work together before I became an officer."

"So, they're fighting because you used to work with her?" Louise grinned and grabbed him by the cheeks. "Come on Jack, was I born yesterday?"

"Who said they're fighting? They may just be merely debating."

Steve laughed. "Jack! Mate! They're fighting, and your name's being mentioned."

Jack felt under extreme pressure as Steve and Louise smothered him for an answer.

"Alright! Alright! We *did* see each other for a short period when we worked together, but I didn't know she was with Chris. Honest, I didn't."

Louise knew he was telling the truth but now seemed annoyed with herself at not being able to use her woman's intuition sooner.

"And I take it Chris doesn't know?" she asked, glancing at the wall between both rooms.

"I've not seen her since I left the hospital...Today has brought back memories that I thought were dead and buried."

"Holy shit!" Steve whispered.

Louise rolled her tongue inside her mouth and counted her fingers. "No way!" she shockingly said.

Jack didn't need to ask what she was thinking. He knew, but Steve had no idea.

"Don't keep me in suspense, tell me," Steve asked.

Louise didn't tell him, but a punch on Jack's arm caused him to give in.

"The child is mine," he said, sweating after letting out the bag that he was the father of Rose.

"You're fucked!" Steve said before choking from an eruption of giggles.

"That's not nice," Louise replied. "This is serious."

Jack stared at the ceiling as thoughts on what was being said in the other room smothered him. He hoped Rachael hadn't told Chris about the affair, but had a feeling, even if she never, he now probably knew.

CHAPTER THIRTY-FOUR

The sound of vehicles closing in on the police station had most of the occupants racing for windows to see the cavalry arrive. They watched Harvey slam his car door, looking annoyed to the point of screaming as he entered the station; not speaking as he walked towards a table and chairs. He was close to kicking one but Walter arrived, preaching the word on how wonderful his rats were.

Maybe I should kick him instead? Harvey thought, glaring at him. *If he keeps droning on about how great those furry fucks are then he's going to feel my boot.*

But the sound of Ray barging his way in snapped him out of his glare.

"Can someone make me a coffee," Ray said, feeling pumped.

"These people aren't your slaves you know. You can make the coffee," Alice replied, entering the station.

"Alright, calm down." Ray gave her a cheeky smile. "Is it your time of the month or somethin'?"

Alice flipped and clenched her fist but Harvey stood in her way, as Ray smirked before heading off towards the canteen.

"Hiya," Trey said, greeting him as he entered the room.

"Oh! Hi buddy," Ray politely replied.

"You come to save us?" Trey asked, yawning into his hand.

Ray smiled at him, as Nathan said, "Let's see your gun."

"Gun?" Ray questioned.

"Yeah! Your gun." Nathan ran around him in an attempt to get a peek at what weapon he was carrying. "Where's your gun, you nitwit?"

"I don't have one."

"But the female police person has one."

Ray was confused by this. "She does?"

"Yep! We saw her with it." Nathan nudged his brother. "Trey, didn't we?"

Trey just nodded.

"Thanks for letting me know. You've been most helpful."

"Everything okay in here?" Alice said, appearing in the doorway to stare at Ray as if he'd just been teasing the boys.

"Nope," he replied, scrunching his lips. "Did you know Louise has a gun?"

"Don't be silly, she's not authorised to carry one."

"These two squirts just told me."

Alice saw the boys cheekily smile at her, leaving her to partly think they were lying, but the other part made her worry they weren't.

"I'll have a word with her."

"You do that," Ray replied, now upset that he'd missed out on the whole gun thing.

Alice nodded and left the room.

Ray helped himself to a well-needed cup of coffee as the boys played the hand-slapping game. He stared at them, glad to have them around, as his mind drifted back to his childhood when he too played that game.

Alice closed in on Louise, spotting the gun holstered. She stared at it and pointed, but Louise looked at her puzzled.

"What?" she whispered.

"The gun!" Alice whispered back.

"Fuck!"

"Fuck indeed."

"If Harvey sees it he'll *fire* me," Louise said, now trying to hide the gun within her clothing.

But the word 'fire' caused Alice to almost burst into laughter.

"I'll *cover* you," she said, smirking.

"What? Cover me with gunfire?"

Now both of them were laughing.

"You two okay over there?" Harvey asked from the other side of the room.

"Yep! We're all good," Louise replied as he continued with what he was doing.

Alice urged her closer to the armoury cabinet as Steve spotted them. He didn't speak but did wink towards them after Harvey turned his back before tossing the spare set of keys at Louise. She caught them and wiped her brow, miming - Thank you - as Steve gained Harvey's attention, happy to see Alice join her at the cabinet.

Louise entered the key inside the lock as Alice watched the men, nodding her head to let Louise know it was safe to replace the gun. She removed it from the holster with a sweaty hand and put it back inside the cabinet, but, before she had time to close the door, Harvey had turned around.

"What are you two playing at?"

"Nothing," Louise shyly replied, wiping sweaty hands down her uniform.

"So why are you wearing a gun holster and have the armoury cabinet open?"

Alice backed away as thoughts of Louise getting sacked for real for using a firearm caused her to cringe, while Steve shook his head at her cowardly behaviour.

"I was just showing Alice how to place a gun in its holster," Louise nervously said.

Steve placed a hand over his mouth, hoping to stifle his childish laughter towards Louise's reply, knowing she wanted to run out of the station for coming up with a lame excuse.

"Is that right?" Harvey asked Alice. "You don't know how to holster a gun?"

Louise pulled a face as Alice replied, "No, I don't."

Harvey stared at her sympathetically before shaking his head at Steve.

"Why hasn't she been taught?"

"She's not done weapons training yet," Steve quickly replied, sucking in the need to giggle.

"But still." Harvey shook his head again. "She should know how to holster a friggin' gun." He turned to Louise. "But now isn't the time, so shut the cabinet and put that holster away."

Louise, still shaking nervously, quickly did what was asked. She expected to be suspended as Alice snuck off to stand next to Steve, but Harvey just tutted before turning to walk over to a map of the town attached to the wall. Steve followed with a notepad in his hand, writing down names and ripping them off before pinning them on the map.

"Right! I don't know much about this town, but I figure, if we split into groups, we should be able to force the rats into this area," he said, pointing to a certain spot.

"Why there?" Alice asked.

"Because it's the most isolated of people."

"But what about the people that live there?"

"Yeah! What about them?" Harvey asked, eager to know more.

Steve froze for a second, feeling like he was treading on Harvey's toes, but Harvey just watched him before nodding for him to continue.

"Some of us will knock on doors to get the people out while others will force the rats into the area so they get caught in the net."

Steve looked at everyone, waiting for some sort of a backlash, but no one disagreed with him as they stared at the names on the map.

"I see you've teamed me up with Ray again," Alice said, annoyed. "Nice one, Sarge."

"You may moan, but you work well together. I did it because I know you won't screw up."

"The only thing she wants to screw is me," Ray said, laughing out loud upon returning with his coffee.

Alice had no comeback, so just gave him one of her death stares.

"I don't think you're capable of screwing in a light bulb so cut out the harassment chat," Harvey snapped at Ray.

Alice smiled at him for sticking up for her, leaving Ray to sulk as he sipped his drink.

"Anyway," Steve said, now becoming the centre of attention again. "I've double-teamed all of us, except of course Rachael and the kids." He then moved the pieces of paper around the map to find places of interest for everyone. "Adam should be here soon, so he can help find the rats with Alice, Ray, Louise, and myself."

Harvey smiled at him weirdly as he helped to navigate the pieces of paper. "Steve's right, if some of us go here," he said, placing names next to the targeted spots. "We can move out the residents and take them here." He pointed at the local church. "And others will go here." Again, the names of the chosen were placed in the area. "And force out the rats so they run into the net that'll go here." He slammed his finger on the chosen spot. "Is everyone okay with that?"

"Will I get some weapons?" Chris asked anxiously, now appearing from behind the officers.

"Of course." Harvey looked at Walter. "You'll get some weapons as well."

"Believe me, I don't need any," Walter replied. "My rats won't hurt me."

Harvey choked. "Hurt you? They won't hurt you, mate, they'll just rip you to pieces instead. Hey! But it's your choice."

Walter kept strong, defending his rats all the way. "I'll be just fine."

"Okay. It's your funeral, pal!" Steve shouted.

Harvey sighed after it sunk in whom he was teaming up with. "So, I'm going with Walter to get the people out?" he asked Steve, hoping he'd made an error.

"Yep! Seeing as Walter, and Chris aren't uniformed men, I figured they would be more equipped at helping than rat hunting. And with Jack being injured, and you're not exactly young, I thought it was the best plan."

Harvey was close to changing the plan but knew it wasn't about him and whether he thought Walter was a complete idiot. He glared at the man again, sucking up all feelings of anger towards him before agreeing with Steve.

But Jack stared at Chris thinking - *What would happen if he was given a baton and a Taser?* –

He had a feeling Chris knew more than he let on about whether Rachael was sleeping with him nine months ago, but Chris wasn't acknowledging him. He wondered why Steve chose him to team up with Chris, seeing as he knew the truth, but right now didn't want to cause a fuss in case Harvey sussed something. He waited for Chris to look at him, hoping for a sign, but still, there was nothing, so silently prayed that Chris wouldn't lose it and attack him instead of the rats.

"Are we going to do this!" Ray shouted, feeling anxious. "I'm getting bored stuck in here."

Louise agreed with him, loving his enthusiasm.

The pair were alike in the way they thought, so she now wished she was teamed up with him.

"Yeah! We're going to do this," Harvey replied, motivating everyone. "Right! grab a baton and fire up a Taser. Let's get out there." He stared at Chris and Walter. "You two need to get suited up. There's a locker room past the canteen area."

Walter shook his head. "No! No! No! I refuse to be protected against my babies."

But Chris disagreed, accepting the offer of more protection.

"Nice to see one of you isn't being a nuisance," Harvey said to Chris before glaring at Walter. "Just go to the locker room, please."

Walter tutted as he slowly followed Chris out of the room. He bowed his head like a naughty schoolboy, reaching the lockers before tutting again after seeing protective suits on hooks, but he didn't move; he just watched Chris reach for one to put it on.

"You'd better hurry before they leave you behind," he said, grinning.

"Leave me behind?" Chris smirked at him. "You're not staying here. They'll still take you with them even if you don't put one of these on."

"I'm fine with that!" Walter snapped, tutting for the third time.

Chris wanted to say more about what he thought about

the rats, seeing as he'd been close to death and had seen someone die, but something else occupied his mind.

———

'Project Rat-catcher' was coming together as Walter looked at his watch, seeing the time now reach *8:40 pm*. He sat inside the van with Kelvin, explaining the best areas to put the net, but Kelvin ignored him to concentrate on Harvey after seeing him through the driver's side mirror waving a hand back and forth. He walked backwards as Kelvin reversed the van before placing up a hand to stop him.

———

Jack and Chris eye-balled each other as they walked towards the houses across from the police station. Jack's gaze was nervous, while Chris' looked disgusted. Neither passed on a word as they reached a house where a family of four were watching television. Jack approached the door, knocking on it, feeling Chris' glare as a very tall man opened it.

"Hello, reverend, can we come in?" Jack asked.

The reverend's name was *Michael Cross*. A sixty-five-year-old man who'd been the reverend at the local church for two years. He smiled at Jack as he escorted the men into the living room, where *Martha*, his wife, and their children, *Isaac*, and *Mary* sat.

"What's the matter?" Michael asked Jack.

"We need your church," Chris bluntly butted in.

"My church, you say?"

"It's hard to explain, but right now there's a pack of rats roaming around outside attacking people."

That's all Chris had to say before the family panicked.

Martha froze, as the children, although twenty, and twenty-five years old shivered in their seats.

"We've been hearing stories all day about missing rats from the lab." Michael stared hard at Jack. "It's all over the TV. On the news. So, are you saying they came here?"

"Not only came here, but they've been killing people," Jack replied, still aching from the injuries.

He knew now wasn't the time to sugar-coat everything, so, if he had to tell everyone about every death recently he would, just to make sure they were safe.

"...I need to get everyone inside the church. It's the most secure building in this town, but I need you and your family to help." Jack winced after attempting a smile. "Will you?"

"I'm lost to what's going on, but I must help," replied Michael, moving over to comfort his family. "I'll get the key."

"Thanks," Chris said, butting in again to annoy Jack.

———

The night sky blurred Ray and Alice's vision as they walked in the direction of Peter's house. They'd heard about Brendan's death from Louise but never knew where he'd died, so, as they closed in on his faceless corpse, a creepy feeling brushed over them. Alice was the first to mention it, but Ray ignored her, not bowing down from the macho man he wanted to be.

"But you felt it, yeah?" Alice asked.

"I felt nothing. It's just cold out here. That's all."

"Whatever!" Alice said, laughing behind his back.

The sound of rats squeaking nearby gained Ray's attention, and, as he stared hard into the night, with his torch lighting up a hedgerow, noticed the bushes rustle.

"It's like they're talking to each other," Alice whispered, gripping her baton extra tight.

"Talking to each other, my arse!" an anxious Ray replied. "They're just fuckin' big mice. That's all. Big fuckin' mice." He stared at a fence to the left of the hedgerow. "I think I see one of the bastards."

He was off before Alice could reply, chasing after what he thought was a possible kill.

"You can't kill them!" she shouted out.

"Don't listen to that mad scientist freak, they're better off dead than alive. Trust me."

"Whatever!"

Alice knew he wouldn't listen to her. He never did when he was all pumped up and angry, so she left him to it.

Maybe, if I don't say anything he would give in trying to kill the rats and just do what he's supposed to.

She shone her torch in Ray's direction, but the vision inside her head of him trying to crush a rat with his baton wasn't what she saw. Instead, she saw him doing nothing.

"You get one?" she said, smiling cheekily.

"It must've scarpered off."

Alice walked over to sarcastically pat him on the back as he angrily kicked up dirt from a nearby garden.

They walked in silence until hearing a frantic voice nearby.

"Where's that coming from?" Alice asked, releasing her taser in case she was set upon.

"Who's out there?!" Ray yelled.

They stared ahead of them, seeing streetlamps glow circles of light on the ground, but no one was to be seen.

"...I said, who the *fuck* is out there!"

"Help us! Please help us!" a whimpering reply arrived.

Alice spotted a woman's shoe about twenty feet ahead of them, so shone her torch over it, feeling confused as she bent down to pick it up.

"...That'll be mine!" a voice from above cried out.

Alice shone the torch into a tree to see a *woman* shivering.

"What are you doing up there?"

"Keeping away from those pesky rodents," the woman replied.

"You said help us, but you're the only person up there."

"My boyfriend ran off, chased by some large, deformed rat."

"What direction?" Ray butted in. "Those rodents are pissing me off."

Alice saw the rage escalate in his eyes so feared he was losing it, but she hoped it wouldn't cloud his judgement whilst searching for the missing person.

"Just be careful," she said.

"Shucks! Alice, you almost sound like you care."

"Shut up!"

Ray laughed as he walked off the path in search of the woman's boyfriend.

"This direction?" he asked, turning to face her as she climbed down from the tree.

She nodded, still spooked as Alice grabbed her.

"Go to the church," Alice told her. "And if you see anyone else in the street you tell them the same thing."

"But what about my boyfriend?"

"We'll find him and take him there." Alice nudged her to get going. "Go! Run!"

Alice turned to see Ray's torchlight fade off into the distance, but the woman screamed to spook her. She shone the light over the woman as four rats circled her.

"Don't move," was all Alice had time to say before the rats jumped the woman like a pack of lions bringing down prey.

Alice broke down, struggling to breathe as the woman ran in circles, screaming before falling to the ground to be bitten by the rats. Alice tried to shout, but nothing came out as two rats tore at the woman's throat. She wrapped her hands around it as her blood covered the pavement, but the other rats chewed at her thumbs.

Alice found her voice but her words made no difference, as the rats still attacked. She shone a light on them to cringe after seeing their eyes glow red, creeping her out to think they were some form of vampire rat as the glow almost hypnotised her. She stamped her feet in a frenzy to get them to stop, but they weren't bothered by her presence. They just carried on feasting until the woman died.

This can't be real. They can't be vampire rats, surely? Alice thought, shaking her head as they ran around on top of the woman.

Her courage was fading and her feet became numb as flesh hung from the rats' mouths, scaring her even more as she turned up the brightness of the torch. It temporarily blinded them to make them run away, giving her time to race over to the woman to bow her head. She kneeled to close the woman's eyes, feeling sick to her stomach for not being able to save her, searching for the rats as she grabbed her phone.

"We're back at Chris' house," Steve replied after Alice reached him. "Why? Where are you?"

"Where's Chris' house again?" Alice spluttered out.

"Sorry, you weren't with us earlier when we rescued his family." Steve looked over at Louise, miming the words - There's something wrong.

"No, I wasn't." Alice almost crumbled after spotting Ray's torchlight aiming towards her. "I'm on Canal Street."

Louise flinched as soon as Steve repeated the words.

"You okay?" he asked her.

"She's near Peter's house. Near to where Brendan's body

is." Louise gulped. "Tell her she's about ten minutes away from us."

"Will do," Steve replied, hearing another voice over the phone. "Who's with you? Ray?" he asked Alice.

"Yeah, he's just been looking for a recent victim's boyfriend," she said, sounding drained of energy.

"Recent victim?"

Ray grabbed the phone from Alice's hand. "Yeah! Recent victim! Some woman's been killed by those little bastards and her boyfriend has run away. I can't find him anywhere," he told Steve, hugging Alice to stop her from staring at the dead woman. "I told you we need to kill those mother-fuckers."

"I know, but..."

Ray turned the phone off before Steve could finish his reply.

He glanced at the body before wiping tears away from Alice's eyes. "You okay?"

"Yeah. I'll be fine," she replied, raising a smile. "Let's just do our job before I have a nervous breakdown."

"I had my breakdown the minute we set foot in this town."

Alice laughed, even though she knew at this moment it was wrong too. Ray had a way of making her do that, to smile or laugh during unexpected times, so she hugged him again, thankful that he was there with her right now.

CHAPTER THIRTY-FIVE

A screeching car pulled to a halt outside the police station as Adam furiously exited. Kelvin saw him as he put the finishing touches on the new location for the net, but, before being able to say anything, Adam was slamming his car door to rush over to him.

"Where's Walter?!" he shouted in rage.

But Kelvin just stood there, too shocked to reply.

"...I said, where's Walter?" Adam calmly asked after noticing he'd spooked the man.

"He's gone off with Harvey to round up the townsfolk." Kelvin pointed a finger. "I think he's somewhere in that direction."

"You think? Shouldn't you know?"

"I was setting up the net again so didn't see where he went." Kelvin moved towards the van. "As far as I know, the plan is to evacuate everyone from the nearest houses and get them inside the church. I was setting the trap up for them to lure the rats into."

"And how's your plan going so far?" Adam asked, knowing the answer after seeing Kelvin shrug his shoulders.

"Anyway, it doesn't matter." Adam stared in the direction of where Kelvin was pointing. "Right, I'm off to find Walter. Just be careful as you guard the net."

"Sure thing," Kelvin replied, watching Adam pull out his baton as he walked away.

———

Alice and Ray froze after the shock of seeing something so horrible made one of them puke.

"You okay now?" she asked him.

"Nope," Ray replied, staring at the mutilated body of Brendan. "I didn't expect him to be so mashed up. Those things tore his face off."

"We were warned, Ray."

"I know, but I didn't think it wasn't going to be as bad as this."

Alice raced inside Peter's house to leave Ray feeling anxious. He shone his torch at a window as she sadly pulled down a curtain, racing back out again to cover it over Brendan's body to leave him smiling at how kind she was.

"Now we find the bastards that did this!" she said, choking from the thought of what the rats were capable of.

———

Louise and Steve stood back-to-back as they searched Chris' house. So far there'd been no sighting of a rat, but just one would be a bonus right now.

"You sure they'll still be here?" Steve whispered.

"Now I'm not so sure."

They moved slowly along the downstairs rooms, sweating from not knowing when and where the rats would strike before climbing the stairs to find Marie lying where she'd fallen, with the duvet still hiding her body. Steve shone his torch around the bedroom to light up the bloodstained cot and the rat he'd killed, staring at it on the floor to feel annoyed at not finding any more or any fresh droppings.

"I think they've vanished from here," he said.

"Yeah, it's like they knew we were coming."

———

The reverend stood inside the doorway of a very tall and very old stone church, opening the door that was in urgent need of a good sanding down and a fresh coat of varnish.

He watched his family slowly enter to nervously walk towards the main hall, but Jack and Chris were walking away.

"Where are you going?" Michael called out to them.

"We need to round up the townsfolk for you to look after," Jack replied. "So, just see this as you attending to your flock."

"Just make sure you keep safe," Michael replied.

He watched the men walk further away from the church before closing the door, as Chris glared at Jack again to leave him feeling the glare claw at his neck.

"You okay?" he asked, turning to face Chris.

"For now."

Jack grunted as he faced the front again before walking over the road to be swallowed up by the brightness of a street lamp. He listened out for Chris, becoming nervous as thoughts of Chris being behind him sent bad thoughts zipping through his mind. But seconds later, Chris shuffled beside him.

"Harvey should be over there somewhere," Jack said, glad to see him in his eyesight. "So, we'll just head for those houses."

"Whatever!" Chris replied, staring at Jack pointing.

He didn't want to drill Chris about his recent change in attitude because it wasn't the right time and place, especially when he knew rats were nearby, their cunningness to not be seen putting him on edge as he shone his torch along a path.

The men held batons tight as they carried on walking, but Jack suspected Chris was more nervous than he let on, as fear for the man's safety overtook his mind. Chris' hands sweated as he tossed his baton from hand to hand, seemingly unhappy with the grip before suddenly stopping, as the dark sky left a silence in the air; a silence that worried the men to wish they were somewhere else. They whipped their torches from left to right to stare in every direction at any faint sound before Jack raised a hand. He suspected a rat was close, but Chris wasn't impressed by his sudden movement and just wanted to keep walking.

"Over there," Jack whispered, pointing towards a recycling bin sitting outside a house.

"Okay," Chris nervously replied, almost wetting himself.

"We need to spook it so it runs towards the net."

"But aren't we meant to be getting the people out?" Chris asked, breathing faster now.

"Yeah, but we can help do this as well..."

Jack was close to telling Chris to go back to the station after seeing just how frightened he was, but somehow knew he would refuse.

"...Look! You don't have to be here, but you are, so let's work together to rid this town of the rats."

Chris nodded. "Okay. But how do you know it'll go towards the net?"

Jack shrugged his shoulders and sighed. "I don't know, but that crazy professor guy said the net was dipped in some kind of liquid that attracts them."

"I hope you're right."

"I don't know if I'm right, but I overheard him tell Harvey back at the station."

"Yeah, that was probably when I was with my family in the other room." Chris raised his eyebrows as if making a point, leaving Jack to back off.

He sighed before walking towards the bin.

"You see anything!" Chris shouted.

"Shush!" Jack replied, knowing Chris probably shouted on purpose to piss him off.

He quietly and carefully moved around the bin to shine light all around it but was on the verge of giving up after no rat was seen. Then, the loud *crash* of Chris' baton colliding against the side of the bin spooked Jack into almost falling over. It annoyed him to the point of yelling at Chris, but a rat pounced on his leg.

"Fuck! Not again!" he screamed. "I don't want to be bitten anymore tonight."

He tried to shake the rat off before slamming his baton against its back; knocking it off to see it run into the darkness, as he became livid towards Chris, who right now was becoming more of a nuisance than the dreaded rodents.

"What's wrong with you!" Jack hollered, checking his leg. "That rat could've killed me."

"Stop being so dramatic," Chris replied, almost smirking. "It wouldn't have killed you. I've not seen or heard of just one rat killing someone. There has to be a gang of them to do that."

"So, tell me this, smart arse, why did you throw your baton at the bin?"

"I was aiming at the rat." Chris scrunched his face. "I'm just a bad shot," he said, turning to walk away.

"That's bullshit, and you know it." Jack wiped his leg, as

thoughts of the rat still being on it caused him to shiver. "What's your problem?!"

But Chris stared right through him as the emotions building up inside desperately tried to come out.

Finding out that his baby girl wasn't *his* baby girl, and sick thoughts about Rachael having an affair with the man standing in front of him were pushing their way to the front of his mind. Now, all he saw inside his head were images of Rachael having sex with Jack all those months ago.

"Are you going to tell me what happened, or do I have to beat it out of you?"

"What are you talking about?" Jack replied, closing in on him. "What happened?"

"You sleeping with Rachael. That's what I'm talking about." Chris came close to punching or at least trying to punch Jack. "I overheard you all at the station, so don't deny it."

"You weren't meant to find out."

"Is that the best answer you have?"

"It's the only one..."

Chris burst into tears as Jack gulped.

He knew this wasn't the right time to explain things, *but when was there a right time to talk about it?* So, with one eye focused on what was around them, tried his best to explain the story to Chris. Not the bit about him having sex with Rachael, but the whole story that started way back when they worked for the hospital.

"...You see, it was only a fling. And I left the hospital after I found out she was already with someone."

"Left the hospital or left her?" Chris replied, sniffing.

"Both!" Jack inched a few more steps towards him, knowing he was now distraught. "I didn't know you couldn't have children."

Chris backed away. "Who told you that?"

"She did." Jack stared into the darkness. "She said she so badly wanted a child with someone, but it wasn't happening. I didn't know it was you. Honest."

"So, you thought you would father a child for her?"

"It wasn't like that. I didn't know about the baby until recently when I helped you fight the rats in your house. It was a shock to me as well."

"So, Rachael's to blame for all of this?"

"No! You can't blame her. She just wanted you to be happy, I think, and persuade you that you were the father." Jack raised a smile. "I bet you were so happy when your baby girl was born?"

"My baby girl? Don't you mean yours?"

Jack knew Chris could keep this up for a long time, but he needed to steer him away from the topic and move on with the plan.

"I'm sorry. Truly I am. But we need to do our jobs before the rats regroup and attack more people."

Chris shook himself and agreed. *This isn't over, but I'll allow it to be put on hold for a while.*

He walked over and picked up the baton before catching up with Jack as he made his way towards the chosen house.

———

Harvey and Walter were still in combat over what to do with the rats. Walter kept denying any blame for the chaos and that his rats were timid creatures, so Harvey had to bite his lip a few times.

His speech to every household they'd visited so far was the same, and that was to go to the church. To most it was okay, but the odd few, the awkward few, would ask the dreaded question: Why do they have to evacuate their homes because of a few rats running loose? - Some, especially small children, hadn't seen a rat before unless they'd visited the university laboratory, so were gullible to the question, but older people, especially males who wanted to stay at home to finish off a can of beer whilst watching some repeated sports programme, were stubborn to move, and it took a while to get them motivated.

In the latest house they were in, the dreaded question was also asked, but, before Harvey could ramble on with the same speech, a large, black rat appeared on top of a shelf near where the *father* of the household sat. It looked evil, even though Walter would disagree. It glared at the man to prevent him from asking another question.

"It's time to leave!" Harvey yelled, grabbing the overweight man. "Get what you need and let's go!"

But Walter smiled at his creation as more rats appeared from the kitchen.

"...Wal---ter!" Harry raged at him, as the man's *wife* raced out of the house with their seven-year-old *son*. "Get moving!"

He did, but he was reluctant to. If Harvey hadn't pushed him out the door he would still be there, and be amongst the things he created.

The overweight man wasn't rushing to escape but instead was laughing at the rodents in his living room. "They're just rats," he said, pointing at them.

"Told you!" Walter shouted, feeling pleased to finally find someone who agreed with him.

Harvey shoved the overweight man to one side before firing his taser at the rats, but the man kept laughing as the taser missed. Harvey glared at him as more rats ran across the furniture.

"Move it *now!*" he blasted.

The man was now frightened after realising it was real, but for some reason still wasn't rushing to escape. Harvey sensed that the man had a serious health problem that left him slow to move, so the rats picked him as their next target, swarming all over him before Harvey could fire the taser again. His wife heard him scream but was too frightened to help as Harvey kicked out at the evil creatures, but one bit the man's arse to make him scream even louder. He fell to his knees as more bites appeared; his scream becoming high-pitched to sound more like a child's than a grown man's.

"YYYYYEEEEHHHAAAA!!" he repeated, falling onto his side.

His wife yelled out to him, pleading with him to leave the house, but he couldn't lift off the floor.

Harvey shook as the rats covered the man. He held his taser like he was tempting to shoot them, but somehow they knew he wouldn't risk it. He kicked out again before using his baton to smack one across the room, but it got up and ran over the man to bite his face.

"Help me! Please help me!" he pleaded, as blood gushed out.

Harvey panicked after overhearing Walter talk to the woman outside, his words sounding like he was trying to stop her from re-entering the house. But she did, and she witnessed her husband's downfall. Her son nervously clung to her as the rat bit into his father's neck, ripping flesh away to leave a scared Harvey firing the taser into the man's ribcage. Three rats fell off him to smoke on the carpet before collapsing to die, as the others raced towards the door, whipping their tails against the legs of the boy and his mother as they passed.

Harvey quickly released some padding from a small, first-aid kit attached to his belt before pressing it down hard against the man's neck, but other wounds bled out just as fast to leave the wife and son crying from thoughts of the man dying.

"Snap out of it and help me!" he shouted at the woman. But she was too far gone with shock to move.

Walter horrifyingly watched from the doorway after seeing the rats disappear into the night again, close to puking from the sight of Harvey's bloodstained hands trying in vain to save the man.

"...Help me! Please," he softly said, but Walter didn't move. "Get in here and help this man!" Harvey blasted.

Walter slowly walked past the distraught family members as they stared blankly at the man on the floor. He saw Harvey point to where he wanted him to be, but it took longer than Harvey hoped before he knelt next to the man's legs.

"What do you want me to do?"

Harvey sighed. "Just help him. Stop the blood for God's sake."

He dropped the first-aid kit next to Walter but the man screamed his last breath, his lifeless eyelids open to spook them as Harvey pushed Walter out of the way. He tried to revive the man but his attempt failed.

"We have to go," Harvey said to the woman, rising to scare the child with his reddened hands.

Walter cringed as Harvey escorted the wife and child outside before shedding a tear at what his rats did. He now knew they were out of control.

CHAPTER THIRTY-SIX

"Where is the little shit!" Adam hollered, spotting Harvey leading the woman and child away from the house.

"Hey! There's a kid here," Harvey replied, unamused by the sudden outburst.

They saw Walter appear, looking faded of energy.

"I want a word with you, you, sick *fuck*!" Adam hollered again, rushing over to punch Walter in the face.

He was left shell-shocked as he fell to the ground.

"I said, there's a kid here, so stop swearing." Harvey left the distraught mother and son to stop Adam from hitting Walter again. "And no punching people for no reason."

"For no reason?" Adam replied, scowling at Walter. "Do you want to tell him what you've done or shall I?"

Walter returned to his feet, his nose dripping with blood. "I don't know what you're talking about." He reached into a pocket and pulled out a handkerchief, holding it against his nose.

"You make me sick."

Harvey stepped in between them. "I don't know what's

going on here but I won't tolerate violence for no reason, especially when those things are out there."

Adam came close to reminding him about his encounter with Ray not so long ago, but erased it as he said, "And why do you think those things are out there? Out there attacking people."

The woman shook as she held her son close, holding hands over his ears as the men argued amongst themselves.

"What's he talking about?" Harvey questioned, glaring at Walter.

"I don't know," Walter replied, removing the handkerchief. "He's lost it."

"I'll give you *lost* it!" Adam snapped, close to punching him again.

But the woman screamed "*Rats!*" to panic everyone.

Harvey grabbed the woman's hand as twenty rodents ran across the road. They closed in fast as she reached for her son, hurrying him towards the church with terror etched on her face as the human daisy chain led by Harvey made some distance.

"Inside the church, *now!*" he frantically shouted after checking to see where the rats were.

He knew he needed to stay in control so the mother and child wouldn't freak out, but, as he pulled them closer to the safety of the church, freaking out was all he did.

Adam felt like leaving Walter to be attacked, especially after seeing him smirk, but knew Harvey would have his badge if he did. He gripped Walter's arm and started running, leaving the professor no choice but to keep up, but, as they turned, found the rats were gone. Walter thought he was the reason why, but Adam knew they'd split up and was keeping out of sight.

"Get a move on!" he shouted. "I don't trust 'em."

Harvey looked ahead to see the reverend holding the door open, thinking he was blessed with the gift of knowing when someone was nearby, but, after seeing other distressed people rush into the church, knew it was because he had been holding the door for them. He got Michael's attention as his little group closed in.

"Quickly!" cried out Michael. "They're coming!"

Harvey pushed the family into his arms as the first rat pounced, but, as it narrowly missed the child, the reverend freaked out to do the sign of the cross. He smiled at the mother and son before leading them further into the church, turning to see more rats close in to feel useless as Harvey fought them off. The mother nodded as she took her son into the centre of the hall, leaving Michael to nervously wave at her as he returned to Harvey's side.

"What's the plan?" he asked.

Harvey just gulped as the woman was greeted by close friends, but, within seconds, they all started crying. They consoled her, fearing her husband wasn't arriving soon and probably wouldn't be arriving at all.

———

A rat almost tripped Adam up as he dragged Walter towards the church, but he swung his leg at it before avoiding more rodents diving at him like balls being thrown in dodgeball. Walter closed his eyes to avoid seeing them up close, as their squeaks sounded like words to make his heart thump fast.

"Harv! I'm on my way!" Adam shouted as they closed in.

Harvey released his gun as he told Michael to stay inside the church, but it took a moment before the reverend agreed.

"Be safe," he said, choking on the stench of the rats. "God will protect you."

LEE ANDREW TAYLOR

He then closed the door to open a peephole, seeing the rats surround the men, as Walter mumbled to himself like he was producing a spell. He opened his eyes and flipped out after the rats hissed, becoming scared to escape Adam's grip, as Michael watched him run away from the church. Adam cursed as the sound of Walter's shoes touching concrete overtook the silence in the street, but he couldn't chase after him while the rats were there.

"Fuckin' chicken!" he hollered, snarling at Walter for not staying to face his creation.

Harvey fired his gun as a rat pounced to knock it out of his hand before bending down to pick it up, but the rat snapped out at him to prevent it from happening. He shone his torch to momentarily blind it before lashing out with his baton, standing upright to sigh after seeing his gun on the ground.

"Are we catching or killing them?" Adam asked, trying his best to keep the rats at bay as Harvey swapped the baton for his taser.

"Hopefully catch. But if they bite us..."

"Say no more. I know."

Harvey glanced into the distance, trying to pinpoint where Walter was. "Go get him. This is *his* mess, so he needs to help."

"But what about you?" Adam seemed concerned, knowing Harvey would struggle on his own.

"What about me?" Harvey smiled as he fired up the Taser. "I've got my best friend with me and we're going to a party..."

Adam watched him act like a madman as he crazily fired it at the rats.

"...Do you want to see these suckers dance?" Harvey laughed, but Adam knew it was a nervous one.

"Have fun," he replied, stamping his boots on the ground to clear a path before firing up his taser.

Harvey watched him chase after Walter but the rats didn't follow. He gulped as they glared at him, wishing now he'd kept Adam with him, but had no more time to think as more rats pounced at him, with the last one landing on the baton hanging by his side to frighten him.

"Why don't you just leave me alone!" he yelled, as his shins were bitten.

He was in excruciating pain as his eyes lit up with rage, but he refused to be defeated. He bit his lip as he tried to fight back as a loud *boom* almost stopped his heart, leaving him close to toppling over as the echoing sound lingered in the night sky. But, as he turned to see what produced the sound, saw Michael reloading a still-smoking shotgun to blast a rat to kingdom come.

"I bet you want to come inside about now?" Michael said, holding out a hand.

"Yes, I do..."

Harvey cringed as he reached for his gun, seeing the blood seep from his shins onto the path as he gripped Michael's hand.

"... I hope you have a license for that," Harvey said, smiling.

They thankfully watched the rats flee back into the darkness before Michael helped him inside the church, watching him hobble as he struggled to walk as the door slammed shut.

———

Adam stalled after hearing the shotgun blast, now feeling confused about whether to carry on or go back, but, as he stared hard at the church, noticed Harvey wasn't there.

It's too quiet, so I hope he's safe.

He wanted to call out to Harvey but didn't want Walter to know he was closing in. But everything changed within a second after seeing the professor pass under a streetlamp.

"Walter!" Adam shouted. "If you don't stop now, I'll arrest you..."

But his words were useless as Walter increased his speed to escape.

"...Fuck you, Walter!"

But the sound of glass shattering nearby made Adam jump.

He shone his torch all around to see a broken bottle on the ground as rats squeaking like they were taunting him made him on edge before flashing light to capture some running along a wall. He knew he had to let Walter gain more distance as the rats now became the top priority. He saw them sniff the air to tease him, but he was ready for them, as a reminder of what Walter did intensified his anger.

"Your time is coming!" he yelled, glaring in Walter's direction to hear the faint sound of his shoes.

But the rats ran at speed to escape the torchlight, frightening him to brace himself for an attack.

He held his taser tight as he cautiously kept moving, flashing the torch from side to side in the hope of finding the rats, but the sound of people talking in the distance disrupted him, confusing him into walking backwards towards the voices.

"...I'm coming to get you, Walter!" he shouted after hearing Walter's voice blend in with another.

He panicked after seeing the shadow of a rat illuminate on the wall, making it appear larger than it was.

"Fuck!" he whispered. "Where is the little bastard?"

He flinched, feeling more on edge as the broken bottle rolled towards him, his taser shaking in his hand as his throat tightened like he was experiencing a panic attack. He carried on walking backwards as his torch lit up the wall again, feeling faint as he made some distance. But was pleased that no rats were seen. He breathed deeply as he turned to run towards the station, closing in to see a bright light glow from one of the windows, feeling thankful to be one step closer to safety, but the rats raced in front of him. *One* sprung at him to squeal as it just missed his head, as *two* more attached themselves to him before he could react. He cursed at them, keeping his focus as they tried to bite into his suit before tasering one as it leapt at his face; its head exploding over his riot gear as he knocked another one away. But the last one clung on to climb up his chest.

Adam laughed at it from beneath his visor as its teeth searched for weakness within the padding, his legs still moving as the light from the window appeared closer and closer. He tried to ignore the rat as thoughts of finding Walter suffocated him again, but two more jumped on him to slow him down. He stopped to fight them off, but they were moving towards his back, leaving his breathing to become erratic from fear that they would eventually find a gap. He knew if they bit him then other rats would sniff the blood and get involved, making him defenceless to fight back. He dropped the torch and reached for his baton, knowing he was running out of time to break free, pushing it against the rat on his chest to hear others close in. They tried scaring him into making a mistake but he drowned out the noises and carried on moving.

"Have you come to take me down?" he nervously said. "Well, you can't."

He screamed at them upon lashing out with his baton, taser, and legs, connecting a boot and the baton simultaneously to the sound of them squealing. It pleased him to enjoy the moment but their squeals soon creeped him out as the rats swamped all over him. He now feared for his life more than before as sweat stormed down his face, but bright lights from a fast-approaching vehicle gave him a chance to escape. He watched it pull to a stop before slamming his back against the side, knocking the rats still clinging on off before smacking the one on his chest away.

"Get in!" Kelvin shouted, lowering the passenger side window.

Adam kicked out at the rats some more before picking up his torch and opening the door, diving inside and shutting it before they could follow. He smiled at Kelvin, almost breaking down as the rodents jumped at the windows.

"...Hold on!" Kelvin hollered, spinning the van around to squash three rats under the wheels. "Let's get you back to the station."

"How did you know I was here?"

"Two reasons. One, Walter told us you were nearby, and two, we heard you screaming at the rats."

Adam laughed. "Oh yeah, I forgot about that."

Kelvin laughed back. "Thank God you have a loud voice."

"Thank God, indeed."

The van pulled up near the net as Walter stood close by, seemingly anxious as he waited for the men to leave the van. But Adam set on him again.

"Are you going to tell me what you did to your assistant?" Adam said, pushing him.

"Will you please stop pushing me!" Walter replied, backing away to avoid being shoved again.

He saw the anger rage in Adam's eyes but still didn't give in and say what he'd done.

"Does the name Edward Munsun ring a bell?"

Walter stared beyond Adam as his mind worked overtime.

"Of course, it does. Edward was one of my top people." He shrugged his shoulders. "Why?"

But Walter's ignorance filled Adam's head with more hatred.

"What happened to Edward?" he asked, knowing Walter was soaking up the question. He waited for a reply, but Walter wasn't rushing one, so turned to speak to Kelvin. "Get inside the station. It's safer inside than out."

Kelvin never questioned the order. He just did what was told as

Adam turned back to glare at Walter.

"...I'll ask you one more time, and I want an answer." But Walter was staring at something Adam couldn't see. It was like he was looking at a ghost. "What happened to him?"

But Adam's words weren't working. No matter what he said it couldn't shake Walter's mind from becoming lost in a time zone. Whatever happened before Edward's death was easy for Walter to talk about, but nothing came out relating to the death or what occurred after it.

"He was working with me on a new idea to increase the potency of the rats' blood."

"What was the idea?"

"I can't tell you."

They heard rats lurking close by to make Adam feel on edge again, but Walter was too far gone inside his mind to worry. Adam needed to stay alert but wanted to find out the truth before giving in to enter the station. He knew the rats could win, killing them both before that happened, but he was prepared to risk it.

"Why can't you?" Adam kept calm. "I need to know."

Walter snapped from staring as the rats now scared him. "Shouldn't we hide?"

"*Now* you're scared." Adam shone his torch. "Why are you

suddenly scared now? Is it because you know what those rats can do? Or because you know what you did to Edward?"

"Please shut up about Edward. He was my friend." Walter shed a tear as Adam's words finally sunk in. "It was an accident. I never meant to hurt him."

"Never meant to hurt him? You fuckin' chopped him into pieces!"

Walter cried. "He just kept on pushing me."

Adam had him where he wanted him, with a signed confession only minutes away, but knew the rats could attack to stop it from happening. He could easily drag Walter back into the station to get it done but somehow wanted him to fear his creation. He watched Walter, knowing he had him beaten.

"Pushing you about what?"

Walter backed off some more as squeals left him checking the ground. "About my decision to use human flesh for food so the blood would speed up the healing process."

Adam choked, almost throwing up. "So, you killed him and made him a guinea pig for your sick project."

The tears kept coming. "It wasn't meant to be him, it was meant to be someone already dead, but he kept on pushing me to not go through with it." Walter slapped himself around the head. "I had to try it. It was for the benefit of the people, the sick people." He pleaded with Adam, but he wasn't falling for it. "He tried to stop me and we fought. That's all. We had a fight but he fell and cracked his head."

"So, what about the bloodied knife that Victoria found in your office?"

Walter looked away. "Maybe I stabbed him before he fell?" He acted lost. "I don't know what I did. You have to believe me."

"So, the meat I found inside the barrel of rat food was human meat, Edward's cut-up corpse?"

Walter's heart beat faster as Edward's name haunted him. He freaked out again as more noises closed in, but, as Adam shone his torch towards it, Walter was off again, running away. But the rats surrounded him to stop him in his tracks. He tried talking to them, but they hissed at him, as their anger increased towards him for keeping them caged.

"Get them away from me!" he cried out.

"Not until you tell me that you killed and cut up Edward."

"Please! Help me! I'm sorry for what I did."

Walter felt the eyes of every rat penetrating him as Adam cruelly laughed.

"It's too late to be sorry now, so just say hello to your little friends."

"You have to help me, you're the law." Walter shivered as he cowardly stared at the nearest rat. "You have to help me... have to!"

But the rat pounced on his head and scratched his scalp. He screamed as blood slid down his face.

"Just admit to what you did, and then I'll save you."

"Okay! Okay! I stabbed him and cut him into little pieces, feeding him to the rats so they'd hunger for human meat." Walter screamed again. "I'm sorry!"

Adam braced himself to charge the rats after receiving the words he needed, but Walter suddenly retreated again to leave them chasing him. He stopped when reaching the net, but rats bit him to release more blood. They climbed over him to bite him some more, but he wasn't trying to knock them off. Nor was he eager to escape. It was as if he'd come to terms with his fate. Adam shouted at him as the rats clawed at his arms, legs, neck, and face, but all he did was cry. Adam tried to reach him but knew it was no use. If Walter wouldn't help himself then Adam was just fighting a losing battle to save him.

"Run back to the station!" he shouted, lashing out at the nearest rats.

But Walter's body fast turned red as his bloodstained teeth showed. Adam couldn't turn away as Walter fell into the net, sticking to it like a fly being caught in a fly-catcher, but no rats landed in there with him. They'd jumped off him as if knowing the outcome before landing on the ground to lick the blood away from their bodies; their Devil-red eyes glowing to freak Adam out as he prepared himself to attack again. But they turned and scurried off into the night as Walter groaned. Adam closed in to rescue him but he had breathed his last breath.

CHAPTER THIRTY-SEVEN

Chris and Jack were back walking the streets, but eerie sounds echoed around them, causing the hairs to stand on their arms. Jack sighed after checking his watch to find it was just after nine. They had evacuated several people, with most being sociable towards them, but the ones that took more persuading finally ended up giving in before things got out of control. So far there had been no casualties, unlike the incident where Harvey was left with blood on his hands. He had recently phoned Jack to tell him he was inside the church with many rescued people and was pleased with the progress so far, but he never mentioned his injuries. Harvey intended to keep Jack motivated and not to panic him more than was needed, so the call ended with just the positives on the rescue mission.

"Where are we off to now?" Chris asked.

Jack concentrated on the houses on the street. "Most of these homes have been evacuated," he said, walking onto the road. "So, we cross to the other side to see what houses are still occupied."

"Wasn't that the area where Harvey was meant to do the

evacuating?"

Jack stopped walking. "Yep! But he's at the church now. Something about a spot of bother with Walter and some rats." He waited for Chris to catch him up. "Adam's back, but he had a go at Walter over something."

"Serious?"

"Serious!"

Chris looked at Jack like a confused boy, speaking no more on the subject as he shone torchlight at the church bell to watch it glow.

"Do you want to pop inside to speak to him?" he asked, keeping the light on the bell as he reached the other side of the road.

"Nah," Jack replied, passing the main doors of the church. "He's told us what to do, so we just do it."

"Okay."

Jack noticed Chris' attitude had changed towards him, but the boy scout act still wasn't convincing him that Chris had quietened down. He could still feel Chris' breath all over him after his shouting accusation about Rachael, so knew there was a chance he could resume where he left off and still want to fight him. But right now, this side of Chris was welcomed.

Jack pointed at the parked van in the distance as it was lit up by the lights from the station, but it was blocking their view of the net.

"You want us to head for the station?" Chris asked, now eager to get the job done.

"Nah! But we can head for the street behind it. Go to the houses with lights on." Jack smiled. "Yeah! That's where we'll start..."

But the silence in the street was interrupted by his groans after each step sent stabbing pains shooting through him. He allowed Chris to take the lead so he couldn't see him flinch but knew he wasn't stupid and had probably noticed. They entered the street, approaching the first lit-up house as Jack's teeth gritted loudly. Chris heard him groan again as they reached the door but pretended he hadn't upon knocking, not looking at Jack as he waited nervously for someone to answer.

"...Knock again," Jack asked.

Chris did, but there was no sign of movement coming from inside.

Jack felt another sharp pain in his back as he annoyingly slammed his fist against the door, but still, no one came.

"We'll go around the other side," he said, leading the way.

They heard rats scurry close by, but the noise immobilised Chris' efforts in feeling brave.

"You've got this. Just keep focused," Jack said, moving ahead of him to clap his hands in front of his face. "I've already noticed them but didn't want you to worry."

"Not to worry? I think I'm past that now."

He followed Jack towards the back of the house, but a part of him wanted to run away. Jack could feel Chris' fear coming back so knew he wasn't cut out for something like this, but then again, was *he*?

"Let's just keep moving," he said, as they turned a corner. "If it gets too much for you we'll just hide inside the house and wait for them to either go away, get killed, or get caught."

Chris shook. "You will let Adam and Harvey know if they get too close, won't you?"

Jack smiled, reaching for his phone. "I'll let Harvey know now where we are. Is that okay with you?"

Chris nodded, holding his baton close to his face as Jack made the call. He tried to listen in but the rats made him more apprehensive; his torch shining towards every sound as Jack explained to Harvey where they were.

"Don't forget to tell him about the rats."

Jack placed up a hand as he returned to the call but Chris was freaking out from the amplified squealing now penetrating his eardrums. He pushed himself against a wall to frantically search for the rats, as Jack finished the call to aim for the back door, opening it to rush Chris inside before using the key still in the keyhole to lock it.

"Why are you locking it?" Chris asked, staring at him oddly. "It's not like they will open it to get in here."

Jack shook his head. "Force of habit."

He watched Chris race to a window before flipping a curtain to one side to stare at the garden.

"See anything?" Jack asked; his worry increasing by the second as he rested against the door.

"It's hard to tell with the lack of light, but I think there's movement."

Jack's agony wasn't faltering but he remained strong upon reaching Chris. He closed his eyes to soak everything up, breathing heavier upon opening them again to see what he thought was a group of rats racing towards the side of the house.

"We have company, so be prepared."

"Be prepared? I didn't sign up for this," Chris said, as Jack's words sent more shivers down his spine to leave him on the verge of running for the front door. "I'm only the fuckin' milkman you know. I'm not a rat killer."

"You have two choices." Jack grabbed him. "One is to fight them."

"What's the other choice?"

"*You die!*" Jack shouted.

Chris almost dropped his baton as the thought of running away faded. He knew he had to face the rats. He sucked up some much-needed air and nodded as Jack walked out of the room, seeing him aim for the stairs before turning around to smile. He knew Chris wasn't over his frightened state so was happy to see the courage he now gained.

"...I'm just goin' to check upstairs!" Jack yelled. "Are you gonna be okay down here?"

"Sure! I've got this," Chris replied sweating.

Jack was glad to hear it.

He walked up the stairs, smiling, but, as he reached the middle step, a pack of rats leapt at him from the top. He lost his balance and fell back to the bottom, crashing against the floor as Chris heard the frantic squeaks closing in; his heart thumping as the sweat increased before slowly leaving the window to move towards the room. But he panicked after seeing the rats snapping teeth at him.

"Get away from him!" he hollered, noticing Jack wasn't moving. "You okay, Jack? Speak to me!"

But he received no response as the rats hovered next to Jack like they were guarding their prey.

Chris shouted his name again and this time, the first sign that Jack was still alive arrived. It was only a slight movement of a leg, but it was enough to convince Chris that he needed to get the rats away from Jack. He screamed at them with every ounce of energy he could muster, looking right through them as they viciously glared at him, suddenly running at him as his stare stayed strong. They closed in to almost biting him, but the stare faded in time for him to lash out with his baton, avoiding their attacks before running back into the other room and slamming the door.

Jack opened his eyes to see the rats scratching at the door, knowing this was his chance to get up. He watched them climb over each other in a frenzied attempt to get inside the other room as the sound of their scraping claws made his teeth hurt. He fought the terrifying moment just like he'd fought the others, so reached for his taser, but it had fallen off his belt.

Chris sat with his back pushed against the door, crying out loud as he listened to the rats scratch and bite it, knowing that soon they would reach him and claw into his back. He scanned the room, hoping to see something better than his baton to fight them off with, praying for either a farmer's gun or a fancy replica sword, but was left downhearted to see neither. He saw an immaculate kitchen dresser with plates stacked perfectly on it, with a Russian doll ornament nearby, but the plates put him off after thinking back to when he used them inside his house to scare off the rats. He sighed because he'd failed miserably before lifting off the floor to grab the doll, as wood splintered away from the door to leave tiny holes.

Jack watched the rats viciously rip away the wood, being fuelled by the person on the other side of the door. Neither looked around at him, but that didn't stop his heart from beating faster than it should. He searched for his taser as his sweat dripped to soak the floor, trying hard not to make a sound as the noise coming from the next room escalated to make the rats crazier. He wanted to punch himself for letting the situation get out of hand, knowing he needed to rescue Chris urgently. He checked himself to find no more injuries, happy that his protective suit cushioned the fall as he moved slowly around the room, keeping one eye on the rodents as their squeals continued.

Chris saw a rat head appear through a hole in the door so nervously pulled off the largest doll, throwing it at the rat to see the doll crash against the door. He tried again with another one but it did the same thing, leaving him nervous after throwing the third and fourth dolls to swear at more rat heads appearing before backing away as the first rat squeezed through the hole. He stumbled as he threw the last doll in fear, seeing it smack the rat on the head to send it shrieking to the floor; its face dazed as blood trickled down. Chris waited for it to attack him, but other rats coming into the room set on it, ripping its face and body to shreds. He stepped back further until crashing against the dresser, not able to stop the plates from shaking before crashing to the floor.

Jack heard the noise so moved quicker until spotting the taser underneath a coffee table. He reached for it as he looked at the door, feeling a sense of dread to find no rats on his end to make him think he could be too late. He raced towards the door in the hope of seeing Chris alive, but, as he opened it, the first thing he saw was the dresser crashing to the floor. The next was Chris jumping on it to swing his baton like a lunatic.

"Do you need help?" Jack spluttered.

"Very funny!" Chris replied, lashing out at the first bunch of rats to join him on the dresser.

His legs swayed like he was on a surfboard, but he wasn't panicking. He knew that one mistake would leave him on his arse, and leave him an easy target, but right now he was pumped up to fight back. Jack saw the effort he was putting in but couldn't see the remaining rats anywhere.

"Where'd they go?" he asked.

But Chris didn't reply. He was too busy fighting the rats springing for his face. Sweat dripped from his brow like it was raining inside to soak the dresser in seconds, but it creaked as his foot crashed through. He tried to pull it free but couldn't as the rats circled him.

"Jack! Help me! Please!" he cried out.

Jack raced towards the dresser to cringe as a rat landed on Chris' head, but he was quick to knock it off as Jack booted another one across the room.

"Hold on to me," he said, grabbing Chris' arm.

Chris did, but the other rats found a way inside his suit to bite him. He clenched his teeth and took the pain as Jack pulled on the arm, freeing the trapped foot to leave Chris back on the floor again, but blood was seeping through his clothing.

"...Let's get out of here!" Jack shouted, but the rest of the rats set on him. "Get these mother fuckers off me!"

But Chris hesitated as thoughts of what Jack did with Rachael raced back into his mind. He glared at Jack as his screams belted him around the face before shedding a tear as the rats frantically hacked at Jack's suit, leaving him struggling to fight them off.

"...Help me!" Jack shouted again.

Chris nodded.

He grabbed a rat from Jack's back and threw it across the room, not caring if it bit his hands as he reached for another.

"We have to find help," he said, tossing the second rat to see it return to its feet.

"We don't have time," the reply came, as another rat jumped on Jack to find a spot not protected by his suit.

It bit down deep and hard to force a heavy blood flow, as its freshness drove the other rats into a frenzy. Chris was shocked at how easily they attacked Jack now, as their bites became fiercer to fill the floor with his blood.

He saw Jack fall to the floor like a tree being cut down as the rats covered him like a blanket of evil before seconds later a hand reached out from amongst them, but it flopped down before Chris could grab it. All he heard was Jack yell his name as a rat bit into his face, but no more yells followed.

Chris stared at them feeding on him, crying inside as he planned his escape. He shuddered as they fought over Jack's eyes, looking away before backtracking towards the door, turning the key to open it to guide him to safety.

CHAPTER THIRTY-EIGHT

Adam sat exhausted inside the police station, closely observed by everyone there. But none wanted to ask about Walter. He looked at Rachael, who was doing a great job at pretending to be a mother for Cortney, Trey, and Nathan before his droopy eyes almost closed. But he shook himself as Kelvin sat opposite before reaching for his phone. And the others watched on as he held it against an ear.

"How are things?" Harvey asked softly after answering the call.

"Not good," Adam choked. "Walter's gone."

"Gone where? You didn't let him escape?"

Adam wiped a tear from his eye. "He's dead. But he was a dick anyway." He looked over at Rachael and apologised for swearing, but she just shook her head before escorting the children into another room.

"A dick he may be," Harvey replied. "But he was a dick who knew the answer as to why the rats are violent."

Adam rose from his seat to take the conversation away from the staring men inside the room. "I know why."

"How? What did he tell you?"

Adam turned to see no one watching him before telling Harvey whom the rats had been eating. He heard Harvey cough up spit, so knew he was finding the information tough.

"Anyway, how are things inside the church?" Adam calmly said, hoping to change the topic slightly.

Rachael returned to listen in, feeling weak upon praying to hear Chris' name; her worry intensifying because he'd not had any police training. She watched Adam nod his head a few times, but Chris' name wasn't mentioned.

"...At least you're in a safe place," Adam said. "I'm back at the station with seven people...How many you got there?"

Rachael's heart almost jumped out of her chest as she eagerly waited to hear Chris' name before studying the movement of Adam's mouth to see if he at least mimed it. But all he did was nod again.

"...Yep, okay, will do," Adam finally said before putting his phone away. He looked over at Rachael to leave her guessing an answer. "You okay?" he asked. "Because you're staring at me like I've stolen something from you."

"What's happening?" she softly asked.

Adam explained that the plan of getting everyone to the church was coming together and that Harvey was okay. He had been bitten, but nothing too serious. He also said that none of the other officers had arrived yet."

"And Chris?" Rachael asked.

Adam shook his head, leaving her to fear the worst.

———

Steve, Louise, Ray, and Alice finally met up again, as the sad encounter with the woman in the tree became the main topic of conversation. Steve and Louise's journey to reach the other two had been much easier, with neither having to use force on a rat.

They were shattered as they walked side-by-side along the dark and silent street, brightening up the area as the rats avoided the light. Steve held his gun, feeling more confident to use it as the others held shields.

"I hope this is the end," Louise said, angrily smacking her shield against a lampost.

"Me too," replied Alice.

But Steve's phone rang to spook everyone into almost jumping out of their skin.

"What's up, Harv?" he asked, still shaking.

"I need you all at the church."

Harvey was gone to leave Steve holding his phone whilst confusingly scratching his head with the tip of his gun, but Alice gently grabbed it and lowered his hand before sighing at him until he realised what he'd done.

"Fuck!" he said. "I could've blown my head off."

Alice hugged him, hoping his lack of concentration was a one-off.

"What did Harvey say?" she asked.

"He wants us all to go to the church."

"But why does he want us at the church?" Louise asked.

"Because we need to fuckin' pray," Ray said, laughing out loud.

"Shut up!" Alice cried out.

"Everyone quiet," Steve said, turning his head.

They did, including Ray which was a first.

They stared in the same direction as Steve, each following the light from his torch as it lit up everything it touched.

"...I thought I saw something move over there," Steve whispered.

"Something big or something small?" Ray replied.

"Does it matter?" Louise said, feeling anxious again now the adrenaline was seeping from her body.

"Does it matter, you ask?" Ray bounced about like a hyperactive child. "I tell you why it matters. It matters because big means no rat. You idiot!"

Louise raised the butt of her torch before coming close to striking him with it, but Steve intervened to stand between them.

"No!" was all he said before walking off in front.

They heard *someone* shouting in the distance to leave their torch beams shooting out thin lines like light sabres, but the shouting confused them, with neither knowing in which direction it came from.

"...Does anyone have an idea?" Steve asked before spotting a teenage girl running from a house.

They found her slumped and bleeding by the side of the building as Alice closed in on her.

"Are you okay?" she asked, feeling stupid because she knew the girl wasn't.

She cringed from the painful scratches on her face, shivering as if she'd just taken an ice bath; not speaking as she stared at the house like she feared something was coming out of it as Alice helped her off the ground.

"Ray! I want you to come with me to search the house," Steve said, as Ray grinned. "You two stay with her. We won't be long."

They moved slowly and stealth-like towards the door as the heart-wrenching sound of another person screaming from inside the house shook them before everyone raced towards the building.

"...Me and you around the back," Steve said to Ray. "You two take the front."

There was no time to be scared when the person inside

needed their help.

Alice turned to smile at the teenage girl as she slumped back to the ground, sobbing into her hands as Steve took Ray around the back. Louise and Alice rushed to the front to open the door with ease, entering the house to see the men appear from the kitchen.

"No one's here!" Ray shouted angrily.

"So, who screamed?" Steve asked as loud noises bounced above them.

They looked at the ceiling as footsteps THUDDED against it before Steve led the way towards the stairs, his gun ready as he climbed them, but they creaked to make his knees knock together. The others closed in on him as the noise increased until suddenly something fell.

"What does that mean?" Alice curiously whispered after hearing something drip.

"Is that a tap?" Louise asked.

But no one could answer her.

Steve walked a few more steps but a sudden thump stopped him again. He tried seeing ahead of him but a wooden railing was the only thing in sight; the dripping constant as blood fell onto Louise's head.

"What the fuck!" she shouted, touching the sticky liquid.

Steve raced to the top of the stairs to frown as Louise looked at her hand.

"Another dead body," he said, cursing under his breath.

"And rats?" Alice replied, wincing at the thought of seeing them again.

"Not here," Steve said. "But they seem to have feasted recently on this victim, so I doubt if they'll attack us for a while."

"But shouldn't we still look for them?" Louise asked, begging for another adrenaline moment.

"Harvey told us to head for the church, so that's where we're goin'."

"Come on, it won't take long to search."

Louise seemed pumped up again as her eyes bulged. She'd hoped he would say *yes* but Steve just let the body language of the others decide for him. Alice nudged Ray to remind him of what happened the last time he saw a dead body, but he just scrunched his nose at her and followed her to the top of the stairs. He picked a room to check, but another scream hit him in the face before he could enter.

"The girl from outside!" he shouted.

The screams became constant for the next five seconds, but it was five seconds too late to save the girl.

"...I thought you said they wouldn't attack again so soon?!" Ray hollered towards Steve as he reached the body.

"We don't know if it was the same rats that killed her," Steve replied, staring at the mangled girl.

Ray wasn't expecting a reply, especially one that could be true, so just sucked his bottom lip and walked towards the church.

"Where are you going?" Alice asked.

"Where do you think? The fuckin' church. That's where."

Alice sadly watched Ray as he made some distance before Louise closed in on her, nudging her to start walking after seeing she was upset.

But why be upset over him? Louise thought, watching Alice stare at Ray.

Steve remained alert as he walked behind the others, as getting them to the church safely became his only priority. He watched the women quicken up their walk to catch up with Ray before shaking his head at how easily they fell for Ray's bullshit.

Alice was the first to reach him, catching him off guard to

witness tears roll down his cheeks. It freaked her out more than seeing the rats and dead bodies. This was rare. She knew Ray had a heart, but he'd kept it well hidden, and in its place was usually hatred; hatred towards his job, his leaders, and to anyone who disagreed with him.

"You okay?" she asked, holding his hand.

He looked at her sorrowfully, showing signs of a man who wanted to sleep forever and forget about the world, but Ray knew he couldn't, not yet anyway.

"I'm fine. It's just reminding me of my past. That's all."

Alice didn't know much about Ray's past, and to be honest, neither did the rest of the officers back home, but what she did know was that he'd seen death before. It was as a child; the death of his parents. She held his hand tighter as reminders of his saddened childhood pushed their way to the front of his mind. He smiled at her, thankful she was next to him.

Steve caught up with them, shouting out to get a move on, not wanting any more attacks happening before they reached the church. He grabbed his phone and called Harvey to let him know they were close, and, as the phone went silent, the door opened to allow them in.

Harvey happily watched them near but they winced after seeing his wounds.

"Stop staring. I'm fine," Harvey said, staring at Louise. "But you need to sort that cut out on your head."

"The blood belongs to someone else," she replied, frowning.

Harvey smiled at her as she entered the church, but, as the others followed, with Steve closing the door behind him, they were swamped by worried locals demanding answers.

CHAPTER THIRTY-NINE

Troy paced up and down near Victoria, feeling on edge as she closely watched him. She was annoyed for still being at the university as the time reached *9:30 pm.*

"You can go home you know. You don't have to be here," Troy said.

"There's no way I'm going out there while all this is going on," Victoria replied. "And anyway, I've not heard from Adam to say everything is okay."

"Whoooo! Adam is it." Troy stopped pacing. "So, it's on first-name terms now."

Victoria suddenly blushed. "Shut up, Troy."

"What did you two get up to anyway?"

Victoria waved a hand in front of her face to fan her burning cheeks, knowing that if she couldn't change the colour soon then Troy would suspect more. If he did then he would keep on pestering her until she caved in.

"What do you mean? Get up to what?"

"You tell me? You and PC plod were on your own for quite some time after we left the Toade's office, so where did you end up?" Troy grabbed his lunch box from a table and opened it. "Plus, I knocked on Walter's door when you were inside, but you never answered." He picked up a cold bacon sandwich and bit into it. "So, what were you two doing in there before I arrived?"

Victoria thought fast. "We took a walk around the building because I was still upset after seeing the awful find, and we never heard you knocking on the door. Sorry..."

But Troy didn't believe her. He wanted to but knew when she lied. He bit into the sandwich again upon staring at her like she was in a witness box before getting ready to pile the pressure on her to gain the truth, but Victoria was on him like a rattlesnake on a desert rabbit, pointing at the hole in the air vent.

"...Shouldn't you be searching for where those rats could've escaped from?"

"And how do you assume I do that? That hole is small you know."

"I don't know. Can't you make it bigger?"

Troy almost chuckled at hearing those words, but, after seeing the look on Victoria's face he knew she was being serious.

"I can't smash the wall in, Walter will sack me." He closed in on the air vent as thoughts of rats coming through caused him to shudder. "And anyway," he said, changing the subject, "You won't go home because you think they'll bite you." He laughed. "You're scared of the rodents you've raised from babies, aren't you?"

Victoria didn't want to think it was true, especially since she was a part of their existence, a part of the S.T.A.R.S project, but Troy was right, she did feel scared of them.

"Yes! I'm extremely frightened!" She closed in on him with watery eyes. "I knew Walter was up to no good with those behind-closed-doors experiments. I should've put a stop to it when I found out, but I had no evidence to back it up."

Troy watched her become a mumbling mess. "We all should've stopped him, Vic. You weren't the only one who knew what he was up to."

"So why didn't you say anything?" Victoria spluttered and began to cry.

"Because I didn't want to lose my job."

Troy hugged her as she sunk her wet face into his work shirt. He felt weird for doing it but needed this time just as much as she did.

"So, you're not going to knock down the wall to find out what's behind it?"

Troy smiled as he kept her close. "Only if you go outside first."

Victoria's tears faded as she removed herself from his chest.

"Get lost!" she said, laughing as she punched his arm.

"And anyway, we know what's behind the wall: pipes, and more pipes."

———

Adam felt the pressure of wanting and needing to go to the church, even though Harvey had told him to stay put. He knew the police station was secure, so, if any rats were stupid enough to try to get in there was plenty of weaponry to destroy them.

But if I left here who would be in charge of the weapons?

He couldn't guarantee that any of the people inside the station would fight the rodents if they got inside, so the decision to flee was put on hold.

————

A *loud* bang against the church door alerted Michael to go open it, and, as he did, Chris fell inside.

"Where's Jack? Isn't he with you?" Harvey asked, hobbling over to pull Chris to his feet.

But Chris never replied. He was lost to the words.

Harvey asked him again, and this time Chris reacted, as the words slapped him around the head to force the terror of what he'd just seen back inside his mind.

"He....didn't...make it," he stuttered, sinking back into a heap on the ground.

"What do you mean? Is he coming later?" Michael asked.

Harvey knew what Chris meant, and it made him quiver.

"Let's get you inside," he said. "You're safe now."

The other officers stared at Chris as he was helped into the main hall, each waiting to hear good news about Jack. But, after Harvey spoke, they knew it wasn't going to arrive.

"Would you like a cup of tea?" Michael asked Chris, watching him burst into tears.

The whole room stared at him, but Chris never noticed.

Martha looked sadly towards him as she walked towards a room to the left of the main door, entering to switch on a kettle to sigh at seeing paint tins, brushes, rollers, plastic sheets, and turpentine bottles stacked in a pile inside the room, wondering when the decorators were coming back to start repainting the church. She picked up a note attached to one of the tins before sighing again after the date shown was still a week away, silently cursing Michael for agreeing to have the items stored in advance. The room was already too small to be used as a kitchen, so, with the pile erected in the centre, Martha had to walk around it to use the kettle.

"How many of those things do you think are still out there?" Michael whispered, closing in on Harvey.

"Not sure to be honest, but I'm not going outside to count them."

Michael took that as a joke, even though Harvey wasn't laughing.

He patted Harvey on the arm before sluggishly walking to the front of the hall, standing behind the altar as everyone watched him closely.

"Can I please have your attention," he calmly said, holding out his hands.

The pews filled with people in seconds, with each either sitting or standing as Michael prepared to speak again.

"...The danger isn't over yet, but we are safe inside here," he said, performing the sign of the cross. "I want us all to pray for those still outside. Let's hope they're safe." He then looked across the room at Harvey. "And to pray for the people that have fallen to the menace that's trying to destroy this town..."

He clasped his hands together as everyone bowed their heads; fear passing between them as he breathed deeply before saying a prayer, allowing the words to open the eyes of the people to the violence outside. The children, who normally fidgeted during one of Michael's prayer readings remained still, each focusing on what he was saying.

"...I pray this day will end on a positive note, and with you watching over this church, oh Lord, I pray that we'll all be safe, and everyone will be home very soon..."

Harvey lifted his head after Chris cried again before seeing Martha arrive with a cup of tea. She placed it next to Chris before comforting him, smiling at Harvey as Michael ended his speech, but the lights above them flickered, causing most people to panic. Michael soothingly spoke to reassure them that all was okay, but, as his words made a breakthrough, the lights flickered again, and this time they turned off. The people became more agitated as they cried in the darkness, as the children called out for their parents to hold them.

"...Don't be alarmed, it's probably just a power cut," Michael said. "The church is full of candles, so please, don't panic..."

He heard the thumping of footwear as people tried to run, but most either ran into each other or hit one of the pews, screaming as if they'd just woken up from a nightmare.

Harvey shone his torch into the centre of the hall to capture the nervous people, as Steve, Louise, Alice, and Ray did the same, lighting it up the best they could. It seemed to work as everyone calmed down, with most silently heading back to their seats as the mothers comforted their scared children whilst the fathers spoke only of positive things to help ease their stress.

Harvey smiled as the officers joined him at the back of the hall, each keeping the light close to the people as Michael spoke again.

"...This is just a mild power failure. The lights will be back on soon." He looked down to his right. "But in the meantime, why don't you help yourself to one of the large candles next to me..."

He pointed at candlestick holders, containing large, white candles standing a few feet away from the altar as Steve shone his light on them to bring them out of the darkness.

"...Come on, Mrs Moore, why don't you be the first to light a candle? It'll help guide you out of this dark place."

Mrs Moore was the church organist, a retired lady who taught music at the local school. She was liked by everyone, and her gift for playing enjoyable, sing-along church music that the local choir would perform on weekends was appreciated.

"Okay, reverend, I will."

She approached one of the candles, passing through the light beam upon grabbing it, but a creepy sound penetrated her eardrums. It wasn't a sound she'd recognised in the church before but it faded as quickly as it arrived. She shook her head whilst lifting a match from a tray next to the candles, striking it to light one, but her movement alerted a rat nearby. It pounced, biting her nose, leaving her to scream as blood poured out, as everyone became confused and tense. But Steve's torch lit her up to make her stand out like someone on a stage. She was barely standing as her head drooped, allowing the blood to fall to the floor as the rat attacked again. She screamed once more, raising her head as the rat bit into her left eye, leaving the children, who were unfortunate enough to witness it, to cry as they placed their heads against their parent's chests.

Michael fought with the rat as Harvey released his gun, but his injuries stopped him from rushing to help as Steve saw him squirm. He nodded and released his gun before following Harvey as the other officers raised their batons.

"Get out of the way!" Harvey shouted as Michael pulled the rat off Mrs Moore's face.

"Keep everyone safe!" Michael replied, feeling pain from a bite to his hand. He lashed out at the rat but it ran off into a dark corner.

Alice and Louise rushed off to find it, hoping it was the only one. They shared hatred towards the rats now, a hatred that went beyond capturing them. They stood close together as they followed the light from their torches, ready to strike the menace that attacked Mrs Moore.

Ray and Steve left Harvey to try and calm everyone down

again, but nothing was working as they saw the people form into separate groups, with each heading off in different directions around the hall. They lost sight of some as they tried to hide, fearing an invasion of rats was about to attack.

"Where's it gone!" someone shouted, while another said, "I want to go home!" As the words left half of the church residents in a trance.

They hurried for the door, but the sound of rats nearby stopped them; their noses twitching as if smelling *who* was the most scared before pouncing on the chosen few. The yelling left the rest of the people aware of what was going on, but neither was brave enough now to run for the exit.

"Get me out of here!" someone snapped, but the words faded after the rats attacked.

"There's another way out!" a teenage, female choir singer shouted.

Those that heard her raced to the front of the church, but again most of them ran into each other.

Steve and Ray shone a light onto as many people as they could, but they were too fast and too scared to stay inside it.

"Keep calm!" Ray shouted as he was pushed to one side.

The people bumped into Alice and Louise almost knocking them to the floor as their torchlight caught the last person running past, as they closed in on Michael sitting on the ground next to a dying Mrs Moore. He was holding a lit candle, shedding tears as blood poured from her wounds before gripping her hand and closing his eyes. Most of the frantic people slowed down after seeing him, lighting candles for the fallen few, as others were ambushed just feet away from the exit door. The large rat lashed out like it was rabid, biting and clawing its way through the flesh of a victim as Harvey fired his gun at it, the shots sending exhilarating pain through his body as the bullets disappeared into the darkness. But, after his gun was empty, three rats lay dead.

Sweat poured from him as an attack of anxiety made him feel too old to carry on, leaving him slowing down as a rat got close. But a bullet from Steve's gun split it in half before it reached him. Harvey thanked him as he reloaded before shouting out for everyone to light a candle, as the officers gathered the people together like sheep. They followed the torch beams to race for a candle, picking one up like it was a magic wand before grabbing a match from the tray to strike in a synchronised fashion. The candles glowed like fireflies in the darkness to leave the front of the hall flickering like a huge fireball, as the people huddled together.

Mrs Moore died in front of them as Harvey covered her face with his jacket.

"What are you doing?!" he yelled at Steve after seeing him aim his gun at the rats blocking the nearest exit. "There are people injured over there. You can't risk it."

Steve silently cursed before reminding Harvey of his recent attempt at firing off a barrage of bullets in the same direction without hitting anyone, so told him to trust his judgement. But Harvey wasn't having it. Ray stared at them, feeling agitated and annoyed to the point of screaming at them for bickering and wasting time.

"It's okay. We'll go to the other door," he said, grabbing the nearest person. "Off you go!..."

But the person panicked as if not expecting to be chosen.

"...Go on! And keep moving," Ray said, pushing the person to start running, hoping that others would do the same.

Several flickers of light split away from the large fireball to aim towards the other exit as Ray, Steve, Alice, and Louise followed.

"We can't fight all the rats," Alice said to Ray.

He smiled at her, knowing she was extremely worried.

"I won't let them get you," he replied, flicking out his little finger to touch her hand.

She smiled back, feeling thankful, and, for the first time since knowing him truly believed him.

"Where are they?" Louise asked, feeling stressed again.

"At the exits, I think," Steve replied.

"But we're heading for an exit."

The officers gulped as they shone light towards the target. They saw bodies of crying and injured people lying in front of them, with some trying to hide behind the ones killed, but there was no sign of a rat.

Michael let go of Mrs Moore's hand and returned to his feet, his chest covered with her blood as he awkwardly walked towards the others.

"Have you seen my wife?" he whispered, turning frantically because she wasn't seen. "Martha! Martha, dear! Where are you?"

His children appeared from behind a group of shaking people, appearing unhurt as Mary held a candle whilst Isaac held her hand.

"What about us?" Mary angrily asked. "Why didn't you ask if *we* were okay?"

Isaac tried to calm her down, but she was on a mission to find out why her father only asked about his wife. Michael started crying as he reached out to hold her, but Mary backed off.

"Sorry." Michael reached out to hold her again and this time she let him. "Your mother was right there," he said, pointing to the spot where Martha was last seen. "I didn't mean to ignore you. I was just lost..."

He threw an arm around Isaac and held him too as his candle lit up the area where Chris was seated.

"...Where is she?" he asked his children.

Mary cried into his chest, as Isaac gulped.

Harvey stared at Chris after shining his torch on him, but he didn't respond. He shouted at him to still receive nothing, so shouted again before smiling after seeing Chris slightly move. He waited for him to get up, but he wasn't trying to.

"Hey, Chris, come on man!" Ray shouted, fearing the rats could strike again at any time.

Everyone aimed torches and candles at Chris as he squirmed violently in his seat, but the sight scared most of the people into thinking he was having a seizure. Harvey cautiously neared him in the hope he was okay, but Chris shook again to spook him into ordering everyone away. He shone his torch at Chris' feet but jumped back in horror after seeing a pack of rats bite into them, close to puking after seeing the pew covered in blood after Chris' arms and stomach were attacked before gulping after spotting his abdomen laid out on his lap.

Harvey backed away to swallow hard as a *woman's* screams attracted the rats' attention. They stopped feeding on Chris to glare at her, frightening her, even more, to lose her bearings before running off towards the confession booth. The rats chased her to follow her in, but, as she pulled the white curtain across to hide, a line of red splashed across it and she screamed no more.

CHAPTER FORTY

Adam seemed fidgety, as staying inside the station to watch over everyone became harder to do. The horror of seeing Walter die kept surprising his mind, making him see visions that weren't there; visions of Walter appearing inside the police station with his face a mangled mess.

He phoned Harvey, but the phone wasn't picked up. He tried again, but it was the same, so started to worry. He stared at the people around him who seemed none the wiser to what was going on outside the police station before rushing to the main door, close to leaving as he phoned Harvey again. And this time he answered, but Adam couldn't hear what he was saying because people were screaming inside the church. He held the phone away from his ear as the latest scream rang out before noticing Rachael turn pale as the scream blasted through her. She shook upon waiting for a voice to come through the phone, but all she heard were different levels of squeals and shouts.

"You have to go and help," she said, shedding a tear.

"I know."

Adam disconnected the call as he stared at his riot gear, hoping it wasn't too damaged, shaking more than he'd shaken before, as thoughts of Harvey and the others being taken down by the rats made him angry.

"Be careful," Rachael whispered, closing in on him.

She grabbed his helmet and passed it over to him as pleading eyes sent out a message for him to end what was happening outside.

"Keep everyone safe," Adam said, putting on the helmet before releasing his taser and baton. "This ends now."

He left the station to walk slowly like someone about to die on death row, shaking from nerves the closer he got to the church before taking one last look at Walter's body.

"Your creation won't win!" he yelled, spitting on the ground.

He neared a window of the church as the silence confused him, feeling confused by the lack of light to see just glowing flickers moving around before shaking his head in temper - *You clever little bastards. You chewed through the cables!*

He was prepared for the rats to attack but had a feeling they were all inside the church.

His heart pounded against his chest the closer he got to the door, as a pain strangled his nerves like no pain he'd ever felt. He heard screams slipping through the crack at the bottom to leave his heart skipping a beat upon placing a sweaty hand on the handle, turning it as silently as he could until sneaking inside.

He could smell blood. It was strong, but his vision was dim, so

replaced the baton for his torch before shutting the door and turning it on. But a pile of bodies rooted him to the spot. He shone the light over to his right to capture four people shaking in a corner, none speaking as they stared at him as if they'd just seen the Devil. The light closed in, illuminating their faces, but they were too scared to move. Adam felt lost as he shone the torch to the ground but found the answer to their fear after spotting a few rats guarding them like prisoners. He zapped one with his taser, seeing it explode as the others ran away, but knew soon they would return if he didn't get the people to safety. He pushed the nearest person to get a reaction and their eyes blinked as if coming out of a trance.

"Get out of here and head to the police station," Adam said, as the person walked towards the door. "You'll be safe there."

———

Harvey tried in vain to keep the civilians in order and to keep them safe, but his words were drowned out by their frantic behaviour. After witnessing the lady in the confession booth fall, taking the bloodied curtain with her, the people became manic, as her final breath frightened those that saw. Now the officers couldn't stop them from running around as the rats prevented them from leaving.

Harvey watched on as ten people broke from the pack to run to the middle of the hall, their candles flickering to the point of going out as the rats quickly chased after them. Harvey shone his torch after hearing the rats squeak, but couldn't pinpoint where they were as the ten people huddled together to cry. But suddenly the rats dropped onto them from the wooden beams to spook Harvey into firing his gun, as most of the bullets crashed into the wood.

Alice almost puked after seeing a rat tear at a man's scalp, its teeth pulling it back to leave her swiftly turning away, as Louise and Ray pushed the other people to one side. Steve fired a bullet into a rat's body to leave its hind legs hanging off, seeing it struggle to escape before squashing it beneath his boot.

———

Adam closed the door after seeing the people run towards the station before his torchlight caught hold of a shoe.

"Hello," he softly said, raising the light to capture a female leg.

"Get that away from my eyes!" Martha blasted at him, lowering a hand from her face to show emotional scars.

"Jesus! You scared me," Adam replied, kicking himself for saying the J word.

Martha stared at him, close to collapsing as he hugged her tight, but the sound of her husband shouting out the Lord's Prayer suddenly revived her. She screamed as if she'd just watched the scariest movie ever to cause Adam's ears to ring, but, as he let go of her the ringing faded.

She raced into the main hall like a wild banshee shouting out Michael's name, alerting him to stop praying as his candlelight tried locating her amongst the chaos. Martha saw him, but the rats saw her. They circled her as Michael arrived, but time seemed to slow down as tears slid down his cheeks.

He heard Adam YELL like a roaring lion before seeing him rush over to shield Martha, desperately attempting to keep her from being bitten before squinting as Adam pulled, kicked, and punched the rats away. But Martha cried as they turned on him.

Louise and Alice broke rank to charge the rats attacking Adam, but their aim was off as their batons swiped at thin air. They gulped as the rats hissed at them before a lucky hit by

Louise crushed a rat's skull, as Alice nodded, feeling more confident as she smashed one to the ground.

"Get her to her husband!" Adam shouted through his steamed-up visor.

They dragged Martha away from the danger, moving her closer to Michael as he reached out and hugged her like he hadn't seen her in months. He knew she'd been lucky.

Some of the survivors moved back towards the exit door where the body of Mrs Moore was laid but none saw any rats as they reached it. They watched the officers try rounding up the most terrified of people, seeing the majority still run around like headless chickens as some now hid between the pews. They heard the officers shouting out to them but were too scared to come out into the open, so Harvey, Ray, and Steve moved in to rescue them.

Adam, Alice, and Louise kept the rest of the frightened people close as they neared the exit door, and, as the children cried, those still with their parents were comforted. Alice sighed, knowing soon the door will open and the people will finally be safe.

"Keep moving," Louise said, smiling at her.

"Yeah! Everyone, keep moving. You're safe now," Alice replied.

They saw two people nervously close in to open the door, but they collapsed within seconds of each other, screaming as they hit the floor. Adam tried to rescue them, but his frantic attempt didn't work as a third person fell next to him, shouting that a rat just bit their ankle.

"Shine your torches on the ground!" Adam shouted, searching for the rats.

Louise and Alice did it without hesitation, but the rats were fast and avoided being spotted. They leapt at more people from the darkness, picking them off with ease.

"…Use your candles to burn the fuckers!" Adam yelled, moving his taser from side to side.

A few candles lowered to the floor, leaving the flames hovering above, as the people holding them shivered in fear at seeing another rodent. They swung the candles like sparklers on Bonfire night to brighten up the ground, but it didn't stop more attacks as the remaining people aimed for the door. They were so close to finally being free but were now running in the opposite direction, as the dancing candle flames aimed towards the front of the hall before haunting screams followed.

The rest of the group slipped between the pews to avoid the recently fallen, their hearts set on reaching the front while the rats chewed on the others. One person headed towards the small kitchen where Martha had recently made Chris a cup of tea, lighting up the door with their candle before opening it to race inside. That person was *Laura Worsopp*, a helper at the church on weekends. She shook as she waved the candle before cringing after feeling the wax drip onto her hand, spotting the kettle to touch it to let the warmth revitalise her body. She felt at peace, but scratching sounds coming from behind her scared her again.

"Who's there?" she whispered as her eyes filled with terror. "Please tell me who you are?"

She whimpered as the noise intensified, until feeling a pain she didn't recognise, seeing a vision dancing between the hot, colourful flame to leave her thinking something awful was going to happen. She heard teeth snapping together, getting closer by the second, but couldn't see anything as a scurrying sound caused her to jump. She moved back towards the door but a rat darted across the floor to bite her ankle. She gritted her teeth as more bites occurred, each feeling worse than the one before, but she wasn't screaming out for help. Instead, she was trying her best to burn the rats that were ripping at her flesh, but her efforts made her tired as the rats now taunted her. She hobbled over to the other side of the room to try and shake them off, but her wounds hurt too much, causing her to stop. A rat pounced on her face to tear at it until she fell to the floor, dropping the candle onto a pile of work overalls left by the decorators to squirm as they set alight. She was unable to move to prevent the flames from growing tall, seeing them ignite a curtain before spreading quickly to become just as frightening as the rats.

"Get off me!" she choked as flesh hung from her cheek.

She watched through painful eyes as the decorating equipment was engulfed in flames before reeling around in agony as more bites released her blood; spitting some out as the rats attacked again.

Alice arrived outside the room to witness the smoke escape from underneath the door, feeling horrified as she opened it to find Laura dead. She felt the hotness of the fire building up around the body before panicking to see the tins of paint bubbling nearby, thinking only of getting everyone else away from the area. But, as she turned to shout - "Run! Fire!" - spray cans from the pile exploded. One hit her in the back, sending her crashing into a wall as two civilians were hit by flying debris. They died as flames now surrounded the door frame.

Adam saw the explosion but was left unable to cope as Louise ran to Alice's aid, but she choked on her hand after seeing smoking pieces from the can stick out of Alice's protective suit. And she wasn't moving.

"Don't die!" Louise shouted, checking for a pulse as Adam stared at her.

"Is she?" he nervously asked, fearing the worst.

"She has a pulse, but it's very faint," Louise said, as Adam helped drag Alice to safety.

"What the hell just happened?" he replied, still in shock after witnessing the carnage the flying debris did on the victims.

"Something exploded from that room."

The fire reached outside the door as the smoke's deadly venom choked everyone nearby, but Adam became alert again after coughing a few times. He gathered people together as Louise grabbed two civilians, but, as they reached down to pick Alice up, Adam panicked.

"We can't move her!" he shouted.

"It's too late to go all protocol on me now!" Louise shouted back. "We've just moved her away from the door."

"But what if her injuries are serious?"

Louise shrugged. "So, what do we do? Do we leave her here to be smothered to death by the smoke?"

"Fuck!" Adam punched the closing smoke as he led the survivors towards the door. "We can't leave her here, so just be careful when lifting her. Support her neck."

"Hey! I've got this." Louise smiled at the helpers before seeing them reach for Alice, holding back tears as she turned back to Adam. "Just get the others outside."

Blood poured from Alice as she was carried away from the fire, leaving Louise trembling as she fumbled with her belt to reach for a medical kit. She smiled as Alice was taken outside before following Adam as he guided the others through the door. The sound of happy and sad crying came from most as they breathed in the fresh air, while the rest coughed and spat on the pavement, feeling thankful to be alive. Adam did the same as he wiped his eyes while Louise looked shattered with worry, kneeling next to Alice to open the kit as she played nurse again.

"I'm going back," Adam said, not waiting for a reply.

He raced back inside the church as Louise awkwardly watched on, her hands shaking as she patched up Alice's back before seeing him pull out the two recent bodies.

———

Steve, Harvey, and Ray remained stunned after the explosion tore up the front of the church, but the rats weren't frightened off by it. They stayed aggressive to block the men from finding a way out before one found a weak spot in Ray's suit, biting the back of his leg to shock his focus into gear as his hand smacked it away.

"Why don't you just *fuck off!*" he bellowed, cringing.

"You okay?" Harvey called out to him.

"Yeah...I'm all good," the sarcastic reply came. "I just want to get out of here."

"We all do mate," Steve said, as a second explosion rattled the main hall.

———

Everyone outside shivered as windows smashed, leaving the smoke to escape the church as the children watched on to imagine fearless dragons after seeing the flames.

Adam rose off the ground to shake off bits of glass, feeling lucky to have not been injured after bringing out another corpse. He shook his head as he looked at Louise, seeing her move after using her body to protect Alice from the blast before miming – Is she okay? - Happy to see her stick up a thumb as he prepared to go back inside.

"Hey! Listen up!" he said, staring hard at everyone as he pointed over the road. "I need you all to stay clear of the area.

The church could explode again at any time, so move to the other side." He stared hard again and sighed. "Those of you not injured, help the people who are."

"What are you going to do?" Louise asked, knowing he was about to crumble.

"I can't leave the others in there," Adam replied, turning to see flames shoot out of the windows.

Louise shook her head. "Did you not hear the recent blast? Look at the church. It's burning to the ground."

"I know it is, but I'm still going back in," he said, running for the open door. "Get hold of the fire station. Harvey needs me."

Louise saw him fight his way through the smoke pouring out the door, as his visor steamed up in seconds.

"Be careful," was all she said, as Adam disappeared.

He aimed for the main hall, coughing behind the light of his torch, avoiding flames to listen out for anyone's voice.

"You need to get out the back entrance," he cried out. "The fire is spreading. It's not safe."

"What happened?!" Harvey yelled, backing away as more smoke filled the room.

But Adam ignored him as he shone the torch at nearby rats.

He wiped his visor before chasing them back into the hall to hear people frantically moving around as Harvey's voice seemed to guide them towards the back exit. But, as some candles burned out, the people holding them tripped over recently fallen bodies to become victims.

Harvey shouted out for the people to fight after seeing how close the exit was, knowing it was their only hope to survive, as Steve and Ray helped the rest of the survivors towards the door. But the smoke was slowing them down.

"Almost there!" Steve shouted, guiding the coughing group away from the rats as Adam yelled in the distance.

He moved quicker towards the main hall as the fire spread, only briefly slowing down to shine his torch over an old man with his throat torn open lying between the pews.

"We can't fight them in the dark!" he shouted, shuddering.

"But we have to try!" Harvey replied, staring towards the worried people. "I want everyone to stamp their feet. We need to squash the vermin."

"You mean, like Irish dancing?" Ray said, trying to be comical.

"No!" Harvey blasted, stamping down to stop the rats from biting him.

The thumping sound of many shoes crashing to the floor brought a smile to his face as rats squealed.

"Right! let's move!" he said, closing in on the others. "Just hold on and keep your nerve. We're nearly there."

But rats dropped onto new victims as the fire now tore through the wooden beams.

A woman screamed after seeing her husband's eyes bleed before breaking rank to run, toppling into the candlestand to set light to the fabric covering the altar with her candle. She watched on in horror as the flames tore through the material, as embers fell onto the dead underneath, feeling lost, confused, and scared as a rat charged to send her falling into the flames.

Ray rushed over to pull her to safety, but she was burning like a wild bushfire before looking away as her face became a glow of hotness as she rolled around on the floor.

"We have to get the rest out!" Harvey shouted at him, looking up to see the wooden beams come away. "This fire will kill us all if we don't do it now."

Ray turned to go back as a rat appeared in front of him, but his glare was vicious as he booted it into the fire.

He looked up to see the door opening before the survivors rushed outside to grasp breathable air, holding onto each other, glad to be alive.

Adam closed in on Ray to grab onto him before he fell over from the pain in his leg, as Harvey watched them exhaustedly close in on the door. They exited the church to leave Harvey feeling the heat against his back as the fire edged closer and closer, but, as he was about to leave, a fearful shriek made him jump. He aimed his gun at the sound as it was swallowed up by the smoke, listening to Adam call out his name, but he wouldn't leave. This was his stand-off, his moment to kill the large rat. He knew it was nearby; he just had to finish it off. He focused on a spot on the floor not covered in smoke until seeing the rat run past, feeling on edge as thoughts of it wanting to keep him there to die tormented him.

"You won't win!" Harvey shouted at it, turning to see Adam re-enter the church.

But that split decision gave the rat time to strike.

It leapt at him to knock him back, but his gun fired as it leapt again. Harvey breathed deeply as the rat ran away before shining his torch on the floor, knowing he'd hit it after seeing droplets of blood.

"You okay?" Adam said.

"I am now."

But the sound of more beams crashing to the floor almost brought down part of the church.

They rushed outside to slam the door, hoping to trap the remaining rats so they burn in the fire.

CHAPTER FORTY-ONE

Everyone inside the police station stared awkwardly at the fire as it ate away the church, with most seeming pleased, thinking the rats were dead.

Rachael stood in the street, watching the rest of the tired survivors gradually move away from the danger as the officers followed before turning to Cortney as she stood on the doorstep. She sadly smiled at her before racing towards the church, scanning the survivors in the hope of finding Chris. But he wasn't to be seen. She slowed down after staring at the bell tower become engulfed in flames, thinking he was still inside the church before crying as she spotted Adam slowly close in. He removed his helmet to see the tears roll down her cheeks, close to doing the same as she stared into his eyes, fearing something was wrong with Chris.

"Where is he?" she whimpered.

"He didn't make it," Adam said, reaching out to hold her hand.

But Rachael became very frantic and she didn't believe him.

"Where was he last?!" she snapped.

Adam never replied as he sadly glanced towards the church.

Rachael was left in shock as the bell tower caved in, but the sight made her angry to run towards the door.

"Chris! Chris! You in there?!" she yelled, closing in to stop after feeling scared by the smoke and flames.

She covered her mouth with a hand to cough into it as the church creaked before Adam appeared to pull her back, holding her tight as he walked her towards the others.

He thought only of Brendan now as the moment to grieve hit him hard.

———

A car pulled up on the opposite side of the road, with the person inside witnessing the church fire. Victoria exited and sighed after fearing her lab rats had something to do with it, but she smiled after seeing Adam, feeling thankful he was alive.

She looked at the crowd of still-shaking people to almost have a panic attack after thinking they could turn on her if someone leaked that she was partly to blame for the rats being there tonight, but, as she neared them could see they were too traumatised to notice.

———

Harvey tried his best to comfort the survivors but knew he was struggling, so let Michael and Martha take over as Ray hobbled past to reach Alice. He collapsed to the ground after seeing her injuries, holding her hand to catch his breath as his heart almost stopped before briefly shutting his eyes after the blood-drenched padding made him feel queasy. But Alice's eyelids flickered to frighten him.

He smiled as she stared at him, not making a sound as he tried to remain positive, knowing she wouldn't want it any other way as he stroked her hair.

"Hey, baby girl. Are you okay?" he said, shaking.

Alice wet her lips with her tongue. "Baby girl?" she replied, coughing.

"You know I'm not very good at tellin' people I love em'. So yeah, baby girl." Ray smiled at her, but her smile back was weak.

"So, you love me?"

"You know I do. Always have."

Alice tried to smile again but she shook, as her eyes closed for the last time. And Ray felt like he'd just died with her.

"She's gone," Harvey said, gripping Ray's shoulder as Louise closed in.

———

Rachael angrily punched Adam in the chest as she tried to blame someone for Chris' death before racing off with her head down towards the station. Adam called out to her but received no reply. He was about to give chase when Victoria neared, leaving him smiling from the last time he saw her, as Rachael gained some distance. He glanced at her and sighed, feeling it best to leave her alone.

"Hey, you. What are you doing here?" he asked Victoria, shaking his head as Rachael reached the station.

Victoria smiled after touching the recent wrinkles on his face. She knew the trauma he'd recently encountered had aged him, but she was so happy he was alive.

"I had to come and find you, see if you were okay," she said, hugging him to stop him from collapsing.

They heard Cortney shouting out her father's name before seeing her run towards them, her shouts getting louder as Adam braced himself for another tear-jerking moment. He waited for her to ask about her father, panicking because he had no answer, but Cortney just pointed into the distance. Adam followed her finger to see Peter walking towards them, looking tired and bitten as he appeared from the next street. And Cortney ran to him, excited to see him okay. Adam nodded as Steve smiled at Peter closing in, but he was curious to know how he'd managed to outrun the rodents.

"Welcome back," Steve said, folding his arms. "Where'd you get to?"

"You don't want to know where I've been," Peter replied, tapping him on the arm.

"But *I* do," Cortney said.

Peter smiled at her before explaining that he'd spent most of the night hiding inside someone's shed. He couldn't outrun the rats and one had bitten him, so had barricaded the shed door with what he could find. He still thought they would get in but was glad they didn't.

"When I thought the coast was clear I left to see the church on fire. I assumed the rats came here." He kissed Cortney on the forehead, happy to be standing in front of her.

They stared at the burning church to find people gathered in prayer, but a look from Steve caused Peter to worry about John.

Victoria also stared at the church, as her mind worked overtime to come to terms with what the rats did.

"Do you think they were all killed in there?" she asked Adam.

"I hope so."

Victoria knew the S.T.A.R.S project would probably cease to exist after this, with the remaining rats at the lab being destroyed, but, after seeing what they did to the town, she wouldn't want to carry on with the project anyway. She kissed Adam before nudging him to move away from the area.

Ray kissed Alice on the lips before letting go of her hand, rising off the ground to cry in front of Harvey and Louise.

EPILOGUE

By midnight, all was still in the town of Aaronsville. The church fire had been put out and the dead had been removed from the streets. No rat activity had been seen since the church catastrophe, so all survivors--the ones who weren't injured--were back inside their homes. None would find it easy to sleep tonight as the fear of not knowing if one of the deadly rodents was lurking in a corner or was under the bed.

The police officers were silent, with each not knowing what to say or how to say it. The only thought being passed between them was about the rats - *Did any get out alive?*

———

Morning arrived, and with it came the sunshine. The Palmer farm, with its crops glistening from the sun's rays, had now received recent visitors. Five rats, with their bodies stained with blood, raced amongst the fields looking for food. The sewage pipe that had led them to the farm had inside a pregnant rat. It had stayed there all this time while the others had hunted. And next to it lay the large one, looking exhausted and injured. It closed its eyes as the pregnant rat licked the blood off its body.

ABOUT THE AUTHOR – LEE ANDREW TAYLOR

Lee lives in Bedworth, Warwickshire, England.

He writes novels that read like movies playing out on paper, taking the reader into an imaginary world that he created. He adds comedy moments in his stories to break up the horror, with silly characters who will make you laugh.

Lee wants readers to see inside their minds the stories he writes, and to live with the characters as they battle the enemy.

Lee's stories are not written to confuse, but to entertain the reader, and to make the reader smile.

———

His novel - *Clifton Falls* - was originally released as *Zombies (Morgue of the Dead)* around 2011, but he changed the name to the movie script version. He has rewritten the novel as a 2 part story, releasing Part 2 in the summer of 2022.

mybook./cliftonfalls2

Part 3 is scheduled for release in 2023.

––––––

Lee has also written a novel based on the old saying – "Night, night, sleep tight, and don't let the bedbugs bite." It's titled – *BEDBUGS (Can you see them?)*...It's a sci-fi-style, alien, horror/comedy story about flesh-eating insects. It was released in 2021 and is available for sale from Amazon Worldwide.

mybook.to/Bedbugs

––––––

Lee also writes movie scripts, with 11 written to date. And he's also written a Sci-fi, horror TV pilot for a British Production Company.

––––––

To keep tabs on Lee's progress please LIKE his Facebook author page –

facebook.com/mrwritermanauthor

or check out his website –

taylorlee544.wixsite.com

Ingram Content Group UK Ltd.
Milton Keynes UK
UKHW010857060623
422954UK00001B/10

9 798223 763369